A Voice in the Wind

The Will and the Wisp
BOOK 2

James Armstrong

A Voice in the Wind
The Will and the Wisp–Book 2

\~\~\~\~

\~\~\~\~

This is the second book of The Will and the Wisp series. This is a work of fiction based on the true story of the Armstrong family.

Sharon Kizziah-Holmes–Publishing Coordinator
Edited by: Sandy Armstrong

Paperback-Press
Springfield, Missouri
an imprint A & S Publishing, A & S Holmes, Inc.

ISBN -13: 978-1-951772-92-5

ACKNOWLEDGMENTS

Special thanks to Douglas Pricer for taking the time to read A Voice in the Wind. Your feedback was priceless and very much appreciated.

Sandy Armstrong, without you putting such great effort into the editing of this book, it may not have ever been finished. Thank you.

Thank you to Mr. James Hussy for allowing me to use his beautiful artwork, HIDAWAY, for the cover of the original The Will and the Wisp and also for this second book in the series.

To Susan Armstrong, thank you for allowing me countless hours in front of me computer, writing, re-writing, editing and more. Without your support I may not have completed this project.

Sharon Kizziah-Holmes, thanks for helping me publish book 2. Without you, the original Will and the Wisp may never have come to fruition.

INTRODUCTION

Many stories were told at the Triple A ranch–some true, some cowboy yarns. After all the day's work was finished, people would take turns telling tales in between much music and dance. Charles Armstrong, an educated and established writer, tried to capture some of the stories in his writing.

Other stories were repeated from one generation to another until modern-day author, James Armstrong, a descendent of the Armstrong family, recalled bits and pieces from the stories he was told as a child. Armstrong recreated some of those remarkable stories and you will read them in this book.

Some tales are fascinating and bold, while others will bring tears to your eyes. Life was raw and dangerous in the Old West, and survival was an uphill adventure.

A Voice in the Wind is the sequel to Amazon bestseller *The Will and the Wisp*. Previously untold stories come to life, as the adventures continue.

CHAPTER 1

The Journey North

In the spring of 1868, three years after the white man's Civil War, Little Boy Horse, Johnny One Horn, and Kicking Wind rode to the top of the hill overlooking the ranch in western Kansas. They had packed well for the trip and would rely on their intuition and experience to carry them through the trials they were about to endure.

Horse gazed upon the Triple A spread. "The Armstrong boys are men now, my brother. They seem to handle things well," he observed.

"Yes," Johnny agreed. "They are smart. They will make it without us now. It is surely a long way from the life we once lived together in the swamp."

Kicking Wind, now a maiden of sixteen seasons, brushed back tears as she gave a final wave to the owners of the ranch that had been her home since childhood. As the trio turned their horses northward, the vision of the ranch shrank in the distance.

Johnny shifted on his horse. "It's hard to leave our good friends–they are like family to us. But I am looking forward to seeing the country in the north that I've heard so much about."

Wind sniffed. "I am too. I was only ten seasons old when Chief Running Bear demanded that you must bring me back to the tribe when the leaves turned and started to fall. I am glad, although I was sad then, that O.C. talked him into waiting until I grew to this age to return."

"Yes, I was pleased they made the decision to let you finish your childhood years here. You have many siblings, and your mother will be overjoyed to see you, my dear one." Little Boy Horse's gaze settled on the girl who had become like a daughter to him. "I am proud of the maiden you have become. You are smart and you are strong. You can shoot an arrow like a warrior and ride like the wind."

"You are making my cheeks burn with heat by telling me that, but thank you." She sighed. "Time has gone so fast," she lamented. "I feel I am so close to everybody at the ranch–even young Carl seems like a brother. Now we are leaving. They have all become family and it is very hard."

"I understand," said Johnny. "We can always turn around. It is your choice."

"No, it is not my choice. I am supposed to return now. If I don't, the chief and my parents will be angry," she answered emotionally. "I do miss my mother and father, and all my brothers and sisters. But it has been so long. I wonder if they will remember me. I think of them every night and I can hear their voices in the darkness."

"They will remember you, my little one," said Johnny gently. "A mother never, ever forgets her child. I hope they will accept Horse and me. I know they are our brothers, but we are of different tribes."

Kicking Wind smiled. "My people are friendly. But we have been fighting the Crow for many years, and they do not like us. I remember they stole women and children from our people. We never saw our loved ones again."

Horse raised an eyebrow and looked at Johnny. "How do we know these Crow when we see them? Do you remember what they look like?" he asked Wind. "And what should we say?"

"You don't say anything to a Crow. You just run or fight. They paint half of their faces black and half white, sometimes red. You will know when you see them. They will try to kill us."

"These sound like very bad people. What makes them so mean?" Johnny wondered.

"My father Grey Wolf told me of these people." Horse glanced at Johnny, then his eyes scanned the prairie. "War makes them like that–many years of war with the Sioux and the white man. Remember the fireside stories my father told of the places he had visited?" Horse realized that Wind could not know these stories, and hastened to include her. "Father was a marked man. Cursed by an evil medicine man. He was told to leave and never to come back."

Johnny explained, "Grey Wolf taught us some of the Sioux language. That's why the other tribes in the swamp were different from ours. We are fortunate to be able speak to the Sioux."

Horse nodded. "Even though my great grandfather was French, my great grandmother was half English. After they died, my grandfather went to live with my great-great grandfather, Tom Red Blair. Red Blair was English and taught my grandfather to speak it well. He in turn taught my Indian grandmother. That is why we know the language of the white man so well."

Wind frowned. "That is confusing."

Laughter escaped Johnny. "That is what my little friend Carl Armstrong said when I told him the story." He smiled at the young woman. "My mother gave me the French name of Jean La Beau and the Indian name One Horn."

"So, you put the names together and became Johnny One Horn."

"That is right."

Boy Horse straightened his back. "I told you she was smart, Johnny."

"Earlier you mentioned the swamp. Will you ever go

back to the land of water?" asked Wind. "It seems strange that you would leave your home forever. I can't see why anybody would leave a place they had been all their lives."

"We didn't leave for our sake, but for the sake of the young Armstrong brothers." Johnny cleared his throat. "They have Chickasaw blood. Their mother was accepted as a member or our tribe, even though her blood was different from ours. The boys were determined to leave after her death, and we decided to help them. They are family to us. We helped them on their journey to the home they call their ranch. Now we will help you safely get back to your home."

"I remember how far away it is," said Wind. "I hope you will like it. I also remember the winters are very cold and there is much snow."

"I have heard of this frozen rain," Johnny remarked with interest. "But we only saw it one time in the swamp. It only lasted a few minutes." He turned his attention to Horse. "We must get ready for this cold. We must gather furs along the way to survive."

After a time of riding in silence, Johnny turned back to the girl. "I have never asked you or Horse why you were with those people that were killed at the water's edge so long ago. Did they take you from your people?" He glanced at his friend to make sure it was all right to ask.

Horse gave an affirmative nod. "I have never heard the full story either. When she was younger, I thought it would be too painful." He glanced at Wind. "If you don't want to talk about it, that is fine."

"No, I will tell you," she answered. "I was taken by two buffalo hunters while I was fishing in a creek near our home. One was crazy. He thought I was his little girl that had died years before. So he kept the other hunter, an awful man named Old Zeke, from bothering me. I learned to play the part of his girl to survive. Old Zeke would try to take my clothes off, but I would scream for my Daddy. That is what the crazy one, BoJack, wanted me to call him. I didn't understand a lot of the white man's tongue then, but I knew he wanted me to call him Daddy."

Wind was quiet for a time as the horses plodded steadily on. It was evident that long-suppressed memories were being painfully awakened. "Zeke was afraid of BoJack, that's the only reason I'm still alive. They were both killers though. They said those people by the river were carrying gold. They hid me in the brush while they robbed and killed them, but I worked the rawhide loose from my hands and crawled into a hole. When they saw Joe and Charles Armstrong and the foreman Nate coming on horseback, they couldn't find me, so they left in a hurry."

"I stayed in that hole most of the night. Then three men, two in wagons and one on a horse, came and got the white people's bodies, and Joe and Charles left. I climbed out of the hole. I was so scared and alone, but I was hoping BoJack wouldn't come back after me. The next thing I knew Horse was picking me up."

Horse spoke to Johnny. "They thought those people were the Armstrong boys. They must have heard it from those other two snakes I killed on the prairie that night. They were after the gold, too, Johnny. This is not good. They might still be out there looking for the gold. Maybe we should try to find these two no-goods before we go north."

"Horse, let's just go on like we planned," said Johnny. "The boys have O.C., Nate, Shorty and the rest of the crew. They can take care of themselves. It's been so long ago anyway. Those two so-called mountain men might even be dead by now."

~ ~ ~

In the afternoon, Johnny stopped and dismounted. "I think we should give the horses a rest. Let's walk for a while." While walking, Johnny took in the quiet majesty of the plains. The day was beautiful. The tall prairie grass undulated like an ocean in the mild breeze and creatures of the plains–ground owls, prairie dogs, and prairie chickens–bobbed and ducked in and out of their dens. The animals chattered an incessant country symphony in the bright sun.

"This is truly a grand and beautiful place," marveled Horn. "There are many whispers in the wind."

"That yellow rock–gold–you talk about," Horse informed Wind, "contains bad spirits. Many people will die because of it. I believe the boys have learned that a little at a time." Suddenly he stopped and faced the breeze. "There is something in the tall grass. Something injured. I smell blood."

Johnny sharpened his senses. "Yes, I smell it, too."

"It must be an animal."

Johnny let Horse take the lead as they slowly walked toward the scent. Presently they came upon a wounded young wolf lying in the tall grass. Frail and emaciated, the frightened beast growled at them as they approached.

"He is too weak to hurt us, Johnny," said Horse. "He's been shot or maybe trampled by a buffalo. It is hard to tell. We can camp here tonight. I do not think the wolf will mind."

Johnny grinned and pointed to the wolf. "Maybe he has a story to tell." He picked out a piece of dried beef and pitched it to the hungry animal. "There, my friend." The wolf snarled but grabbed the morsel and limped further into the tall grass.

Johnny felt for the Arkansas Toothpick he kept sheathed at his side. "I think I'll go get a couple of those prairie chickens to eat tonight. I like them and they cook fast."

Gathering some dried buffalo chips, Horse placed them on the ground. "We will make camp while you are gone." He instructed Wind, "Pull all this grass up a few feet around us to make a clearing. We do not want to start a prairie fire. Remember O.C.'s scars from that grass fire? It's a very bad thing to deal with."

Wind nodded and began to clear the campsite as Horse went in search for more buffalo chips.

Before long, Johnny returned with two fat prairie chickens. By the time they were dressed and cleaned, the fire was ready. He suspended the birds from a tripod over the fire. "I like these metal sticks Joe gave me," he smiled, proud of the gift. "They work very well and make me a great cook!"

While their supper slowly roasted, the two men began to tell Wind some of the many stories of their journey to the ranch, and the gold they had taken from the depths of the unforgiving swamp. Johnny enjoyed hearing and telling the tales again. But he could tell it was the story of the great Mississippi River that intrigued Wind most of all.

Wind settled back as she began to eat. "I am fascinated by the thought of a stream so large that one could not see its other side. The vision of the city called St. Louis is almost unbelievable! I have heard stories from many white men before, but I thought they were just tales." She shifted her gaze from Horse to Horn. "Now that I know there is such a place, I want to know more. Is the place called the City of St. Louis as big as mountains?"

Johnny smiled at her youthful curiosity. "Yes, little one, it is. It is huge, with huts that reach in all directions."

"All those white people," she marveled. "Did they not likc you? Did thcy try to kill you?"

"No," Johnny replied. "They just looked at us and tried to figure out what we were, I guess. The ladies acted funny. They blushed and waved a lot. And they all seemed to smell good. They were like flowers. Some were pretty, with red cheeks and color around their eyes. Some kind of paint, I guess. Some were not so pretty."

The little campsite flickered in the fire light. Johnny glanced up. Overhead, the moon was a great ball of light that was reflected by the dry prairie grass. The south wind was warm.

Wind sighed contentedly. “I am comforted by the warmth in the air. Your stories amaze me. I want to hear more but I’d like to tell you again: I’m so grateful the Great Spirit sent me to you, Horse.” She glanced at Johnny. “You too, Johnny One Horn. You were the answer when I asked the Great Spirit to help me. You saved my life.”

As they sat and enjoyed their prairie chickens, Johnny told Wind more of the things he had seen in the white man’s cities. “Once I lived in a white woman’s… I shall call it a… playhouse.” He recalled the good and bad times he’d had in Garden City at Eula May’s Saloon and Brothel. It brought joy and a broken heart at the same time. “I was a card dealer, and learned more of the white man’s ways.” He thought of the schoolteacher Sue King. She had been the light of his life. He had to force himself to tell them about her. “I lost my true love there. A couple of players didn’t like that I had won their money. They were rotten, like the Crow, I guess. The men that killed my love were dirty snakes!”

Johnny stopped. This was a recollection he didn’t want to go into. It still hurt too bad. “I will tell you about it one day, but for now, while the grass is quiet, get some sleep. I’ll take the first watch. Horse, I will wake you up when the moon is high.”

Wind yawned. “Why don’t we all sleep, Johnny? There’s not a person in sight.”

“No, little one,” he said. “We learned a long time ago from Grey Wolf never to let our guard down. That is what happened to me in Garden City when the fat woman Eula May saw me. I was careless. We are in a strange land and someone or something can be watching us as I speak!”

~ ~ ~

Alone with his thoughts, Johnny watched the moon in the eastern sky. Its reflection grew brighter than he had ever seen it. He remembered how Grey Wolf often told him of the circle in the sky. As he gazed at the millions of stars, he wondered how it was all tied together. The Great Spirit was truly amazing.

In the celestial glow, the wind flowed like a gentle river through the prairie grass. He saw the eyes of an antelope reflected back at him as he scanned the horizon. He noticed the wounded wolf lay close by. He took some of the leftover prairie chicken and pitched it toward the animal. The creature painfully limped over and ate it, all the time watching him warily. Johnny wondered if he could make friends with it.

How anybody could shoot this amazing spirit, he did not know. He pitched another piece of meat, and the wolf came closer. Apparently, the poor creature had not eaten in days. Trying his luck, Johnny moved a little closer, but the wolf backed away and snarled at him. "Well, my little friend," he said gently, "I guess I should not ask you to join us just yet. You are too frightened." To Johnny, the Great Spirit lived in all things and he spoke to the frail wolf as if he were another person. "We will be leaving when the mighty sun comes up. I wish you would come with us." Going back to his bed roll, he sat and met the gaze of the wolf. "Thank you for listening. If you go, you are young and I think you will be fine."

As the moon rose to the center of the sky, Johnny saw Little Boy Horse sit up and yawn. "I see you are awake, my brother."

"Yes." Horse grinned. "I have been listening to you talk to the wolf. I think those fat women and their firewater have made your mind go in circles. Kind of like that woman that ran around in circles at the ranch." He sat in

Indian fashion and stoked the fire. “Tell me,” he went on, “how do those fat women compare to ours?”

Johnny smiled at the memory. “They are loud, and they give all the orders. The men seem to be scared of them. Eula and Pickles are very smart. I wish you could have met Eula May. She would have taught you a lot of things. She is a woman that will shoot you dead if you cross her.” He glanced at his friend with a knowing look, raised his eyebrows, then cocked one side of his mouth into a smile. “I think she would like you.” Johnny remembered how she’d looked at him when she’d come into his room and he stood there naked. Boy Horse was built the same. Though *he* had refused to fulfill her fantasies, she might be able to convince Horse to. This thought brought a grin to his face.

“Of course, she would like me. I am big, strong and better looking than you.”

Johnny laughed and lay back on his buffalo robe. “I am tired.”

“I will sit away from the fire and watch for anything unusual.” Horse stood and studied the expanse of land. “I often think of the swamp, and family in the tribe we left so long ago. The journey we’ve made, the lives lost along the way–where will we end up? What will tomorrow bring?”

“Only time will tell, brother. Only time.”

Little Boy Horse stepped into the shadows. “Sleep. I’ll wake you if there is a reason.”

Knowing that was true, as soon as he put his head down, Johnny was fast asleep.

CHAPTER 2

BoJack

BoJack sat on his haunches a few hills away from the ranch, glaring down on the quiet buildings and corrals of what he'd learned to be the Triple A–Armstrong a–ranch. He'd searched for years for his little girl. Many times, he'd nearly given up, but rumors on the prairie and gossip in cow towns had finally led him here. Now he would have his chance to claim her.

"Stupid mountain man. BoJack, you're driving yourself crazy. Why don't you stop drinking that rot gut for the night?"

"Zeke, you sorry, no good bastard. You know those sons-a-bitches got my little girl down there. There's no tellin' what they've done to her over the years. She needs to be with me, her daddy."

"She ain't no little girl no more. She's nigh on sixteen years now. Forget about her–'member, they've got gold, too."

"I don't care nothin' about the gold! I just want my girl back. If you think I'm gonna just walk away and leave her with those shitheads, you've got another think comin'!" BoJack threw the empty whiskey bottle to the ground, opened another and knelt by the fire. "I'll kill ever' last one of 'em!" He grabbed the cold end of a burning stick and threw it as hard as he could. "Including those sorry-assed women and kids of theirs!"

"Stop screaming, BoJack. Damn, if they have someone on lookout, you'll damn sure alert 'em we're here." Zeke stepped forward.

"Shut up and come on, we're gonna go get her."

"You're not in any shape to go ridin' down to that ranch now. Besides, that swamp Indian that has her is a killer and I've heard tell O.C. Armstrong and his boys are no men to be trifled with either."

BoJack took another swig of whiskey. "If you're too scared, I'll do it myself." He stood up and stumbled backwards.

"Hell, it's the middle of the night and you're stumbling all over the place. You ain't in no shape to–"

At that moment, BoJack took a tumble forward and fell into the brush. The bottle dropped from his hand and the remainder of the contents poured out.

"BoJack?" Zeke went over and rolled his friend to the ground and onto his back. "Passed out cold. Somebody must be looking out for you. This way you can sleep it off and, in the morning, we can make a real plan."

~~~

Unable to sleep, Shorty, a hand on the Triple A, walked out of his cabin and looked calmly around the ranch. On a distant hill, he noticed the flicker of a campfire. "What's somebody doin' up there?" Immediately suspicious, he stepped back inside the cabin, quietly dressed, and strapped on his gun belt.

He started up the hill on foot. "It's probably one of the new hands slipping off to meet one of the Mexican or Indian girls," he said to himself. "Can't say as I blame 'em. I'd like to take a run at Marianna myself. Shoot, eighteen years of age, long black hair and full of Apache spirit. No
~~~

wonder she drives the ranch hands crazy." He chuckled.

Silently, Shorty walked toward the firelight. When he reached the top of the hill, he saw a man lying on the ground by the fire.

"What the hell is this?" he thought, drawing his single-action Colt forty-four and walking toward the still figure.

Shorty bent over and nudged the man with the toe of his boot. "Hey, fellow, you all right?" Then he noticed the empty whiskey bottles.

"Drunk." He snickered and stooped to help the man to his feet. "I'd hate to be you in the morning."

Shorty heard a rustling noise behind him, but before he could turn around, he felt a savage blow to the back of his skull and the world went dark.

Zeke quickly secured the short man's hands and feet with rawhide. Next, he poured water from his canteen over BoJack's face until he came to. So drunk was he, it took some time before he was sober enough to talk intelligently.

"Who the hell is that?" BoJack asked when he noticed a man's unconscious form on the ground.

"I caught him trying to slip up on us," Zeke whined. "He's one of them cowhands, I'm sure."

"Well, just kill him," BoJack blurted. "Cut his head off or something." Still slurring his words and slobbering, BoJack staggered to his feet and drew his skinning knife. "Never mind, you're probably too chicken-shit. I'll do it," he bellowed at Zeke. "You're nothin' but a worthless fool! I ought to kill you, too!"

Zeke drew his skinning knife in a defensive posture. "Go ahead and try," he said. "You're still drunk and it'll be easy for me to cut your balls off and hang them around your neck, you damn fool! Don't you see? This guy can tell us where Wind is, and maybe even the gold."

This stopped BoJack in his tracks. "Well, I'll be damned. For once you're right." BoJack steadied himself. "Let's tie him to the tree closest to the fire."

BoJack cinched Shorty's hands and feet tightly to the trunk, then emptied his canteen on the ranch hand's head.

Something cool ran into Shorty's eyes and onto the back of his head. Confused and half-aware, he gradually realized it was water. He glanced up at the two men that stood in front of him. One was the guy that had been drunk on the ground.

His head hurt like hell but when he tried to rub it, he realized his hands were bound to the tree. "What the hell are you doing?"

"If you don't tell us what we wanna know, we gonna kill us a little cowboy," BoJack sneered as he grabbed Shorty's hair. "Then we're gonna burn you alive while you're tied to this tree. You see, little man, you need to tell us about my girl Wind. You don't and I'll do just what I said I was gonna do!"

Shorty's heart raced. He was in a spot! He moaned and recalled how Wind had told Marianna about her abduction. Marianna had told him in confidence. Realization hit him. "You're the two bastards that kidnapped her from her people. Aren't you?"

Fury glinted in the drunk man's eyes as he lunged toward Shorty. Suddenly Shorty was overwhelmed by pain as the man cut off part of his left ear. He screamed, "You son-of-a-bitch! I'll kill you!" But really, he wasn't in any position to make threats. He feared for his life.

Now the man looked even more crazed. Shorty felt the knife blade when it whacked off the little finger of his left hand. Blood trickled down the side of his head and slithered down the tree trunk. What had he gotten himself into?

"BoJack. Stop."

BoJack turned toward the other man. "You want a little of this, Zeke?"

Zeke held up his hands and backed away.

Shorty shook his head to clear his thoughts. Why would

Zeke let this BoJack fellow keep torturing him? "Help me, Zeke, please." The man just shook his head.

Then BoJack turned his attention back to Shorty. "You call me another name," he roared, "and I'll cut your marbles off and dangle 'em where you can see 'em on this tree."

His face with its vile whiskey breath and rotten teeth was only inches from Shorty's face. Gasping for air and in terrible pain, he realized BoJack was nothing short of a maniac who'd probably kill him in any event. In order to live, he had no choice but to comply. "I'll tell you anything you want to know." Shorty's voice was just above a whisper. "And help you if I can." He knew this was a lie, but he had to try to fool these men.

"Which one of them cabins have they got her in?" BoJack growled. "Tell me quick, boy, or I'll cut two more of them fingers off!"

Stuttering and terrified, Shorty struggled to explain. "She left with the Swamp Indians." "They're taking her back to her people." The unbelieving BoJack whacked off another finger. Was he going to die tonight? Shorty tried to catch his breath.

"You're lyin'. Tell me the truth!"

"Please, I'm not lying. Horse and Horn are taking her home. For real!" He feared he would pass out. The agony of his injuries was intolerable.

"You mean them Injuns from the Mississippi swamp?" BoJack's eyes glazed with a murderous gleam. "I'll kill 'em all for this!"

"You gotta understand, mister," Shorty sobbed, unable to help himself. He had to try to get through to this unreasonable person. "They love Wind. They won't hurt her. It was just time to take her home."

Unsatisfied, BoJack became even more frenzied and Shorty realized that anything he said would be wrong.

Now Zeke stood up and turned to Shorty. He drew his

filthy knife from an even filthier leather sheath. "Shut up, you idiot! You're making BoJack worse. Hell, I'm gonna kill you myself!"

Petrified with fear, Shorty closed his eyes and braced for his demise. Suddenly the shriek of a bullet ripped through the air and part of Zeke's head exploded. Blood and brains scattered and he dropped dead on the ground.

BoJack froze for a moment and then sprinted for his horse and mounted as a second bullet slashed through the night and smacked into the crazy man's hand, leaving part of the appendage in a bloody lump on the ground.

Shorty watched as the villain wheeled the horse through the thick brush and galloped into the night. He searched the dark brush trying to find who'd done the shooting. Finally, he saw a figure emerge into the clearing. "My gawd, I'm saved," he whispered as Nate approached.

"What the hell?!" Nate yelled. "Good gawd, man! Who the hell are these guys?"

Shorty squirmed and could hardly hold his water. He was going to live.

"Hold on, Shorty. Be still while I cut this rawhide."

Free of his bindings, Shorty scooted away from the tree and stood on shaking legs. "Did you kill them both?" Shorty asked hysterically, knowing the answer. Pain wracked through him. He grabbed Nate's shirt, his body trembling in fear.

"I killed one." Nate gestured at Zeke's lifeless form. "That one there's had his last ride. I hit the other one in his hand. There's part of it over there. I heard his yelling. Maybe it hit him somewhere else. Just don't know how good I got him."

"I didn't think anyone was going to show up," blubbered Shorty. "I thought they were going to kill me for sure. Look, Nate," he went on, now shaking so hard he found it difficult to form the words. "He cut off my fingers and my ear too!" Darkness began to descend on him and he dropped to his knees, then to the ground, and everything ceased to exist.

"My, oh my," Nate sighed. "I know you can't hear me, old friend. But I'm taking you home. We'll get you taken care of."

One Week Later

O.C. Armstrong wiped sweat from his brow. It was branding time at the ranch. The day was hot and dry. Dust, sounds of bawling cattle, the smells of singed fur and burning cowhide permeated the air. Today he was running count and branding, while Shorty, sporting bandages on his head and left hand, stood by and let Marianna pamper him like a newborn baby.

Joe had purchased the livestock directly from cattle drives as opposed to the higher-priced brokers in Abilene. He had learned that he could save substantial money that way, not to mention getting the pick of the litter.

O.C. leaned up against the cattle chute and watched, amused. "Shorty, I'd keep getting the fingers cut off if I were you. It seems like you're getting the royal treatment." He and Nate both grinned.

"I'm going to track that bastard down when I get better," Shorty retorted. "I'm going to skin him a little at a time."

Nate shook his head. "Shorty, you need to stay here and forget it. Besides, that old boy might be dead by now."

"Naw," argued Shorty, "he's alive and he's going after Horse and Horn. You didn't see how wild he was. I never saw a man that crazy before."

"Well, he's crazy for sure if he goes after Horse and Horn. They *will* skin him alive, especially if he touches that girl." Nate glanced at O.C.

"Hell, yeah, they will," O.C. smiled. "Those two boys can smell a rat a mile away."

Joe walked over from the corral to where the men were talking. “Pete, get over here and take over for Pop, please.” He looked at his father. “How many head, Pop?”

O.C. slapped his oldest son on the back. “Four hundred eighty-four.”

“Hell, that trail boss said it would be six hundred. I swear you can’t trust anybody these days. He and his men are waitin’ at the house. He will only get paid for what we got.”

“I’m surprised he got any here at all, especially coming all the way from Texas,” said O.C. “Looks to me like most of his hands can barely ride, much less control a herd.” He turned toward Joe in bewilderment when he heard the young man’s next words.

“I think we should go after that outlaw.”

O.C. followed Joe’s gaze. He was studying Shorty. Now the injured ranch hand wasn’t the only one that wanted to go after the man–Joe did as well.

“It’s not right to let him get away with it. I bet he’s killed a lot more people than we know about,” Joe insisted.

O.C. shook his head. “No, he’ll be watching for just that thing. He might kill a few of us, and I’ve seen enough of my friends die. People like him don’t care about life. He’s a good four days ride from here, anyway. Besides, he’s crazy.”

“Just thinkin’ about Horse and Horn, and mostly the girl.”

“Let it go, Joe,” advised O.C. “Hell, nobody slips up on them. They always have an eye out. They’ll see him before he sees them. You know that. Those two are the last ones I’d ever try to second guess.”

Joe sighed. “You’re right, Pop. If he’s as crazy as Shorty says he is, he may be dead already. Not only that, but probably skinned if I know my friends.”

O.C. turned and walked to the small shack that contained the moonshine still. “Hey, boys.” He pulled out a jug. “Drinks are on me!”

The sun had dropped behind the western hills and with their workday over, the men set to cleaning up. While some of the hands preferred to ride downriver and bathe in its deep clear pools, most of the boys congregated at the rough-hewn shower stalls they’d built beneath the main water tank. Employing the principles of simple gravity, the men had run a horizontal water line from the base of the main tank that extended over each stall. Suspended above each stall was a wooden bucket, the bottom of which was shot through with holes. When the signal was given, a valve at the base of the tank was opened, allowing a steady stream of fresh, cool water to flow to all the buckets, creating a shower for the men beneath. It was an idea they’d gotten from a visit to St. Louis. Each day after a refreshing shower, they all agreed that there were some good things to be found among the city slickers.

O.C. studied the ranch, which had become more like a village. Construction was never-ending, with structures going up in all directions. His old friend Levi had abandoned his culinary duties and taken on the role of organizer and planner. Under his strict and precise direction, the small community grew at a steady pace.

Levi had also built a general store. Joe staked him enough money to stock the modest enterprise, and showed him how to order inventory from St. Louis, have it shipped by rail to Abilene, and thence transported to the ranch by wagon.

The little store was the only one of its kind for miles around. It hadn’t taken long for scores of people, from local settlers and ranchers to traveling drifters, to hear about the establishment. They all stopped to purchase needed items from Levi’s Mercantile.

O.C. loved the nights at the ranch that were a combination of fiesta, barbeque and grass-roots music. Each evening at dusk folks began to gather for supper.

Everyone pitched in, and soon one could smell all kinds of delicacies cooking. The men traded off cutting firewood and the women brought freshly cultivated produce from the nearby fields.

Music was a constant at these gatherings. It seemed that nearly everyone could play an instrument of some kind. And many were the nights the air was teeming with home-spun melodies and ballads played on banjos, guitars, fiddles, jugs and wash boards, by the tough and hard-working people of the plains.

Security was always a concern at night and several ranch hands rode the perimeter. On balance, there wasn't much trouble and O.C. was proud of that. Once in a while a passerby, or desperate folks traveling by wagon, would steal a calf. But more often than not, these people chose to stay in the ranch's comfort zone.

~ ~ ~

The ranch was growing exponentially. Joe and Nate were buying livestock as fast as the suppliers could deliver, and an organized management team was crucial. Nate assumed the role of ranch foreman, seeking to hire able-bodied men from the trains of immigrants heading west. Most would stay just long enough to re-supply, but many elected to stay on.

Charles handled all of the clerical affairs, including payroll and banking. His education lent him enough knowledge to serve as a legal consultant, and this he did with an iron hand. Some of the cowboys disagreed with him, but law and order were vital to the operation. His enforcer was Pete, who did a fine job as ranch security man. In fact, Pete was a natural because of his unique ability to calm people down.

There were more than a few Mexican couples on the ranch, and a number of unmarried Latinas who loved to flirt. This led to some hot domestic disputes, but Pete just had a way of defusing these flareups.

Through it all, Joe and Charles never forgot where they came from. And on the quiet nights when they rode down to Carl's grave, they could honestly tell themselves that the ranch was becoming a reality. They knew there were many tough days ahead, but they also knew that their lives had forged them into strong, confident men. They also knew in their hearts that there was nothing in the future they couldn't handle.

The North Platte River

"This land is very different," mused Little Boy Horse as he scanned the horizon. "The deer seem bigger than in the place called Kansas. The trees seem to be larger. Look at the river–it is very blue and does not have the color of mud in it. It's peaceful. Maybe that's why that wolf keeps following us. I think I will give him a name, although I don't know what it will be yet!"

"It is very nice here," agreed Johnny. "I could love this place."

As the trio dismounted and walked their horses down to the water's edge, Horse kept turning around and peering behind him. "I feel like we are being watched," he said to Johnny and Wind. "Something is not right about this place." Just then a reflection on a faraway hill caught his attention and the wolf started growling and snarling in the direction of the hill.

"You're right," exclaimed Johnny, pointing, "there–someone's there!"

The three did not panic. Instead they calmly mounted their horses and rode slowly across the river. "Let's not hurry," said Horse. "They are all around us in the brush."

Four Sioux braves, dressed in beaded buckskin and armed with rifles, quietly stepped in front of them, blocking their path. A second later, several more, mounted on painted war ponies, emerged from the brush.

The warriors were expressionless and silent, but their eyes glowed with vigilance and their stoic presence exuded violence. Finally, the leader edged his horse forward and slowly circled the strangers.

Wind broke the silence. “We are of the Sioux,” she said respectfully. “We mean no harm. I am trying to get home and my friends are trying to help me.”

The leader listened with caution. “I am Blue Feather,” he said quietly. “I wonder why someone would undertake such a mission in such a dangerous land. Who are these men?” he continued, pointing his rifle at Horse and Johnny.

“We may also be of the Sioux,” Johnny answered. “But we were raised far to the southeast of the big river and have never been sure of our tribe.”

“I know of no Sioux there,” said Blue Feather. “I think you are lying.”

Sensing danger, Little Boy Horse knocked Blue Feather from his horse to the ground, prompting the other braves to advance toward the trio with bows drawn and rifles cocked.

“No!” Blue Feather shouted, waving them back. He motioned for Horse to dismount. When Horse stood facing him, Blue Feather drew his hunting knife. Declining to draw his weapon, Horse beckoned his quarry to come on.

The two warriors grappled and then went to the ground. For a short time, they rolled and fought in mortal combat, until Horse had gained the advantage and sat atop the Sioux leader, pinning him to the ground.

Horse pulled the intimidating homemade toothpick knife from his belt and waved it in the face of the now-terrified Blue Feather. “If you ever call me a liar again,” he snarled, “this will be the last thing you see, my friend.” Horse rolled off the man and stood up while several braves stepped forward and helped Blue Feather to his horse.

Blue Feather smiled. “I don’t think I’ve ever been

whipped that fast," he said. "You are very brave. I welcome you to our camp south of the river; you will be our guests."

The Sioux camp was orderly. The hunt had been good and large slabs of buffalo calf roasted on each of the several campfires.

"Come," said Blue Feather, "let us sit and talk of your journey."

They sat down in a traditional way around one of the fires.

"You have a long journey ahead of you, Little Boy Horse," warned Blue Feather. "There will be many dangers. The white man's army of hundreds roams the plains. Their sole purpose is to kill or capture us. You must stay in the trees and away from open plains."

Horse nodded and then smiled. "But you, my friend–you were traveling in the open plains."

"That is true," said Blue Feather. "But we have scouts watching from four directions. I tell you it is certain the white man's army will try to kill you or worse."

Johnny and Horse looked at each other in surprise. "We have been to the big city across the great river, and no one even looked at us," said Johnny. "The women smiled and waved and were friendly."

Blue Feather was puzzled by this; he shook his head in disbelief. "Why would they be friendly there, and not here?" he wondered.

"We were with some boys who were half white," Johnny explained.

One of the elders sitting by the fire beckoned Blue Feather away. Together the two walked away from the fire, where they stopped and talked for a moment. When they were finished, Blue Feather returned to the group and addressed them.

"We have heard of you men and your half-breed brothers," he said. "You helped Running Bear with meat for the tribe. We have heard that they are good men, and we know the story of Wind. A messenger says an evil snake of a man is following you. This man we know very well. He has killed many of our people.

Kicking Wind gasped, and started to cry on Johnny's shoulder. "Why don't you just kill him?" she cried.

"It is not easy to do so," Blue Feather frowned. "We have tried many times, but this man is elusive. He seems to travel with the dark spirits of the night. You must be careful of the dark, because this snake lives there and has no respect for life.

"If we could, we would have killed him already. We know what this girl has been through, but the snake follows you, so beware of dark and stormy nights. That is when the snake will strike. Stay in our camp tonight. You will be safe here. I see you have a wolf following you. That is a good sign. Remember, when you leave us, be careful of the dark, and we wish good luck to you."

As the camp bedded down, Wind snuggled close to Little Boy Horse. With wide eyes, she stared up at the endless darkness of the prairie night.

CHAPTER 3

BoJack

Riding north, less than two miles from the North Platte River, BoJack was desperate. He'd ridden nonstop for days, driven by his lust for Wind. Now he slumped in his saddle, wracked with a burning fever and a left hand so grotesquely swollen and covered with dried blood that it was unrecognizable. His last conscious thought, before he fell to the ground, was a blurry recognition of a dust cloud in the distance.

The dust cloud arose from seven prairie schooners carrying a band of twenty-one Mormon pioneers. Led by a man named Bud Flint, the cadre of Latter-Day Saints had been sent by their prophet, Brigham Young, to explore and populate the regions west to Salt Lake City in the territory of Utah. As the group drew closer, Flint's son Andy galloped ahead and approached the motionless body.

"Here, Pa," he shouted. "I think this man is dead."

Quickly Flint rode up, dismounted, and knelt next to BoJack. "No, he's alive," he told his son, "but he is very sick. You did well, my son," he continued as he got to his feet, brushing the dirt from his knees. "We'll see what we can do for this poor soul."

Unaware of the danger they were putting themselves in, the party of good Samaritans gently loaded BoJack into the shade of a wagon. Now conscious, the outlaw recognized an opportunity for evil gain and never moved or opened his eyes.

The group was governed by the edicts of the Mormon church and was accustomed to helping all men. Quietly, they gathered around to discuss the helpless man. Bud's wife Betty, an ever-practical woman, spoke first.

"Mercy!" she exclaimed to her husband. "He stinks so bad! Do you think this is a good idea, bringing him into our wagon? We don't know this man, where he's been, or what he is."

"But Betty," Bud answered, "we don't know what he's been through. He may be a good man." With that, Bud carefully began to clean BoJack's wounded hand. BoJack moaned with pain as Bud gently worked. "Looks like he's been shot," observed Bud. "He's got two fingers missing from that hand. I don't know if we can save him or not–he's really bad--but we'll do what we can."

Bud cleaned the wound as best he could with warm, clean water, and bandaged it with white cotton strips torn from a pillowcase. When he was finished, he had BoJack sip a small amount of laudanum to stave off the pain and to induce sleep.

Having done all that he could for the moment, Bud stepped down from the wagon and glanced north to the hills. There a lone Indian sat astride his pony, his figure cast in silhouette against the afternoon sun. Just then a shot rang out, driving the lone brave from view.

Bud whirled around. "Do you have to shoot at everybody you see?" he scolded the sentry. "God help us if we believe every man we see needs to be shot!"

"But you said these natives are dangerous," the man retorted defensively.

"Well, they're not all killers," Flint responded. "What are we turning into? Instead of thinking the worst, we should pray for all men!"

~ ~ ~

Late that night when the camp was bedded down, a thunderstorm rumbled across the prairie, bringing a torrential downpour. The pilgrims had experienced many thunderstorms on their journey but this one lasted all night and blocked the sunrise. The once dry, firm land was now a quagmire unable to support the heavy prairie schooners. The Mormons were now stopped where they were with no alternative but to wait until the earth dried.

"It will be a day or two before this mud dries out," Bud concluded. "We might as well make the best of it. Get some of the tarps and make some lean-tos from the wagons."

While all this was taking place, BoJack plotted his next move. Lying in the bed of a wagon, conveniently moaning in pain while the Mormon ladies fed and washed him, he patiently waited in comfort for his body to recover.

BoJack was a very tough man with extreme cunning and cruelty, having survived many encounters with the Sioux and the Crow. The Indians understood how dangerous he was, and had tried, to no avail, to kill or capture him.

The outlaw was like a snake and until now had avoided capture. Using a scoped Sharps buffalo gun, his favorite hit and run tactic was to take cover at an extreme distance, shoot one or two women or children, and then disappear into a well-camouflaged hiding place.

These tactics terrorized hunting parties, driving them off so BoJack could hunt the area unchallenged. Many of his attacks were conducted at night, so few were able to recognize him. Like other white buffalo hunters with whom he rode, he also had a string of false identities.

To the north, Red Cloud had organized a search party of six warriors whose sole purpose was to hunt BoJack down and bring him in alive to be judged for his crimes.

To the south, Running Bear was also looking for him, seeking revenge for his murdered sister and niece. But despite all efforts, BoJack had always managed to slither away. Now, both leaders, aware that the outlaw had been shot at the ranch, hoped that his wounds would eventually kill him.

The lone scout on the hill that Bud Flint's sentry had shot at thought the man the Mormons had rescued could be BoJack. He had galloped off to report his find to Blue Feather. After two days of hard riding the exhausted scout arrived at the camp of Blue Feather and told his story. Immediately several warriors were dispatched to alert the party searching for BoJack. To their chagrin, Blue Feather asked Johnny One Horn and Little Boy Horse to stay behind in camp with Kicking Wind.

~ ~ ~

Blue Feather's riders rode without sleep, hoping that they would find their comrades in time to stop the desperado's next murderous move. They found the search party quickly and together set off in the direction of the Mormon camp. Within two hours the warriors spotted a lone wagon driving across the plains. At the reins was a white man dressed in the Mormon fashion, with a woman sitting beside him.

The leader of the search party was a brave named Tomah. Sly and cautious of the unpredictability of the whites, he knew that he and his companions could draw fire.

"Should we go closer, Tomah?" asked one of the braves.

"No, we can track them later," he answered. "For now, let's finish our mission."

After another hard ride, the Sioux search party paused atop the hill overlooking the Mormon encampment.

"Something is very wrong," frowned Tomah. "No one

moves there."

The party slowly descended the hill and entered the silent camp. Their worst fears were realized. Dead Mormons lay all around them. Behind one of the burned-out wagons a small group of survivors were mournfully burying their dead. One of the women was searching for her fifteen-year-old daughter to no avail; she was almost certain that BoJack had kidnapped her. Another woman was holding her two dead children and deliriously screaming and crying and talking to them as if they were still alive.

When the survivors saw the painted Sioux warriors, the women screamed in terror and ran to the brush for shelter and the men stood silent, too traumatized to move. They looked terrified and bewildered.

Their language prevented communication, but Tomah bowed his head slowly toward the men to indicate he felt their sorrow. The ghastly scene was more than even the hardened Sioux warriors could take.

"This is the work of BoJack," Tomah told his braves. "He probably killed them while they were asleep."

"Why would he kill young children and women?" asked a young brave.

"He comes from a dark world. He is not like a man but like a beast," replied Tomah. "I will kill this devil and hang his head for all to see."

"The other wagon we passed," he continued, "carried this snake. He took captives with him to complete his disguise. The woman we saw must be the daughter that is missing, but I doubt if she will live long. The night is closing–we must hurry. When they stop for the night, he will probably kill her for fun."

~ ~ ~

The sun was getting low in the sky, and BoJack was

enjoying himself immensely. High on laudanum he had pilfered from the Mormon's medical supplies, he grinned with morbid satisfaction at Bob Flint who was tied to the base of a tree, immobile and helpless. Nearby, Bud's wife Betty and their young daughter lay dead in the dirt. Just moments before, BoJack had forced Bud to watch as he raped and beat the powerless woman before turning on the little girl.

Bud had screamed to the point of passing out as he watched his wife fight with all her strength. But Betty was small, and BoJack was a crazed mountain man, his mind growing more deranged with each passing hour. When Betty had begged for her life, he had only laughed louder. The screams of the mother and her little girl wailed unanswered in the prairie wind.

~ ~ ~

Tomah and his warriors found the bodies the following morning. Tomah dismounted, cut Bob's lifeless form free, and lay it next to the mutilated bodies of his wife and daughter.

The entire band stood in horrified silence, sad and puzzled by this scene of cowardly violence.

"This poor man doesn't have a scratch on him," Tomah observed. "I think his heart stopped. He saw terrible things and his heart just stopped."

Then the scout on the hill overlooking the scene called out, "Soldiers! Many soldiers!"

"Mount up," ordered Tomah. "The Long Knives will think we did this and they will hang us all."

"What are we going to do about the Snake?" one asked as they started off.

"We will have to let him go for now," replied Tomah. "There are too many soldiers here. We must return to the north quickly."

Chapter 4

Two days later

Tomah reported the horrific things he had seen to Blue Feather, and explained how it had shaken his warriors. Blue Feather was furious at the thought that this devil had escaped their grasp once more. He put his hands to his face in rage, just thinking about it.

"That is not all, my brother," sighed Tomah. "There were many soldiers there. We were outnumbered many times and had to leave. Our people will be blamed for this massacre. We must move farther north or the Blue Coats will find us and many of our people will die."

"Bring me the traveler–the swamp brother–the one called Horse," ordered Blue Feather.

Little Boy Horse and Johnny One Horn were rubbing down their horses as Tomah approached. Kicking Wind lay nearby, asleep in her bedroll.

"Blue Feather wants to see you, my friends," Tomah announced.

Little Boy Horse and Johnny One Horn turned silently and accompanied Tomah back to the fire, where Blue Feather respectfully asked them to sit. Even so, both men kept a wary eye, prudently doubting even this seemingly safe situation.

"My friends," began Blue Feather, "I have heard stories

from my people in the south of your cunning, and your ability to move like the wind in the night without being seen. I ask your help in killing this terrible devil that haunts our people. He has killed so many people, and his lust for blood never ends. The party has returned and told of a terrible slaughter of a wagon train to the south, but again the evil one escapes us. He may have a hostage, probably a young girl or boy, that he will eventually kill. We thought he was gone. But now he is back and is searching for you. You need to find him before he finds you. You will need this," the chief concluded as he handed them a rifle.

"I will go, and I will find and kill this devil," said Little Boy Horse. "But I will not take your rifle. You may need it." Turning to Johnny One Horn, he advised: "Keep traveling north until you can find shelter. Be on guard at all times and keep Kicking Wind close to you."

~ ~ ~

Word of Horse's departure quickly spread among the women, and a traveling kit of dried hide containing jerked buffalo meat and bread was prepared for him to stave off his hunger on the trail. It was a warm gesture, and Horse thanked for their kindness as he mounted his horse. With a slight motion of his hand he turned and headed south to the hills and toward the river.

Johnny and Wind watched as he faded from their sight. Tears rolled down Kicking Wind's face as she watched her beloved Little Boy Horse disappear in the distance.

Blue Feather mounted his horse and rode up alongside Johnny. "I hope he's as good as his legend tells, my friend," he said. "I have seen many men die trying to kill BoJack. Horse will need the help of the Great Spirit. We will all ask that he is safe and is able to kill this demon."

"He will kill him. And if he doesn't, I will be the next to go after him," Johnny confidently assured Blue Feather.

"Take care, my friend."

Johnny turned his horse to the north. He looked at Kicking Wind. "Don't worry, my little flower," he said reassuringly. "Horse has the insight of ten men and the eyes of an eagle. He will find this devil and remove him from this land."

They rode away from Blue Feather and the others, and soon were out of sight. At the top of the next hill, Johnny stopped and turned his eyes southward to a never-ending expanse of plain. He marveled at the beauty of the river bluffs below. The great ocean of prairie grass seemed to reach forever. His mind drifted back to the times he and Little Boy Horse as small children were playing in the ghostly and unforgiving swamp. It seemed as though it was just a dream, warm in many ways, but in many others an unsettling truth.

Johnny observed Kicking Wind, her smooth cheeks wet with tears of fear and uncertainty. "Don't be afraid, little one. We'll make our way north until we find a safe place. Little Boy Horse will come to us. We'll all be together again. You'll see."

Back at the Triple A Ranch

As the legend of the gold spread across the prairie, the hired hands became increasingly curious about the fortune. In response, Joe would tell them it was just a legend. "We found a few gold coins in the swamp," he would say. "But our money came from a rich aunt in Vicksburg, Mississippi. The rest we have, we made by trading cattle and horses and developing land." He was consistent with this story to both newcomers and veterans, firmly repeating it to halt their inquiries.

"If I hear anyone telling or talking about this fairy tale or spreading such gossip, they will be fired on the spot," he told his employees.

This seemed to work with most of the hands, but for some, curiosity remained unabated. Many a night in the bunkhouse their conversation centered around the lost treasure, and during the day they remained on the lookout for it.

~~~

Nate had hired two families that had been traveling west. Like so many pioneers, they'd discovered that the journey to the gold fields of California was much more arduous than expected. The wives especially had quickly come to appreciate the comforts of the ranch and wanted to settle there. Their husbands, two brothers, John and Wayne Bennis, were close to each other. Both had been degenerate gamblers in St. Joseph, Missouri, and on occasion had gambled everything they had, leaving their wives and children hungry and destitute. But the brothers were good with horses and they were welcomed to stay and work on the ever-busy ranch.

Even as cabins were being planned and built, demand for sleeping quarters seemed always to exceed supply. As a result, John and Wayne slept in the bunkhouse with the hands while the women in their family stayed in the overcrowded cabins. The men spent time on Sundays with their families and for a few weeks, things were going well. Their wives, Judy and Carol Bennis, helped teach the children, and the other women really enjoyed their company.

Both John and Wayne were knowledgeable workers and seemed like honest men. But there was a sneaky aspect to their ways that made O.C. suspicious. More than once John had brought up the subject of the missing gold, and while it had been during casual conversation, O.C was becoming annoyed.

When he confronted John about his curiosity, John
~~~

smiled and said, “Well, it’s an exciting story, and people around the camp are looking for it.”

O.C., being the sly individual that he was, knew that John Bennis was just trying to divert attention in somebody else’s direction. His warning to John was right to the point. “Never ask me about that gold any more, John, or you will be gone from this ranch,” he said firmly. “Make no mistake, it will get you killed, and that’s something I don’t want your pretty wife and those beautiful children to have to go through.” O.C. hoped he got his point across, but he was not really sure.

O.C. was riding the perimeter of the ranch with Nate when he spotted a young Sioux scout on a hill not too far from the boundary. “Nate, you see what I see?” he asked.

“Yeah, I sure do, and almost every day lately I see one or two spying on us. I sure hope they are not planning to steal our horses or cattle.”

“Not them,” smiled O.C. “Those are Running Bear’s scouts. He told me they would be watching. It’s just normal; we are the strangers in their land. They don’t really want to harm anybody. That’s why they let the wagon trains go through all the time.”

It wasn’t too long until Joe and Shorty met them from the other direction.

“Hey, boys, anything unusual go on?” greeted O.C.

“Well, looks like the coyotes got a couple of calves over the hill there,” said Joe. “We better keep a couple of riders up here to try to thin some of those varmints out. We also saw a Sioux scout to the south there.”

“Yeah, we saw him too, and I’ve seen one or two almost every day. I really think something’s up,” frowned Nate.

“Well, I don’t think it’s anything, but if it will ease your mind, Nate, I’ll arrange a meeting with Running Bear,” said O.C.

“O.C., you’re the dandiest old man I’ve ever met. Old Running Bear will tie one of them buffalos to your marbles," smiled Shorty.

"Nah," Nate laughed. "His marbles are probably all shriveled up. But I got to admit, Running Bear might have a hard time doing that."

Joe laughed, "Hell, I guess we'll just stand here all day and talk about somebody's marbles. Mercy sakes alive, let's get to work–last I checked it's not a holiday."

"You know, Joe, you need to take a good swig of Nate's moonshine, and smell the roses," smiled O.C.

"I've tasted Nate's moonshine before, and as I remember, Cindy wouldn't let me in the same bed for three days. Besides that, Pop, there isn't a rose within fifty miles of here!"

"Yeah, I remember, and that's another thing–you're henpecked," laughed O.C. "Nate, you and Shorty go on now. I want to talk to our boss a few minutes."

Nate and Shorty, still laughing, shook their heads and headed back towards the ranch.

Immediately, Joe noticed O.C.'s expression change to a look of concern that he had seen many times before. "What's wrong, Pops?" he asked. "I know you don't really want to go into how henpecked I am."

"Well," said O.C. anxiously, "John Bennis was asking questions about the gold again. I think he's looking for it. I know you think he's a good hand, but I don't trust him. There's just something about that man I can't figure out." O.C. shook his head. "You know, Joe, the place you and I stashed that gold would be really hard to find, and I don't think it will be found, but there's always a chance it could happen if someone were to have too much access."

"The only way it could be found is if Johnny One Horn would tell somebody, and I don't think he even cares. After all, it was his idea to put it in the bottom of that water tank."

"You know," O.C. continued, "if something were to happen to the three of us, I bet no one would find it for years. The tank would have to rust out or be taken apart. Besides that, there's enough to last ten lifetimes under my cabin. I just can't feel easy when I hear the men bringing it up all the time."

"Well, we'll keep an eye on him," Joe assured him. "Let's not let him know we're watching, and just see how it works out. He's a damn good hand with horses, and I hate to lose him as long as we don't have to. I'll tell Shorty and Nate to get with Pete and keep an eye on him. If he's not actually doing anything, Pop, we need to leave him alone. Make no mistake, though, I will take care of it."

That evening Joe and O.C. met with Pete and Shorty and devised a plan to watch John Bennis as much as possible. They would watch him even when he was working with the horses, because he could cover a lot of ground doing that kind of work.

That night, most of the ranch was peaceful and quiet, except for the bunkhouse where the hands were playing cards and sipping whiskey or moonshine from Nate's still.

In the three large cabins where the women and their children lived, Cindy and Marianna were putting all the children down for the night.

As O.C. was coming back from his evening walk to the cemetery by the river, everything seemed normal. Then, when he passed the bunkhouse, he saw Joe going in the front door.

"All you men drinking that moonshine better be ready to work at first light," he bellowed. "Anybody and I mean anybody–that can't do his job will be fired on the spot. Be smart about it, or be gone."

CHAPTER 5

The next morning as the sun came up, Joe walked out onto the porch of his cabin. He stretched and yawned, then turned to go back inside, but dropped his coffee mug. As he reached to get it, he noticed blood everywhere.

"What the hell?" he thought. At his feet lay the decapitated head of one of his prized horses. He strode to the bunkhouse and banged on the door just as Pete was coming back from his morning patrol around the ranch. Inside the bunkhouse the men were up and mostly dressed, drinking their morning coffee.

"What happened here?" Pete yelled when he saw Joe and the bloody horses head. "You men get your horses–we got some outlaws on the ranch!"

Hearing the commotion, O.C. came out of his cabin with his buffalo gun. The ranch hands were quickly gathering their guns and horses.

"Pops, look at this!" wailed Joe. "Who would do a thing like this?"

"See anybody?" O.C. responded.

"No, it was just there, and from the looks of it it's only been there a few hours." explained Joe.

"You boys take a ride around the boundaries of the ranch. Split up and see what you can see," O.C. instructed the hands. Then he turned back to his son. “This ain’t the work of thieves or anything, Joe, this is a warning from the Sioux. I’m not too sure what it means yet, but saddle your horse and let’s take a little ride.”

The two mounted up and O.C. led the way at a slow and cautious pace.

“Where are we going, Pops?” Joe finally questioned. But his father remained silent.

Twenty minutes later they dismounted in front of the Mound of the Sioux.

“Just as I thought, Joe,” said O.C., shaking his head. “Somebody’s been digging in the mound. Running Bear warned us never to trespass there.”

“How do you know it wasn’t the Sioux?” asked Joe. “Maybe they buried somebody.”

O.C. scanned the site carefully.

“I don’t believe it’s a burial ground,” he said. “I think it’s just a sacred place they use to pray to the spirits. Whatever it is, it’s for damn sure they don’t want it messed with. When we get back tell all the women and children never to come here.” He shook his head. “Hell, we might be in over our heads already. Ask everyone if they’ve been here. I’m going to talk to Running Bear. I might be gone all night, and I hope I’ve still got my hair when I get back.”

“I’m going with you, Pops,” protested Joe as he wheeled his horse around.

“No, Joe, I don’t think he’ll try to kill me or anything. I think we’d all be dead by now if that was his intention. I’m hoping it’s just a warning. Go on now, Joe, you’re needed here. I’ll be back when I get back. Don’t sit up and wait. Before I head out, I’ll go to Levi’s and pick up a few days grub and some bullets.”

As they rode back to the ranch Joe argued with O.C. to no avail. O.C. got off his horse at Levi’s. As usual old Levi was sitting in his rocker in front of his soon-to-be store. O.C. gathered things with Levi nagging away at him all the time he was there.

"Old man, you're going to get your scalp tied to one of them sticker trees out there," warned Levi. "They might strip your gonads too. Here, take these two bottles of whisky with you. It goes good with them beans, that is, if you sleep with the wind in the right direction."

O.C. couldn't keep from laughing at old Levi–he was so grouchy, but he was damn funny. "I'll keep an eye on my gonads, Levi," he chuckled. "You do the same."

As he mounted his horse, Old Dan, Levi hobbled up and grabbed O.C.'s hand. The smile had turned into a sad, concerned expression. "You take care, my good friend," he said softly.

O.C. had never seen such a concerned look from Levi before. He smiled and patted his hand. "You too, my old friend. I'll be back soon, and if I'm not, you take care of all the ladies for me."

"You can be sure I will, old man. And if you don't come back, I'll take care of yours, too," he laughed.

"I'm sure you can, Levi. But make sure you don't get mine mixed up with somebody else's. Hell, you can't even see 'em anyway."

They both seemed to get a lot of fun out of trying to best one another. At last, O.C. turned his horse around and started riding up the river's edge. He knew it would get dark before he arrived if he didn't keep a steady pace.

As he rode along the trail O.C.'s thoughts flashed back and forth from the past to the future. He knew Running Bear was a person you didn't want to cross. After he had thought the situation through completely, he realized there was a very good possibility that he would not be coming back.

When he arrived at the place where he had delivered the cattle, O.C. wondered if Running Bear would even show up, or if he would just send his braves to kill him.

As the sun went down in the western sky, O.C. readied

his camp with a fire and laid out his bedroll. It was a clear night and the air was full of the scent of pine and cedar.

He sat back for a while and sipped on a bottle of old Levi's whiskey. He was not much of a drinker anymore, but on this night the fiery liquor acted as a poultice to calm his nerves. He dozed off. After a while, Old Dan grew restless and began to whinny.

O.C. woke with a start and scanned the horizon for any movement in the moonlight. The shadows of scattered clouds crept across the dark ground, while overhead the brightest moon he had ever seen hung in the sky.

When he knelt to stoke the fire, he heard a clear voice from behind. "It is the Moon of the Wolf that you see."

Shaken, O.C. kept his eyes on the fire. He recognized the voice of Running Bear and spoke without turning around.

"Is that what they call it, my friend? I hoped you would be here."

"I see you got my message. Some of my braves wanted to send the head of one of your ranch hands. But I was more kind."

"Well, it was a good horse, my friend. But I need to know a little more about why you made me a gift of his head," O.C. jested as he stood and faced Running Bear.

"The reason I chose the horse was to tell you that the men who work your horses have desecrated our sacred ground," replied the war chief. "It is my thought that they look for the yellow iron. I came by myself tonight, because many of my people would kill you for such a thing. My braves are watching us as we talk, at a distance."

"Are you sure it was them?" O.C. asked.

"Yes, we are sure. We watch the place day and night, and we are certain of what we know. It's the law of our people that they must die for their crime. They must first leave the ranch in two moons or many of your people will die. Some of the young braves are restless to fight the white man."

O.C.'s suspicions were confirmed. He knew Running Bear would not lie about such a grave matter. He pondered how he should deal with the chief.

"I will give you ten more cattle in the fall," offered O.C. "And I will tell the Bennis brothers what a mistake they have made. I'm sure they will never go around the mound again. I give you my word, my friend, and I'll see to it myself."

"I wish it was different," frowned Running Bear. "But it is our law of life, and we will not change our thoughts. They have the greed of the yellow rock and they will not stop. They must die."

"But they have children, Running Bear. What will be done with them?" pleaded O.C.

"They will not be harmed. But the men called Bennis must die, and the things they took from the sacred hill must be returned. No more about this."

Running Bear paused. "I will still demand ten more cattle in the fall to help feed our people, and from this day on, anyone caught north of the river will die. You keep the entire ranch south of the river, or our peace will be broken and all will die. Tell the great One Horn I send him my friendship, and look forward to seeing him when he returns. It is a very good thing to return Kicking Wind to her family as we agreed. I'm sure she is in very good hands."

"Build a fire the night before the men called Bennis leave the ranch," he finished. "We will give them until morning before we track them down."

With the matter settled, Running Bear turned and mounted his pony. Without saying another word he gave the sign from the chest and slowly rode north.

About one hundred braves came out of the darkness and followed him. O.C. had never known they were there. The bright moon was reflected off the dust rising from their ponies' hooves as they disappeared into the night.

When the Sioux had gone, O.C. was frustrated and angry. He threw his whiskey bottle against the rocks by the fire. The following morning, he arose at sunup, cinched the saddle on Old Dan's back, and began a slow ride back to the ranch. He wondered how he would tell Joe and the Bennis brothers of Running Bear's dreadful decision. There seemed to be no way out for the Bennis brothers.

CHAPTER 6

The Ranch

As he arrived at the ranch, O.C. saw Joe on the hilltop roping a steer. He walked Old Dan to the top slowly so he wouldn't spook the cattle.

"Hey, Pops," Joe greeted anxiously. "How did things go? Did you find Running Bear? I've been worried sick about you. I wish you weren't so damn bullheaded."

"Running Bear found me in the middle of the night," answered O.C. "He said them Bennis brothers have been digging in their sacred hill. You know, Joe, I've never trusted John Bennis. Wayne seems to just go along with everything he says, but John's kind of sneaky."

"Well, did you tell Running Bear that we would make sure it never happens again?"

"Yeah, I told him, Joe, and even offered more cattle as a guarantee. But he wouldn't have it. He says they have to leave the ranch in two days, Joe, or he'll attack the ranch."

"Attack the ranch? Hell, we can't have that. We've got all kinds of children there. They will just have to leave and send for their families later. We don't have a choice."

"Running Bear says they must die for their crimes. They will probably be killed the first day they leave."

"Die? yelled Joe. "For digging in a dirt hill?"

"He said they took things from the hill, Joe. Those things have to be returned. It's their law, and nothing I said made a difference. They will have to leave or everybody here will be killed."

The two men rode their horses down the hill toward the corral where John and Wayne Bennis were busy shoeing horses.

"Hey Joe, O.C.," smiled John Bennis. "Kind of a nice day, huh, boys?"

"Yeah, it is a fine day, John, but I've got some bad news for you and Wayne," said O.C.

"Oh? What's that?" Wayne frowned.

"Seems that some of Running Bear's people seen you digging in their sacred hill," sighed Joe. "You know I gave you strict orders not even to go around that place, and now the whole ranch is in danger. I can't believe you two would ever do that, especially having children like you do!"

"Well, we won't lie to you," said John. "We were just looking, and all we took was a little handful of beads to give to the kids. Hell, we'll just put them back."

"It's too late for that, John," O.C. said. "Besides, I think you were looking for that gold I heard you talking about. I told you it was just a fairy tale made up by a bunch of people that don't have anything else to do."

"So, what if we were? Everybody in the camp knows about the gold, and we are no exception!" retorted John Bennis. He reached for the shotgun leaning up against the corral post, unaware that Pete, upon hearing the argument escalate, had walked up behind him.

"I wouldn't do that, John," warned Pete. "I don't want to tell your wife I shot you today."

"Hell, Pete, it was just a handful of beads," implored John, "and everybody's going crazy, me included, I guess. I'll put them back. I just thought the kids could have them to play with. Those Indians–hell, let's just let them know that they can't boss us around anyway."

"Those Indians have about a hundred warriors in that party," said O.C. "They're all skillful hunters, and a lot of them are carrying rifles. And they damn well know how to use them."

"I just came from a meeting with Running Bear," he went on. "He didn't give us much choice. He could kill us all, or you two can leave the ranch before the second moon. That's tomorrow night."

"I hate to lay this on you two, but you boys did break their law, and we can't see these women and kids killed just because of you. I kind of like you and your brother there, but if you leave as fast as you can they won't come after you until maybe day after tomorrow. You can leave tonight and try to get as far away as you can. Your folks can stay here until you can send for them. I'd say get to the next town, maybe Abilene. We'll take care of your family."

Wayne started breaking out in tears, as he chokingly spoke. "You know they'll be watching our every move, O.C. And they'll kill us as soon as we leave."

Deeply affected by the terrible dilemma, O.C. wiped a tear from his own eye. "Like I said, boys, I hate to bring this on you, but there's nothing I, or anybody else, can do. You two will have to leave tonight, and without any help from us. If they see us trying to help you then our word will be broken."

O.C. dismounted and offered his hand. "I know you men didn't mean it to work out this way, but it just did," he said sincerely. Pete and Joe also dismounted and the men shook hands all around.

"Well, so long, boys," said Joe quietly. "Hell, maybe we'll see you in Abilene and play a good game of cards one day. Just stay out of the prairie as much as you can, stick close to the bottom of the hills, and, whatever you do, don't build any fires!" Joe mounted his horse, turned, and slowly rode toward the river.

As O.C. mounted Old Dan, he looked at the men with

sorrow in his eyes. "I truly wish this didn't have to happen, boys; you two better go say your goodbyes. We won't be there so I'll just say so long and good luck. Maybe things will change one of these days and you can come back."

With that he and Pete turned their horses around and followed Joe toward the river.

When the two reached the riverbank, Joe was sitting on his horse staring pensively at the water. Behind them in the distance the Bennis brothers walked slowly toward the bunkhouse.

"You know," said Joe, "those two are as good as dead right now. Those scouts watch us all the time. Hell, we might as well have killed them ourselves.

"Well, maybe not," Pete said. "It may just be a firm warning. But I'm sure if it's not, the outcome won't be good."

The sun was lingering in the western sky by now and the afternoon breeze brought the scent of supper cooking.

"Hell, look there," said Pete. "Cindy's got a fire going. That gal's always cooking something on that fire pit. Let's go see what it is. We might as well relax a little, but it's hard knowing what John and Wayne are going to face."

Nate was riding up from the river with a few of the hired hands, and waved from a distance as they rode past.

"Wonder what Nate's doing there," asked O.C. "Well, I see some dark clouds to the southwest. I think he's probably going to check fences around the perimeter. I tell you, that Nate's a fine ranch foreman not taking anything away from you, Pete–you both are the best at what you do. We couldn't do without you."

"Well then, I guess I'll be demanding a raise in the fall," laughed Pete.

"Well, I wouldn't go that far," laughed O. C.

As they approached the ranch, Bessie was picking a few wildflowers by the trail. O.C. reached and swung her up behind him. She giggled as O.C. galloped Old Dan into the picnic area in a big cloud of dust. They dismounted and he tied Old Dan to the water tank.

Immediately Cindy walked up and handed the men two large towels. “Get to work,” she ordered. “I’m not going to clean up all this dust you just made!” She loved her father-in-law, and was always teasing him, but was very serious about cleaning the tables. She turned away to keep him from seeing her smile.

O.C. pointed to the southwest. “Look there, Cindy, there’s rain coming! It will all wash off in a jiffy.”

“Not unless it blows sideways,” she yelled back. “Besides, I never saw it rain under a roof.”

“Hell, Bessie,” laughed O.C. “She’s trying to make a maid out of me.” Nevertheless, he good-naturedly got to work with his towel.

The hands had built several gazebos in their picnic area. It was there that supper was served each evening, and breakfast every morning. In the case of inclement weather, meals were pre-pared and served in the large cookhouse. The men had also built a large and growing Community Center.

Finally finished with the cleanup, O.C. grabbed a bottle of wine and his jug of corn whiskey, wiped the dust from his clothing and sat down with Bessie at a table beneath one of the gazebos.

From where they sat, Bessie could see John and Wayne Bennis packing their saddlebags in front of their houses down the street. She noticed that their wives appeared anxious, even frantic. Then she watched as Judy and Carol started walking toward her and O.C. “Looks like we’re going to have company, O.C.,” she remarked.

“Yeah, I know,” he responded. “And I’m afraid this ain’t gonna be pretty”.

When the two women reached the gazebo, Judy Bennis addressed them bitterly. “I can’t believe you, O.C.,” she snapped. “Sending our husbands away just for digging a few little beads in a damn dirt hill! They've worked hard for the ranch, and now you're kicking us out like we're some kind of trash."

"It's not just an ordinary dirt hill, Mrs. Bennis," O.C. answered carefully. "There may be Sioux chiefs buried there, and both of your husbands knew that. They were told when they hired on never to go near there. It's an agreement that Running Bear made with us when we settled on this land. I'm sorry–we all like your husbands, but they broke the rules, the law is the law, and we all must go by it."

With her voice trembling and her face pale with fright, Carol Bennis said, "Well, it's not the first time our husbands have broken laws or rules, but if they have to leave, then we and the kids are going with them."

With that, O.C. stood up and waved to Pete and the hands by the water tower.

Pete immediately walked from the tower, drying himself off along the way. "What's up, boss? Something wrong?"

"I want you and the boys to lock Miss Judy and Miss Carol in the bunkhouse," ordered O.C.

"Lock us up? What for, O.C.?" the women cried. "You can't just lock us up! We didn't do anything!"

"Well, Mrs. Bennis, I might be saving your lives," said O.C. firmly. "This is more serious than you think, and I've got to do what I've got to do."

Resigned, the two wives turned and started towards the bunkhouse. Pete waved and six more ranch hands came running. Pete ran past the women to where John and Wayne Bennis were cinching their horses. He drew his guns and asked them to step aside. "Are there any more guns in the bunkhouse, boys?" he demanded.

John Bennis answered that there was a shotgun just inside the door.

Pete motioned for the hands to get it. "They're determined to go with you, boys, and we can't let them do that," Pete informed the husbands. "You need to tell them why, and then saddle up and leave. It will just get worse if you stay any longer."

"So why can't you take us with you?" Carol wailed tearfully. "You can't just leave us here with the kids."

"It's not like that, sweetie," John said in a broken voice. "The Indians said we have to die for taking those beads."

O.C. walked into the bunkhouse. "I'm sorry," he said to the two women. "But if your husbands can make it to Abilene, they can send back for you. We will see they have the money to do that."

O.C. turned to Wayne and handed him a packet of money. "There's about one hundred dollars there. I figure about six month's wages," he said. "Maybe it will help."

John looked down from his horse with tears in his eyes. His children were watching through the window. He and Wayne leaned down from their horses and gave their wives a final hug. By now, both Judy and Carol had given up on the idea of going along.

"Thank you, O.C.," sobbed Carol Bennis. "We didn't know. You won't have any more trouble from us. Besides, I'm sick of running." John Bennis had a strange expression on his face at her words, but it was obvious he knew what she was talking about.

Both O.C. and Pete stared at the ground to avoid eye contact. Neither wanted to share in her grief.

Finally, Pete looked up and extended his hand to John.

"Nothing stays the same for always, John. If this blows over, you both are welcome back. I'm gonna have a hard time replacing you boys."

"Thanks, Pete," John replied with a melancholy smile. "You and the boys try to keep that hair on your head and maybe things will work out."

"Let's go, Pete," said O.C. "Let them say a last goodbye to their people."

As the two men walked back to the picnic grounds, Pete

turned around and watched Carol Bennis walk into the bunkhouse and shut the door. Judy Bennis held her husband's hand as he said goodbye to the two boys.

"Did you see that, O.C.?" asked Pete. "Carol Bennis just turned and walked into the house like John was just leaving for a few minutes."

"Well, Pete, she's been left a lot of times before. To her it's just one more time. John's always been a rover and a gambler, not to mention other things we probably will never know about." Abruptly, his focus shifted and his step quickened. "Look there–that storm's getting closer! We better help Cindy get this courtyard ready for it!"

"Don't you think them boys should wait till that storm rumbles through here before leaving, O.C.? Looks like it might get pretty damn rough."

"They can use the cover of the storm to travel," said O.C. "At least that's what I would do. They got a hell of a lot more to worry about than a storm, anyway. Let's just get busy, Pete, and let it be what it is. They brought this on themselves. Now they've got to deal with it."

Pete looked back once more as the wind started blowing down the road from the cabin. Through the swirling dust he could see John and Wayne riding southeast. Overhead, huge but scattered rain drops started stirring up more dust. He saw Nate with several other ranch hands riding to the south to try to keep the cattle from scattering.

To the north across the river two Sioux braves watched from a cave on the hillside. Silently they began to apply their war paint of death. They were biding their time, waiting for a break in the storm.

~ ~ ~

The Bennis brothers were draped in slickers and moving slow, unaware that they were being watched. As the sky continued to darken, they began to look for shelter.

“Let’s find a cave or a hole in the rocks, John,” Wayne yelled above the torrent. “This lightning and thunder is as bad as I’ve ever seen. We need to get out of it. I doubt if anybody is around for miles, especially in the storm.”

It took them an hour to find a safe outcropping of rocks with an overhanging ledge.

“This will do,” said Wayne as they unsaddled their horses. “Hell, this rain ain’t gonna stop!”

There were a few small trees around the opening near the overhang where they tied their horses. With some dried brush from the front of the shed-like sanctuary, John quickly built a small fire.

The two fugitives warmed their chilled bodies as the fire flickered from the rocks above. Then they broke out a bottle of Nate’s moonshine and began passing it back and forth.

“Feels good,” John smiled as the moonshine began to take effect. “Hell, Wayne, like I said, ain’t nobody within ten miles of here. I’m going to get a little sleep.”

“Well, I don’t think we should, John,” warned Wayne. “The Sioux are used to being in bad weather–they kind of like it. And remember what Joe said about the fire?”

“Hell, how does he know? He ain’t been around near as long as us–he’s just blabbing!”

“Well, he is half Indian and I guess he knows a few things about it. You know he was raised with them.”

By now John was drunk from the potent moonshine and had fallen asleep with his head on his saddle. Wayne covered him with a blanket, all the time shaking his head. He thought of how many times he had listened to his brother and how many times his brother had been wrong.

“I ought to just go on,” he thought. Thoughts about his family and how he would miss them were running through his mind. He also knew John’s wife Carol was fed up with him and things between them had been on a downhill slide for many years.

The rain seemed never-ending. Still wet and scared, Wayne leaned against the rocks and stared out from beneath the ledge. His eyes wandered to the trees where the horses were tied. Through the driving rain he could see that they were gone!

He knew at once what had happened. He leapt to his feet in horror. Then, like apparitions, two Sioux braves materialized from the dark.

Their faces were painted white and their knives were drawn. Wayne instinctively looked across the clearing to where he'd left his weapons and knew at once that they were beyond reach. Frozen with fear, and with no place to run, he dropped to his knees and softly began to pray.

At that moment an enormous bolt of lightning flashed and a clap of thunder rolled across the sodden prairie below and up the hillside with such force that the ground literally shook.

Seeing this as his only chance, Wayne rose to his feet and sprinted into the dark wall of rain. He was clad in his long-handled underwear and barefoot. Immune to the pain of the blackberry vines that tore at his flesh and bloodied his feet, he ran blindly through the night, leaving his brother John behind.

CHAPTER 7

The North Platte Basin

For two days, Little Boy Horse rode back and forth along the north bank of the North Platte River searching for tracks of horses coming out of the river.

After two days he noticed a body floating face down in the current. Horse spurred his mount into the water. When he arrived beside the lifeless form, he realized it was that of a young girl. He gently carried her ashore and lay her down in the soft grass of the riverbank.

"She must be the missing girl from the Mormon wagons," he thought. "How terribly she has been beaten and tortured!"

Horse slowly collected a pile of driftwood and formed a makeshift funeral pyre. He respectfully placed the girl on the pyre and set it afire. The crematory flames and smoke rose into the blue sky. Horse offered a prayer to the Great Spirit for her soul.

"This is the work of a true devil," he said to himself. "And he is following Johnny and Wind. If I am to catch this devil, I must follow them also. This body was not too badly decomposed and that means that I am between them at this point. I'll double back, find their tracks, and wait for them." Within two hours Horse had found their tracks, including those of the wolf, and began to follow their trail.

He decided against catching up to them for fear that doing so would put BoJack too close to them. He knew that BoJack always traveled at night. Horse planned to get him as he was trying to track them at night. He reasoned that the outlaw would need some sort of light. But what would the villain use? Then he remembered something he had learned in his childhood. O.C. and the boys once had a dog that could track anything alive, day or night.

He had never considered that BoJack might have such an animal, but if he did, it would surely explain why he had never been caught.

He must have a dwelling somewhere in these plains, Horse mused. If he did, it was probably close to the river and it made sense that he would have a dog or two. With that in mind, Horse decided to set a trap along the tracks of Johnny and Kicking Wind.

As Horse scanned the trail, he noticed some cliffs with an overhang that he could get above. He dared not get any closer to Johnny's trail because BoJack's dog would pick up his scent. He would have to stay as far away as he could and set a place for his attack.

Horse tread lightly in the narrows of the rocks, keeping upwind so as not to alert the dog. He found a carcass of an antelope in the tall grass alongside the cliff, cut the rotting hide from the remains and wrapped it around his feet. Then he rode the horse about a half mile away and hobbled him to a large bush. As he walked back through thc tall grass, he could smell the hide from the antelope and knew the dog would also. He also considered that a tracking dog would ignore most other scents except the one he had been told to track.

As he moved stealthily along, Horse sensed with greater certainty that BoJack had a hideout along the river. There had to be a place where he kept items with Kicking Wind's scent. The dog would surely know this scent. He found it strange that Wind had never mentioned the dog.

Now Horse stretched a rope anchored around a large rock down the steep cliff from the trail. When BoJack approached, he could jerk the rope and trip him, sending him down the steep twenty- or thirty-foot cliff.

If he could incapacitate the villain in this way, the large Indian reasoned, he might be able to get a killing shot off, or attack him with his knife. The unknown factor was the dog that would undoubtedly attack. He would have to worry about that when it happened, just like he had done with the panthers back in the swamp. In those confrontations one would let the black cat jump into the blade and hope that it would deter the animal. This did not always work, though, and several of his tribesmen had been killed.

With his plans made and his trap set, Horse climbed to the top of the rock overhang and patiently waited for his quarry. He watched the sun set in the west, majestic in purple. How beautiful it truly was! The river off in the distance, and the prairie grass to the south waving in the wind, were awe-inspiring. “This will be a good place to die if I don’t succeed,” he prayed to the Great Spirit.

There was a late moon rising, and it had been dark for several hours. Only a three-quarter moon, but it shone bright against the prairie grass flowing in the breeze. To the south and down the trail he heard a few prairie chickens disturbed by what he thought could be BoJack.

~ ~ ~

As the evil mountain man moved slowly up the hill toward the trap he had laid, Little Boy Horse silently raised his head. He spotted the hound in front of BoJack. “I knew it to be true,” he thought.

Horse watched as the hound methodically sniffed the trail in a sweeping pattern. The dog was well trained.

Warily the animal approached the rope, sniffed several times, then growled. Its eyes moved along the rope until it was looking straight at the outcropping where Little Boy Horse hid.

The Indian flattened his body against the rocks. Then he heard the unmistakable sound of BoJack's massive buffalo gun being cocked. He had no way of knowing BoJack's position relative to the rope, so he quickly raised his head for a quick look, but even that was too much. BoJack saw him and fired a booming shot while simultaneously freeing the hound.

The dog bolted forward with a loud howl as Horse stood up and jerked the rope as hard as he could. BoJack fell awkwardly and with a curse, tumbled down the cliff.

By now the dog had ascended the cliff and attacked Horse from behind. Man and beast rolled down the cliff in a death embrace. At last, Horse managed to draw his long knife and struck the vicious animal a solid blow. With a loud yelp the dog ran off into the dark prairie.

Horse could tell BoJack was badly hurt from the fall. He had thrown down the single shot buffalo gun and pulled out both his revolvers. Shooting wildly in the dark, the crazed man was desperately trying to retaliate.

Horse crouched, hidden behind a rock, and wiped the long knife in the rotten hide he had around his feet. Then in a single movement, he stepped from behind the rock, sized up BoJack's position, and skillfully flung the blade. It was a move that only Little Boy Horse could execute, and true to form, he hit his mark. The razor-sharp blade sliced into BoJack's upper thigh.

The outlaw responded with a scream, shooting blindly in Horse's direction. Horse ducked, but not before a stray bullet grazed his head. The force of the bullet knocked him off his feet and he fell into the wild brush behind a giant rock.

~ ~ ~

The bright sunrise and the damp morning dew awoke Little Boy Horse to the reality of a throbbing headache. He frowned into the sun, disoriented for a moment. Then he took off his neckerchief and tied it around his head.

He looked in the direction he last seen BoJack. Nothing was there but the blood-spattered buffalo gun lying abandoned in the dirt. In fact, everywhere he looked there was blood. But there was no BoJack. He picked up his bloody knife and nodded with satisfaction. He had hit his mark. And since he had wiped the knife on the filthy hides he'd used for foot covers, there was a good chance he'd infected the outlaw as well.

Little Boy Horse walked over to his pony, opened his canteen, and washed the wound on his head. Patting the horse, he mounted and rode back to the overhang to look for BoJack's trail.

Along with the headache, Horse's mind was filled with doubt. "Maybe BoJack can't be killed," he thought. "Maybe the legend is true. Maybe I'm fighting something that can't die."

Horse rode south on the rocky cliffs toward the Platte River. It was an easy trail to follow–BoJack had left blood spots everywhere. But when he reached the river, Horse grew more cautious. He knew that the old mountain man was savvy. Alongside the river Horse would be exposed.

CHAPTER 8

BoJack stuck to the water's edge to prevent his blood from dripping onto the rocks. He suspected he was being followed but had no way to determine how many were on his trail. Still, he was confident. He knew this country intimately and was sly.

Before long, he came upon another mountain man skinning a beaver by the river. BoJack knew the man and called out his name.

"Red Tom," he yelled, "Can you give me a hand?

Red Tom was a friendly man. He'd met BoJack at one of the annual rendezvous the mountain men held. At the time, BoJack had gone by the name of Quick Bob.

"Red, I need your help, my friend," said BoJack as Red Tom approached. "I was attacked by Indians."

Red Tom knelt and quickly trimmed away BoJack's buffalo hide trousers to expose the wound. "Hey, Bob, this went clean through your leg," he frowned.

"Yeah, it was a hell of a long knife," moaned Jack.

Red Tom pulled a bottle of whiskey from his poke. "This is going to hurt, Quick Bob," he said. "But it's the best I can do." With that he poured the whiskey on the wound and started cleaning it. When the wound was cleaned to his satisfaction, he heated his skinning knife on the fire to sterilize it. "You know, my friend. I'm going to have to sear this wound to keep the rot from getting in it. But it might already be too late," he warned.

All BoJack could do was sit and shake his head in pain.

When the knife was white hot, Red Tom applied it to the wound.

Old BoJack bit a piece of leather and moaned. He knew if he screamed somebody down the river might hear it, as he knew he was being hunted.

"What happened to the Indians?" asked Red Tom. "I've seen a few, but they acted just like I wasn't here. I did talk to a hunting party a few days ago. They said they were looking for a man called BoJack. I told them I never knew anybody by that name, but I have heard that he was a cold-blooded killer. Do you know anybody named BoJack?"

"Not me," moaned Bo. "The Indians thought I was somebody else, I guess. I shot at a bunch, but I don't know how many I got."

At that point, BoJack realized that Red Tom suspected him. His eyes narrowed as Red Tom walked back to the horse to put the whiskey away.

"You know, Quick Bob," remarked Red Tom slowly, "I never knew the Sioux to make a mistake like that."

As he spoke, he reached deep into the poke on his horse and grasped his .44. He realized BoJack was the man the Indians had told him about, and that he had killed several wagons full of innocent people. His plan was to get the jump on BoJack before the outlaw could react.

To do so required turning his back. It was the wrong thing to do. BoJack picked up a large piece of driftwood and slammed it into Red Tom's head. The mountain man dropped to the ground unconscious.

The killer dragged Red Tom to the river's edge and pushed his head beneath the water. Red Tom put up a stout struggle, but he was finally overcome. BoJack turned the dead man over, stripped the body, and swapped his clothes for those of the dead man. Then he rammed his knife into

Red Tom's upper leg and let the body drift off in the current.

Satisfied, BoJack walked to the horse and pulled the whiskey from the poke. He took a hard pull, then painfully crawled into the saddle. He rode down the river in the shallows to hide his tracks, counting on the fact that whoever had attacked him the night before had not seen his face. With a little luck, he mused, his pursuer would mistake the body floating in the river for him. BoJack smiled grimly to himself and rode on.

~ ~ ~

Little Boy Horse, who was carefully watching the riverbank from the south side, noticed a body swirling in some driftwood in the river below. He rode out to the lifeless form, dragged it by the feet to the shore, and turned it over.

His mind was racing. Could this be the devil he was looking for? The body had a huge bruise to the side of his head, and, as he looked closer, he saw a knife wound in the upper leg. He didn't exactly know where his knife had hit BoJack. This must be the man. The bruise to the head must be from the fall, and he had probably bled to death.

"I'll leave him here for all to see," he thought. He dragged the body to a nearby oak tree, hoisted it up feet first, and tied it off. Feeling relieved that his job was finished, he would now return to Johnny One Horn and Kicking Wind and complete their journey north. "BoJack is dead," he thought as he gave praise to the Great Spirit.

~ ~ ~

BoJack rode Red Tom's stolen horse to the point of exhaustion. Finally, he reached the hidden cabin he had used for many years. Really, to call the structure a cabin was generous. In fact, it was just a lean-to at the mouth of a cave. Inside were several dog cages, one woman, and three children.

He started yelling from the moment he arrived at the entrance. The sound of his voice terrified the two little girls who ran and hid.

A crippled elderly woman limped from the shack with the help of a walking stick. She was the outlaw's mother. She watched as her exhausted son fell off the staggering horse.

The old woman stood over Bo's prostrate form and noted his heavy bleeding. She knelt and stroked his hair. "What have you done this time, my son?" she asked. She yelled over her shoulder at the boy to bring her a bucket of water and a rag.

The boy brought the bucket and slammed it down beside the pair. "Why does he always come back, ma?" he whined. "Is he gonna get well and beat you and the girls, and me if he can catch me?"

"Shut up, Zack," snapped the woman. "Help me, boy–help me get your daddy into the house."

Together the two half-carried, half-dragged the limp form to the shelter of the shack. It was late afternoon and a slight rain, then a deep clap of thunder rumbled down the canyon.

The old woman gently removed her son's clothing and carefully cleaned his wounds. BoJack slipped in and out of lucidity.

"Is he going to live, Grandma Wicky?" asked Zack.

"I don't know," she replied. "But if he's got the rot, he might lose this leg."

"Why couldn't he just stay gone?" remarked Zack bitterly. "All he's ever done is beat us and stay drunk. He's crazy, Grandma Wicky! Maybe this time he'll kill us all, like he did my Ma."

"That was an accident, Zack," snapped the old woman.

"Your mother fell from the cliff."

"Well, that's what he said, but I don't believe him. I think he killed her."

Wicky stared at BoJack and then her eyes drifted to the dirt floor. Then she started babbling a sing-song chant.

Zack looked at her and shook his head. Then he walked over and hugged his sisters. He loved the girls and knew that, with BoJack back, he would have to watch over them all the time.

The smallest girl was Tina and she was terrified of BoJack. The outlaw had taken the girls from travelers a year or so before. There was no doubt in Zack's mind that he had killed their family. He dared not ask for fear of what BoJack would do to him.

Zack thought of BoJack as a collector of people. And if those people were not to his liking or would not submit to his will, they would disappear, never to be seen again.

He knew Wicky lost her mind at times and blanked out all the things she didn't want to know.

The fire flickered against the wall of the old cabin. BoJack moaned with pain as the rain and storm howled outside.

The small girls got into their makeshift beds and snuggled beneath their buffalo hides. Old Wicky continued to chant and stroke BoJack's head, rocking back and forth as if in a trance. Young Zack stared blankly out the open window.

Below the bluff, the river was rising.

CHAPTER 9

Back at the Ranch

Bessie, , Cindy, and Amy kept busy teaching the students in the new schoolhouse. The children were learning at a very fast pace, much faster than Cindy and Amy had thought they were capable of.

Joe's and Cindy's sons, Carl and Earl, were busy whispering in the corner. Amy sternly reprimanded the boys and they quieted down. But not for long.

"I've told you two for the last time," Cindy finally said. "It's too late today, but tomorrow you two will have to clean the building, while the rest of the class gets to paint."

Carl and Earl looked at each other, then sat down glumly and remained quiet until Cindy dismissed the class. Then the boys ran past her in a huge hurry and made their way to the courtyard where they grabbed their fishing poles.

They scurried past the school and headed to the river. They knew that O.C. and Jack Tunnie would be there in the afternoon. They raced to see which one could better the other, and when they arrived Jack and O.C. were putting a large catfish on a stringer.

"You boys slow down a little–you might fall in the river," laughed O.C. "Then a big old snake might bite your peanut off!"

"Hell, O.C.," Jack smiled, "I wish I could still run that

fast. Mercy, those boys can run!"

"Well, I used to be fast," said O.C. "But you never were, Jack."

"Hell, yeah, I was fast," insisted Jack. "Just not fast enough to catch some of them fillies I used to chase. You know, them gals got the legs for it."

"That's not the idea, Jack–you want them chasing you!" O.C. grinned as he took a swig of moonshine. "You see, Jack," he went on, "if you chase them you just ain't gonna get 'em. You got to make them think you ain't interested."

Both men laughed, knowing that neither of them would get in the last word.

"What would you know about any of that?" teased Jack. "Hell, you were married all those years to Martha!"

"Well, I was twenty-five before I got married," said O.C. "and never regretted it. By that time, I felt I'd been around the neighborhood a few times." He shifted his attention to his grandsons. "Hey, look at them boys drifting that line," he remarked. "They're really good at that. Johnny One Horn has taught them well."

Jack leaned back lazily, watching the eager youngsters. "Hey, boys, what you working so hard at that fishing for? You're supposed to take it easy when you fish."

"Earl Stockman said whoever catches the most catfish for him this week gets a knife he will make for the winner," yelled back Earl.

Just then Carl yelled at Earl to get out of his way. The brothers fought a lot and both had quick tempers, but they got over things fast as brothers usually do, and were mostly inseparable.

"I'll be danged if that old mountain man didn't trick them boys into catching his fish for him again," grinned O.C. "I see he's putting together a still in that shed he built."

"Well," laughed Jack Tunnie, "I saw Rose dash a bucket of water on his old hide before. He better slow down on all that drinking. You know, the two were made for each other, I guess. He sure is an ornery old goat."

"Yeah, but the old boy sure has a good heart. We seen that down in Texas," replied O.C.

"We sure did," said Jack, staring at the ground in front of him. "He risked his life many times to save them women and kids. He's a hell of a good man. You know, O.C., we're lucky to even be alive–that was one hell of a trip."

"Yeah, but the Lord was with us, Jack, or we would have never made it. Look there–Carl's got a big flathead on his line!"

The fish was huge and Carl was struggling to get footing in the sand. The river had many flatheads in it–some grew to a hundred pounds, and more. They were fierce fighters and were seldom caught because they could easily break a line or straighten a hook. Carl's was a fierce one and the boy fought very gamely. Jack stepped forward to help but O.C. waved him off.

"Let's just see how he does, Jack."

"Yeah, OK, but that's a big one."

Finally, Carl yelled for Earl to help him. Earl got hold of the line and both boys struggled on the sand bar. Joe had brought a young black dog from town on one of his cattle buying trips, and now the dog was barking with excitement as he watched the big fish pulling the boys closer and closer to the water's edge.

Just about the time the boys had the big fish to the shore, it snapped the line at the hook.

Earl just laughed, but Carl took it very personally. His head down, he threw his fishing pole to the ground in disgust. "Damn, Damn, Dammit!" he yelled as he started back to the ranch house.

"You better stop that cussing Carl," laughed O.C. "Why, Jack here will tell your dad for sure."

"Me?" Jack smiled. "Why would I?"

"Well, I don't want him mad at me, and better you than

me."

"You're the dandiest feller I've ever met, O.C.!"

"Yeah, but pay attention while you can, Jack–I won't always be around for you to watch and learn from."

Jack just shook his head, smiling. "Well, that was a hell of a fish," he declared. "I don't know if I've ever seen one that big or not."

O.C. stood up and watched as Carl stalked back toward the ranch house. "You know, Jack, that boy's got a heck of a temper. I'll bet he don't ever give up too easy. He's a lot like his dad."

"Yeah, and like another old man I know," laughed Jack.

The Next Morning

Joe was up at sunrise with a pot of coffee steaming on the wood stove. As he looked out the window, he could see Carl fumbling around with some of the fishing poles. "Carl," he yelled, opening the window, "I need you to bottle-feed those orphan calves this morning, and then you have school today."

"I know, but I'll be back before breakfast," hollered the boy. "I just have to do something first."

"You better be or your mother will tan that hide of yours." Joe shook his head. "I wonder what he's up to?" he thought.

Just then Cindy walked up behind him. She had heard the conversation and was also curious. "He's headed to old Earl Stockman's place–probably has some questions for him," she mused. "Well, if I have to go looking for him, he's going to have to scrub floors for a week!"

"He said he'd be back before breakfast," answered Joe. "Let's just see if he can keep his word."

"OK." Cindy smiled and kissed Joe on the cheek. "He's a lot like his daddy, though."

~ ~ ~

Carl ran around Earl's cabin. Earl was outside sharpening his long knife.

"What do you want there, my little friend?" greeted the gruff old prairie man "I don't see you in this kind of hurry very often."

"Earl, I hooked the biggest catfish you ever saw, and he straightened my hook and got away!" responded Carl breathlessly. "I want to know how you catch 'em, Earl!"

"You talk about the big whiskered fish by the willows," smiled Earl. "I often see them there when the sun gets low in the sky. We had those in the river where I grew up. They're very hard to catch. The first thing, Carl, is that you need a big hook, and some real strong line. It has to be a lot stronger that that stuff you're using. Get the hook and line from old Levi–he uses that same line and sets them in the river. He tries to catch the big fish, but he can't. I know what he's doing wrong, but I don't tell him."

"Why don't you tell him, Earl?" asked Carl. "He loves to eat catfish."

"If I told him, he would catch them all, and they take years to grow big," answered Earl, laughing. "He catches a few smaller ones, and I always laugh at him. I will show you, my little friend, but don't you show anybody else!"

Old Earl grinned. He enjoyed playing games with Carl. He seemed so much like his own brother Cody. Earl and Cody had grown up near the Missouri River, and they had been very close.

Earl could hear Cindy calling for the boy now, and told Carl to meet him at the river when the sun got low.

"I will!" Carl yelled as he ran to answer his mother's call.

Earl watched as Carl scurried back to the family cabin. His imagination drifted to his brother, young Cody, and their life by the river. He marveled at how much this boy

Carl reminded him of the brother gone forever. He shook his head and wiped a tear from his eyes. It was a show of emotion rarely seen, and he wasn't going to let anyone see it now, either.

CHAPTER 10

That afternoon when Carl had finished all his chores, he quickly headed for the willow trees by the bend in the river.

Earl Stockman had arrived a few minutes earlier and was kneeling beneath the willow trees, which reached down to touch the crystal-clear water. He signaled Carl to approach quietly, then pointed out the big flatheads cruising around in the swirling current. "There they are," he said, "but they can see you and they're real spooky. See the biggest one? I call him Fat Boy. I sit and watch him chase the perch in the rocks close to the bank. Nobody will probably ever catch Fat Boy–he's too big."

"I'm going to catch him, Earl," declared Carl. "I'm going to catch him if it takes forever."

Earl observed his young friend as he stood and watched the fish. "Well, if you do, Carl, you'll be the best."

"I have to get back, my little friend," he went on. "But I have shown you, and now it's up to you."

Earl mounted his horse Poky and started back toward the ranch. His dog, Old Tuff, sneered at Carl's little black dog and slowly followed the horse.

"Tuffy, you're getting so grouchy in your old age, you remind me of Old Levi," teased Earl. The old dog just growled a little to let him know he heard him, plodding along at its own pace behind him.

As Earl passed the sacred hill, he noticed something different standing at its foot. When he got closer, he saw that it was a decorated ceremonial spear. A bloody scalp hung from the top. Cautiously, he looked around at his surroundings. O.C. and Jack had already called it a day at the river. He could see them sitting in the picnic grounds playing cards. He turned from the spear and trotted Poky back toward the willows. He dared not touch the spear–the Sioux Scouts could be watching from the cliffs above the river. Back at the river, he beckoned for Carl to come to him. Carl knew the signs of danger Earl and Johnny One Horn had often taught him, and obeyed immediately. Earl used one hand to swing the boy up behind him and then rode to the ranch.

"What's wrong, Earl?" asked the boy.

"Nothing yet, my little friend. I just think you should get away from the river for now," answered Earl.

Earl rode back to the picnic ground where he knew O.C. and Jack would be sitting with Bessie and Amy. He called O.C. and Jack over, then helped Carl dismount and told the boy he'd better stay home the rest of the day. Carl was not too happy about this and scuffled off, kicking dirt in the air. His trust in Earl was strong, but he would miss his chance to catch the fat boy catfish.

"I see Carl's as mad as a little bear there, Earl. What happened?" asked O.C.

"There's a spear in the mound, O.C.," answered Earl. "It's a ceremonial spear."

"So?" smiled O.C. amiably. "They put spears in the mound all the time."

"This is not like the rest, my friend. This one has a scalp on it."

There was a teamed wagon in front of Levi's store. O.C. quickly climbed aboard and started toward the mound. Earl and Tuffy trotted alongside.

Levi walked out of his store and blustered at them at the top of his voice. “What the hell are you doing? You ought to be arrested for stealing an old man’s wagon. Hell, I still got beans in there!”

“I’ll be back in a few minutes, you old grouchy buzzard,” O.C. yelled, laughing.

Levi grabbed his rifle from the side of the store and fired it in the air. Then he turned and went back inside, laughing all the way.

“You know, O.C., that old man may just shoot you in the ass one day,” said Jack. “He’s getting grouchier all the time.”

“No, Jack, he’s just playing with us. He’s got a heart of gold.”

“Yeah, I know,” smiled Jack. “He’s a hoot.”

As they approached the mound, they could see Joe and Nate riding from the south.

Joe wheeled his horse up by the wagon. “What’s wrong, Pop? We just heard a shot.”

“That was just old Levi playing with his rifle,” smiled O.C.

Nate and Joe exchanged looks. Then Joe asked seriously, “What’s going on, Pop?”

Jack pointed at the spear. “My God! That IS a scalp! It looks a lot like the red hair of John Bennis.”

“Damned if it doesn’t,” frowned Nate. “I don’t see any others, though. I wonder if Wayne got away?”

“I doubt it,” frowned O.C. “He’s probably dead.” He shook his head as if to clear out the horrified thoughts that were swirling through it. “Joe, you need to have a meeting with the hands,” he ordered. “Tell them not to come anywhere close to this place. We don’t want Carol or Judy Bennis to know anything about this until we are sure whether it’s John’s or not.”

As they headed back to the ranch, Jack Tunnie pointed to the Bennis children playing in a clearing behind their cabin. The men looked down at the ground, then O.C. looked at Jack and shook his head.

"Sad," he said softly. "So sad."

Garden City, Kansas

It was late in the afternoon and a summer squall had just dumped a half-inch of rain on the dusty streets. Jo Bo Hatton was sweeping the wood board sidewalk in front of Eula May's saloon. Miss Pickles, a young lady of the saloon, sashayed out through the swinging doors.

"You know, Jo Bo," she said. "I think one of these days I might just leave this dusty old place and go to St. Louis. This place gets more dangerous all the time. All these people traveling west, and all these cattle people coming up here from Texas–hell, you never know when you're going to get your throat cut."

"Well, you know, Miss Pickles," he responded. "I was in St. Louis once, when I was a lot younger. And I'll tell ya, you can get your throat cut there faster than you can here."

"I should have known better than to talk to you, Jo Bo," she said. "You ain't never got nothing good to say about anything."

"Well," he frowned, "I'm just talking the truth."

Pickles leaned back on the old wooden bench and started fanning herself. "Damn this heat, and what the hell is that walking down the street?"

Jo Bo lifted the brim of his hat and stared down the center of the dirt street. "I don't know who or what he is, and I don't think he does either," he said. "He kinda looks familiar, but all that blood on his face–I can't really tell."

Wayne Bennis staggered toward the saloon. He was clad in a pair of long john underwear. He wore no shoes. His legs were bloody from the prairie thorns and he was struggling to walk. The mud from the storm had completely covered him.

"My God!" yelled Pickles. "Help him, Jo Bo–he's in really bad shape!"

Jo Bo and Pickles ran toward the stricken man. Wayne Bennis tried to talk but was too exhausted to do so. Jo Bo and Pickles each took an arm and helped him across the street to the office of Doc Young, who was quietly sitting on his porch sipping a bottle of whiskey.

At the sound of Jo Bo's shouts of alarm, the good doctor raised his head and said, "I hear you, I hear you. Just take him in and put him on the table." After observing the wretch of a patient, he added, "Hell, he's just another drifter that can't pay me a dime. Looks like he's done some running."

Together Doc Young and Jo Bo lifted the stricken Bennis onto an examination table.

"What in the world happened to you, mister?" asked Dr. Young.

"The Sioux," mumbled Bennis with great effort. "They'd have killed me too if not for the thunderstorm."

"OK, hold still for a moment," said Doc. "Your feet are full of thorns. They have barbs on them, like fish hooks. I'm going to have to tear them out, or they'll get infected with the rot. Hold still. This will hurt."

The old doctor poured a little whiskey on his patient's feet and gave him a generous swallow of Laudanum. Pickles took one look at the man's feet and ran out the door. The doctor started pulling the thorns out. Wayne's screams echoed through the streets and into the saloon. Finally, he passed out from the pain.

Down the street in the saloon, the card players and cowboys were silently staring at each other.

The proprietress, Eula May, stood beside the staircase and leaned against the railed bar smoking a cigar. "Damn, these cigars are good," she said to nobody. Then she walked across the crowded room to the swinging doors and stared at Pickles standing in the street. "You better get your ass back to work, Pickles," she yelled. "This ain't Christmas, as far as I know!"

Frustrated and angry at her boss's insensitivity, Pickles crossed the street and stormed into the bar. The men at the card tables snickered and began quietly commenting to each other.

"That man," Pickles retorted, "is one of them brothers that came through here a while back. Remember, Eula? They lost all their money and stirred up quite a mess."

"Yeah, I remember," the madam frowned. "The one they called John still owes me for four nights with one of our girls. He was a sorry ass. I heard he had a wife and kids that were a few miles out of town–he just left them out there for four days while he was here having a good time."

"Well, he's dead," said Pickles. "Wayne said the Sioux killed him. He was kind of talking in circles, but he said they would have killed him too if it hadn't been for that storm that come roaring through here the other day."

"Well," sassed Eula, "he must have done something pretty bad for the Sioux to come this far south, just to kill those two. That John deserved killing anyway."

One of the card players looked up and shook his head: "The other one's still a dead man if the Sioux want him bad enough. They're relentless. If he ever leaves here and travels through the prairie, he's as good as dead."

"Oh, well," smiled Eula, "just another no-good that bites the dirt, as far as I'm concerned!"

"I can't believe you, Eula May! You're the coldest-hearted person I've ever met!" Pickles frowned and shook her head as she briskly cleaned the tables. "OK, girls, back to work," she snapped as she headed up the stairs. "Or the wicked queen will behead us all."

"What did you say, Pickles?" screamed Eula May.

Pickles turned quietly and replied innocently, "Oh, nothing, Miss Eula May. I was just singing an old song."

Eula May just turned and smiled to herself until she reached the top of the stairs and made it around the corner into one of the rooms. Then she couldn't hold it anymore; she busted out in a loud laugh and had to put her hand over her mouth.

The card players looked at one another and laughed or smiled. One man turned to his table and said, "This is one hell of a place, but I kind of like it."

Three days later at Doc Young's Place

"Well, looks like them feet are a little better today, Mr. Bennis."

"Yeah, I can stand to walk on them now, barely." Bennis replied. "Dr. Young, I don't have any money, I left it there with my clothes when the Sioux attacked us. We had a hundred dollars' pay, but I guess it's gone now."

"You any good with chickens? I have a chicken farm I could use a little help with. At least I could take some off your bill and will give you fifteen dollars a month."

"Well, that sounds fair, I guess. I used to have a bunch of chickens."

"You can start when those feet get better. I'll give you some clothes, take you out there and show you around. There's a shack you can stay in, and a well with good water. You'll need to have a shotgun to shoot the 'possums and other critters though. The dang 'coons can eat their weight in eggs in one night."

The next day Doc rigged up the wagon and Wayne Bennis limped out the door. They walked the mule down the street and out of town.

The farm was about a mile from town, and had a rather large chicken coop. The old shack wasn't much, but for someone that didn't have anywhere to live, it was a welcome sight.

"You can make any kind of improvements you like, Wayne. The only thing is, this land has been in my family long before I was born, and I can't ever sell it. You're welcome to stay if you do your job, and if you want, you can move some gal in with you."

The old doctor took out his bottle of whiskey and took a big swig. He handed the bottle toward Wayne, but Wayne quickly turned it down.

"My first of the morning," laughed old Doc. "It just wakes me up before breakfast. I always go down to Miss Eula May's for breakfast," he explained. "Now," he continued, "you take these eggs to the two grocery stores and to Miss Eula's every morning about sunup! The rest goes to passersby for fifteen cents a dozen."

Wayne agreed to Dr. Young's conditions and the deal was set. One of Eula's girls had been staying in the shack at night and watching the chickens. She yelled at them through a broken windowpane not to leave without her. Dr. Young just laughed and yelled back for her to hurry up.

She raced out of the cabin with just her nightclothes on, and jumped like a horse straight into the wagon.

"They call me Fast Sally" she said to Wayne. "I guess you're the new Chicken Man. You damn sure can have it. I didn't come all the way from St. Louis to babysit those stinking chickens! But if you ever need my services, though, just leave a note with them eggs, and Miss Eula May will give it to me."

Wayne kind of smiled and answered, "OK." Then, "How am I going to get back here?" he asked.

"Well, you can bring the wagon back. Just put the mule in the corral on the other side of the shack."

Wayne wasn't too thrilled about being the new Chicken Man, but he had nothing else. He dropped Dr. Young and Fast Sally off in town and went back to the cabin. He was thinking about how far he had gone downhill since leaving the ranch and his family. He drove the wagon back to the shack and unharnessed the mule and put him away, along with some hay from an old barn behind the shack. He went to the well and drew a bucket of water. As he washed his face, he stared across the plains at the seemingly endless nothing. There were always summer storms this time of year and he was deathly afraid of them.

He entered the old cabin door and it creaked with an eerie sound. He looked around the lonely room, his mind drifting back to his family. How could they ever live there? He thought to himself that John had been the root of all his problems. He also wondered if his family could ever live on the money from a chicken farm. The people of this town would look down on him for being at the bottom.

Most of Wayne's friends were cowboys and horsemen. All his grown-up life he had followed his older brother John like a puppy follows his mother. But he, like his brother, was addicted to gambling. His mind raced back to the times when they had won and he remembered how great it was to smoke fine cigars and frequent the night spots in St. Louis.

As he lay by the window that night, Wayne could see the dim lights of the town in the distance. But, instead of appreciating what he had, he started planning to get out of this situation and get back to the good life. The old cabin moaned and creaked from the prairie wind, and thunder rolled in the distance. Hours went by with his eyes wide open, and he made a plan.

He would work with the chickens, as he had agreed, for a while and gain everybody's trust. While he was gaining their trust, he would also be watching for opportunities–something to give him the boost he needed to get back to the gambling life he had once been used to.

CHAPTER 11

Reunited–The Story Continues...

It was almost sundown, and an orange glow was starting to change the landscape on the cliffs above the campground. It was one of those days when the color seemed to absorb into everything it touched. A small dust devil came down the center of what was soon to be a real street. Earl Stockman was griping about the dust devil that was blowing his clean clothes off the line. Everybody seemed to get a laugh watching him chase his garments across the street wearing just his long-handle underwear. He couldn't catch them all, and some went into the river. The group in the campground laughed even harder the longer the spectacle lasted.

Earl finally stopped and watched as his favorite scarf was lifted at least thirty feet in the air. He lifted the wine jug he was carrying to take a drink, but the jug was dry. "Damn devil winds," he hollered. Just then he noticed he didn't have anything on but long-handles. He looked toward the campground and realized everyone was laughing. At first, he frowned and started to sass them all back, but then he just decided to laugh along with them. His huge laugh roared down the river canyon, and Tuffy the dog turned his head and let out a howl.

Earl stomped his way back to the cabin where Rose

leaned on the porch rail laughing. She just ran out and hugged him, and he popped another jug.

Continues to the North...

Johnny One Horn and Wind found the overlook cave on the side of the mountain, never noticing the signs of the great bear. Johnny made a fire to take away the night chill. Kicking Wind was getting ready to cook a rabbit they had caught.

Johnny One Horn was outside of the cave cleaning the rabbit when he heard something in the brush below. He peered down through the almost moonless night. There was nothing his eyes could focus on. The dark of the moon was complete in the sparsely clouded night that blocked out most of the stars' light.

He listened very closely to a slight noise coming from the brush. Then he told Wind to stay by the fire and went out to ease down the hillside.

Wind was sitting looking around the overhang when, as the firelight brightened, she saw a pile of bones scattered across the dusty floor in the corner. She jumped to her feet and screamed to Johnny below, "Bear! Johnny, it's a bear!"

Johnny never saw the huge grizzly in the blackness until the bear had ahold of him. The giant bear threw him around like he as a buffalo hide. Its huge claws ripped at Johnny's shoulder as the bear tried to get Johnny's head into its massive jaws. Johnny grabbed for his knife and tried to get it in a position where he could use it. When he saw he could not win, he curled into a ball on the ground. Blood was everywhere. He was mauled around the ground for at least five minutes while Kicking Wind hurled rocks at the great bear. Still the bear pawed at him.

Johnny remembered about the black bears in the swamp–if a person would play dead, they would go away.

This bear was different, though. It was twice the size of any bear he had ever seen. He realized that this was one of the Great Bears that his father Gray Wolf had told him of. It was then he realized he had to do something else or he would die.

He pulled the long knife from his side and ran it through the huge paw of the bear. The great grizzly moaned and walked a few steps away. Suddenly the wolf charged the grizzly. Johnny struggled to his feet and watched as the grizzly tried to swat the wolf. The wolf was much faster, though, and the grizzly could not match his speed. He looked into the great bear's eyes, and the bear seemed to look directly back at him. There was a large scar above one of his eyes.

The wolf circled back to where Kicking Wind had loaded the buffalo gun. She had it pointed straight at the bear's head.

"Wait, Wind," Johnny moaned as they watched the great bear turn and limp away into the darkness.

"Why didn't you let me shoot, Johnny?" she asked. "He was trying to kill you."

Johnny stood holding his bloody shoulder. "I don't think so, Wind–I believe I would be dead if he wanted to kill me. The wolf was a sign, I believe. Cha-cha seemed to have known the bear. I don't know, but both are great spirits. It's kind of strange," Johnny mused as he struggled back to the fire. "You had the buffalo gun pointed at the bear, and the wolf attacked the bear. Was he trying to save me, or the bear?"

Wind spent the next hour cleaning the wounds and dressing Johnny's shoulder. The shoulder was cut deep and would need to be wrapped tightly.

About sunup Wind awoke to the familiar sound of a coyote, the sound that Little Boy Horse made whenever he approached. She answered back and the big man entered the cave. She hugged him with a never-ending grip of love and affection. Johnny sat by the fire and smiled when he saw his beloved brother.

"What happened to you, my brother?" Horse frowned, concerned.

"Well, I'll tell you this, brother–don't ever try to whip one of the bears in this country–you will lose."

"You fought the bear they call Grizzly and lived?" Horse said, shaking his head. "I have often heard that no man lives who fights the mighty Grizzly."

"Well, I had some help from the wolf and Wind. I don't think the great bear wanted to kill me, but we were in his home and it made him angry. I believe the wolf attacked him before Wind could shoot him. I ran my long knife through his claw, and I don't think he will be back."

"I will tell of this story one day," smiled Horse. "It will make many children smile, and make many men wonder."

Johnny had a stitching needle and thread from Levi's store, and Little Boy Horse stitched the wound. He then poured on some raw alcohol from Nate's still. Nate had given it to him and told him that it would help heal such a wound.

"Did you kill old BoJack?" Wind asked in a shaking voice once the work was done.

"I am sure I did, and I hung his body up by the river for all to see. We had a fight the night before, and I got him with my long knife. When I found him, it looked like he had bled to death. He was face down in the river."

Wind, wiping her eyes and smiling at the same time, gave thanks to the Great Spirit. Johnny and Horse stared at each other for a second as if they were feeling her relief.

"We need to go. The sun is up and we need to leave this place," Little Boy Horse said, staring down the hillside. Can you ride, my brother?"

"You ask me if I can ride. I think I can. I fought a grizzly bear last night, and you ask me if I can ride." Wind laughed as the two kidded each other as always.

The next hundred miles were spent avoiding Cheyenne hunting parties and Army patrols as Little Boy Horse scanned the horizon for antelope or deer. They did not dare get near the buffalo for fear of hunting parties of both the Sioux and the Cheyenne. It seemed these tribes had become competitive over the buffalo and sometimes clashed with deadly outcomes.

Though the Sioux were not so fearsome as the Cheyenne, they started traveling at night so they would not be seen. Making use of the new quarter moon, they moved very carefully under the cover of darkness. As the days went by, Cha-cha the wolf got friendlier to Johnny, and would even allow him to touch him occasionally.

Horse would often say he felt like he was being watched. He had good reason, because the Cheyenne chief Black Eagle had scouts watching them ever since they had left the Platte River. They had been in the darkness watching the night Johnny fought the great grizzly. They had watched when Horse was on the quest to kill BoJack. The two had become legends on the plains, and even the Army had heard of their exploits. The Cheyenne had also heard of the killing of the men in the Kansas plains from friends that were Sioux. It wasn't unusual for information to pass on from tribe to tribe, and in this day and age one really had to pay attention to his surroundings.

Black Eagle was aware that they were traveling under cover of darkness. The Cheyenne also watched in the night as Little Boy Horse and his group made its way. The nights were getting a little colder the farther north they ventured. But Johnny's shoulder was healing, and the chill didn't bother him too much.

One morning as the red sky appeared, Horse, Johnny and Wind came to the banks of the Missouri River. The water was clear and swift. They stood on the banks of the river and watched the deer grazing in the plush grass.

"I am glad to see this place. It is beautiful here. Is this

where you come from, Wind? I never saw a prettier place than this." Little Boy Horse's sharp eyes scanned the riverbanks until he saw what looked like a nice place to camp. There were plenty of deer and ducks darting in and around the mighty river. The wind was blowing slightly, and the rippling of the water seemed to enchant the place.

As they gazed in wonder at the beauty of the river, Kicking Wind told them they were still a long way from where she had lived.

"I wish we were closer," Johnny said, shaking his head, "but seeing all these beautiful things makes the long journey worth it."

They made their camp and settled down to get a few hours' sleep. The night before had been long and troublesome. Some brush they had encountered was thorny and it was hard on the horses. Several times they had backtracked to make sure nobody was following them.

"We are going to start traveling in the day because this land is a lot tougher than the plains," explained Little Boy Horse. "We will just have to be more careful. We aren't making much time in the dark anyway, and we could stumble upon another one of the great bears."

About the time Johnny had laid his head down, Wind whispered, "It's a scouting or hunting party."

Johnny sprang to his feet.

"There are six of them."

It was too late to run, so Horse just motioned for Wind to stand behind Coattail the horse.

"You must be tired, my brother," frowned Johnny. "You never let people or anything else slip up on us so easy."

Little Boy Horse turned with a surprised look on his face. "They are at the water's edge and it covers their sound," he explained.

The hunting party rode completely up to where they were standing.

The leader gave a peace sign from his chest and Little

Boy Horse returned it.

The lead brave pointed to himself and said the name Seetah, then he said a few more words Little Boy Horse could not understand. Kicking Wind answered Seetah. Johnny and Horse turned and looked at each other, amazed at what they heard. As Seetah talked, he motioned toward a deer strapped over the horse next to him. "My chief Cold Hawk sends a gift to the Bear Fighter One Horn and the brave warrior they call Horse."

Kicking Wind quickly told Horse and Johnny what was said. The two men stared in surprise. Then Little Boy Horse asked her to give thanks to Chief Cold Hawk. When she did, two of the party unstrapped the deer and laid it on the ground by the fire.

"Cold Hawk gives you permission to visit our camp when you complete your journey."

Johnny and Horse thanked them and then the party mounted their ponies and walked away, giving their welcome sign.

The three watched as the party slowly made its way down the river and around the bend.

Kicking Wind smiled. "They are the Lakota Sioux. My family has known Cold Hawk for a long time. He is a fearsome chief, but a good, just man. Word travels fast in our land, and an eye is always upon us. I have known they were watching us for a long time now."

Horse returned Kicking Wind's smile and told her she had amazed him. The small girl he had found was growing up and turning into a woman.

By the time they reached the Missouri River they had learned the ways of the hunting parties and the Sioux. The Army patrols were the easiest because they always traveled in the daytime and were easy to spot. Their scouts saw Johnny and the group many times and would just wave at them and lead the Army in another direction. It almost became funny because the scouts of the Army were all

Sioux and Cheyenne, and they would stop and talk, and sometimes have a cup of the white man's coffee with the group.

The country had changed so much it was like a different world to Johnny and Little Boy Horse. They had never seen the like of the Missouri River basin, but by all means, they must carry on. It seemed to be colder at night and the wind blew a lot more. The moon seemed to light everything up in this country. Johnny and Little Boy Horse were enjoying a beauty like they had never before seen.

"Don't let the beauty of this place deceive you, my brothers–this place can be a monster in the dead of winter. You must dress for it, and the game seems to travel farther south. The people here have learned the way of the winter and can survive, but people that are not from here usually perish from the cold or starvation. My people know the winter and make use of it. The Army won't be here, for it is too cold. The other tribes will be, especially the Crow. They are from the north and are survivors. We will have to watch for them when the snow flies as they will hunt farther south. They don't want a fight with the Army so in the warm months they stay to the far north."

Kicking Wind was letting them know of all the dangers of the country when their friend, a Sioux scout that had visited them on occasion, rode up to them. "Hello, my friends. I ride to give you a message from the south. The Army is looking for you. There were people from the Mormon faith slaughtered in the south, and they believe you were with Tomah and Blue Feather, and took part in the killing. I told them I have word that you are farther south, and not in this country. I just wanted to let you know this, my friends."

As they were having coffee, Little Boy Horse told the scout of his knowledge of the killing–that the real killer was BoJack. "I hunted BoJack and killed him by the North Platte River," explained Little Boy Horse." I hung his body on a tree for all to see."

The scout answered, "The Army has heard of the man by the river, but they are not sure who he was. If it was BoJack, you did a great deed, my friend. We have met several times and you have shared your drink. My name is Sad Hank–at least that is what I am called. The Army gave me that name because I once cried when I saw the slaughtering of the Great Buffalo."

As Sad Hank turned and mounted his horse, he waved and advised them to keep their eyes wide, for "there are many dangers here that are not so easily seen." The group waved as the scout rode back to the south.

Kicking Wind sat at length and discussed with Horse and Johnny the directions to her beloved home, and the route they must take. Even though she had been young when she was taken, she still remembered the ways of her people very well.

It had been their plan to follow the river, but Kicking Wind knew the dangers of the country and offered them a different plan. She warned that the river held many trappers and mountain men. It was also a path for prospectors and renegade Sioux and Cheyenne hunting and war parties They should stay west of the river at what she figured to be about twenty miles. There were many small creeks and rivers running into the Missouri, and they could easily find game and water. So, although the land was beautiful along the river, the places they chose to travel were arid and treeless.

They mounted and slowly, leading their pack horses, walked at a good pace to the north. "It is my guess that I will be home in about a week," the young woman remarked joyously as they set out.

CHAPTER 12

The Chicken Farm

Wayne Bennis carried the eggs into town and delivered them every day just like he was told. However, he was not honest with Dr. Young–he sold a lot more to passing wagons of people going west and kept the money for himself.

He began to frequent Eula May's Saloon in the afternoons to play cards. He was not a very likeable guy. At first he gained sympathy by telling people about his family that supposedly was killed on the trail by Indians. But as he got comfortable with the crowd, he seemed to forget about his family and started playing around with the girls in the saloon.

Eventually, Wayne's greed for money led him to stalk certain wagons on the prairie. He would sneak up to their wagons and rob them at gunpoint during the night. He was fully masked so the travelers could not identify him, and no one had a clue who he was. Even though Marshal Tibbs set out a patrol at night to warn the travelers, the robberies continued.

Bennis was accumulating quite a bundle of money, which he needed to keep up with his gambling. He was an average card player and at times seemed to win a lot by cheating. Nobody realized what he was doing right under their noses.

Nobody really seemed to like Bennis after they got to know him, so he didn't make many friends. But he was wearing expensive clothes and buying things a chicken farmer would never have. Finally, Doug Pricer, one of Marshal Tibbs' deputies, noticed Bennis at the local clothing store spending a lot of money, and brought it to the marshal's attention.

Deputy Pricer was suspicious of Bennis and started watching him. Bennis seemed to be getting rich playing cards, or from some other suspicious source. One day he saw Bennis ride up to the front of the saloon, and thought he would have a talk with what now was becoming quite a wealthy chicken egg farmer.

"Mr. Bennis, going to play a game or two, are you?" asked Pricer.

"Yeah, just a few–I got a date with Miss Lucy. Gonna take her for a moonlight ride tonight," he answered, grinning cockily.

"Well, what did you do, Mr. Bennis? Find a pot of gold out there at the chicken farm?"

Wayne Bennis suddenly became very nervous and just tipped his hat at Doug Pricer before he walked inside. Quickly a number of the saloon girls swarmed around him, and he began buying them drinks as though he were a celebrity.

Pricer looked at the spectacle in amazement. He walked to where Pickles was serving drinks at a table.

"Why, Deputy Pricer, what brings you into our humble place of business?" Pickles smiled. "Are you looking for a little action, or just wanting to play cards?"

"Well, I'd really like to talk to Miss Eula May," he smiled. "And it is about business."

"Well, she's in room six, teaching some of the new girls the ropes, if you know what I mean."

Deputy Pricer went up the stairs and knocked on the

door. The house was packed most of the time, and very loud. It was a rough place and nobody liked to see the Law come through the front door. All kinds of people–ranch hands, buffalo hunters, mountain men, and trail drivers–were in the mix.

At last, Eula May jerked the door open, in a rage, not knowing it was the deputy. She apologized at once when she realized who had interrupted her training session. "Oh! I'm so sorry, I didn't know it was you! These damn trail hands are always bothering me when I get a batch of new girls."

Pricer explained that he didn't want to interrupt business, but wanted to ask a few questions about Wayne Bennis. He asked how good a card player he was, and how he seemed to be getting rich. Eula May laughed and told him she didn't really like Bennis–he reminded her of a worm! She said she surely didn't like his supposedly-dead brother John. She confided to Pricer that Bennis was just an ordinary card player that seemed to lose just as much as he won.

As Pricer walked away, Eula May yelled, "You know, old Bennis is married, and has a family somewhere. He says they were killed by the Sioux, but some of these trail hands say they are alive and living on the Armstrong Ranch northwest of Abilene, close to the Colorado Territory."

"Where are the men who told you this? I would sure like to talk to them," Pricer responded.

"Well, most were only here a few times delivering cattle to what they call the Triple A Ranch, but that's the Armstrong's, I've heard. They tried to talk to Bennis, but he would deny he knew them and leave real quick after that."

"If you see these men again, Eula, be sure and come tell me. There's a dead fish somewhere in this barrel."

Eula May shook her head and went back up the stairs, ordering Pickles, "Get those girls busy, Pickles, or I'll replace you with a wooden Indian."

Pickles sassed back at Eula to just go ahead. "I'd be glad to pack up and head for St. Louis."

Eula just shook her head and laughed.

When Doug Pricer returned to the office, he explained to Marshal Tibbs what he had found out about Bennis. Marshal Tibbs decided to send Deputy Pricer and two other deputies to the Armstrong ranch to investigate what Eula May had just told them. Pricer picked out a couple of good men. They were young, but fast learners, and Tibbs was confident they could do the job. They planned to leave at sunup the next day.

Meanwhile, Wayne Bennis told Dr. Young that he would have to find someone else to mind the chicken farm because he was moving to a room at the Fairview Hotel. Since the old doctor suspected Bennis was stealing from him, he was glad to get rid of him.

Every afternoon, having spent the night before playing cards, drinking, and switching girls at the bar, Bennis would cross the dusty street from the Fairview Hotel and enter the saloon. He knew he wouldn't hear from the deputies for at least a week.

One afternoon Marshal Tibbs was standing at the entrance just looking around for anything unusual, when Bennis passed him. Bennis never made eye contact with the marshal, but tipped his hat with his head down.

"Hey, Bennis, you been doing pretty good gambling, I see. Did you win all the money? I mean, to rent a room at the Fairview, and dress better than anybody in town?"

Bennis looked up and smiled, "Well, Marshal, don't a man have the right to win a little?"

"Yeah, I suppose he does. Tell me, Bennis, I see you ride out of town sometimes but I never see you come back. Do you ride all night, just enjoying the moonlight?"

"Yeah, I like to ride sometimes in the moonlight. Is there something wrong with that?"

Marshal Tibbs leaned back against the horse rail and lit a cigar. Bennis started to walk off.

"One more thing, Bennis. On these rides you take at night, do you see anything unusual out there on the plains? A lot of travelers have been getting robbed by a lone bandit out there." He drew on his cigar for a moment before continuing. "Oh, I also heard you were afraid of the Sioux. Seems there's plenty of danger out there at night."

Bennis blurted back, "Oh, Marshal, I don't go very far when I ride–just around the lights of the town. I keep the lamps in sight."

Marshal Tibbs was a sly old man, with many years of experience. He could tell Bennis was hiding something and he was going to find out what it was.

"You say your whole family was killed by Indians? Would that just happen to be around Abilene? Maybe somewhere northwest of there?"

Bennis made a motion with his hands and pointed east of town. "No, it was over on the plains to the east, out there somewhere. Excuse me, Marshal; I have a date with Lucy. You have a nice day now."

Bennis entered the saloon a nervous wreck. He knew the marshal suspected him of something.

Marshal Tibbs decided he would follow him the next time he saw him ride out of town. He was now almost convinced Bennis was the man who had been robbing the settlers traveling the prairie.

Three Days Later

Deputy Pricer and his deputies had arrived at the crest of the hill overlooking the ranch.

One of the deputies pointed north, where they could see several riders approaching. As soon as Pete and his men arrived, several more came from the south.

"Damn, this place is well guarded! We sure as hell better

watch our step," Pricer frowned.

Joe had been beside Levi's store when he saw the action at the top of the hill. He quickly mounted his horse and rode through the dusty street and up the hill.

Joe, always on the lookout for trouble, rode up with his rifle in hand. Pete and Nate had their guns trained on Pricer and his deputies. Joe pointed the rifle at Pricer, and asked, "What are you men doing here? State your business."

The deputies were scared, and it sure showed as the rough-looking ranch hands gathered around.

"I'm a Deputy U.S. Marshal. I'm here on business. Tell your men to drop those rifles," Pricer said, as he showed Joe his badge.

"Well, we don't get many marshals visiting the ranch. Please excuse us for getting a little on edge, but we don't drop our rifles for anyone." Joe motioned to Pete. "Pete, get the men back to work. It looks all right now."

Pete, being kind of a mean-looking character himself, tipped his hat to the deputies. They tipped theirs back, though they still glanced nervously at the rough-looking ranch hands.

As the other men went back to their jobs, Joe invited the deputies on down to the campgrounds. "We're about to have our nightly cookout, boys–you are very welcome to stay and eat. It's a nightly thing we do and it has brought us all very close to each other. You can clean the dust off of you there by the water tank, and we can talk later. I'll be back after I check on some riders patrolling thc corrals to the south."

As Joe rode away, Deputy Pricer and his men made their way past the campgrounds and cleaned themselves by the water tank. Three of the girls brought them towels and soap.

"Wow," said one of the young deputies as he looked around the place. He started counting the picnic tables. "Wow," he said again. "These people live pretty dang good. I could get used to this. Did you see how pretty those girls were? What were they, Doug–were they Indians?"

Doug smiled, "Tom," he said, "you and Bill better mind your own business here! You can bet them girls got suitors here, and from the looks of some of them, I don't think you young fellows would stand much a of a chance! To answer your question about the girls, well, they don't wear their hair like the Sioux. I think they're Mexican. Anyway, we are their guests and I'm not going to get too damn nosey."

Tom Sheen, the young deputy, was amazed by this ranch. He kept looking at the way it was laid out with the giant sandstone rocks towering above the river. He could see many children playing behind the newly built school. Old Levi was sweeping the dust off his porch. Earl Stockman was skinning a mink he had trapped, and Rose was complaining to him about the cabin roof.

Yolanda, one of the prettiest girls, brought them a jug of moonshine and a big pitcher of cold water. Tom stared at her brown skin and beautiful complexion. He spoke to her in a stuttering voice and thanked her as she put a tablecloth on the table where they were sitting.

Yolanda acted shy, but she was a real practical joker. At first, she acted like he wasn't even there and never looked up.

"She can't speak our language. But look how pretty she is," Tom remarked to his friends, smiling. Confident she didn't understand English, he commented on how hard she was working. Then he motioned Doug Pricer to look at her body as she leaned over to clean the bench.

Yolanda whipped around, picked up the water, and slowly poured it on his head. He just sat there in stunned silence as she spoke. "See that dog standing by that rock?" No one had noticed old Tuffy.

"My God," Tom murmured in amazement.

"One word from me and Tuffy will tear your little dingles clean off." Yolanda turned and walked back to the main cookhouse. Several of the other girls were inside laughing, and she joined them when she was out of sight. "Did you see the look on his face?" she giggled.

Bill Larkin, the other young deputy, was also busting out laughing. "Damn, Tom, she sure learned to speak English fast."

"She sure as hell did!" Tom agreed, sheepishly joining in the laughter. "That's one mean-looking wolf over there! My God, he's big!"

"Actually, that's a shepherd dog of some kind, but he does look like a wolf," laughed Bill. "I wouldn't push my luck with him–he looks mean as hell."

Old Tuffy just sneered at them for a second and then strolled around the rocks in the direction of the river.

"These people keep wolves for pets–that's hard to believe," said Tom with amazement.

"I told you, boys, when we got here, not to get out of line. I've got a strange feeling that you can get into trouble real fast here, if you're not careful." Deputy Pricer sternly put an end to all the fun.

As the sun sank in the sky, the ranch hands started gathering around the water tank to clean up.

"You know," Bill remarked, "this ranching looks like hard work. I wonder what it pays."

Tom laughed at Bill. "Well, why don't you ask that old boy over there that skinned that mink, and if he doesn't skin you, he might invite you for dinner."

Bill glanced at old Earl and looked concerned. "That's one mean-looking old mountain man. I wouldn't want to tangle with him. Why don't you ask him?"

O.C. and some of the hands had cleaned up and were walking around the rock toward the camp tables, teasing each other, popping towels, and laughing.

"Howdy, boys," laughed O.C. as he sat down. "This here's Pete and Nate, our ranch foremen, and, you might say, our police."

"We've met already, but they look different without them buffalo guns in front of their faces," frowned Pricer.

"We're sorry about that," smiled O.C. "What brings you boys out our way? We don't see many lawmen out here."

"Well, there's somebody we need to ask you some questions about," the lawman replied seriously.

"Well, let's all have a drink to settle the dust down first," O.C. laughed as Yolanda sat down on his lap and hugged him. "We'll drink and eat and when Joe and Charles join us, we'll talk about these questions of yours."

The night went on like any other night, with some of the girls dancing and everybody joining in with a little music of some sort. The deputies relaxed after a while and seemed to have a lot of fun.

Tom Sheen so liked the place that, after a few drinks and dancing with Yolanda, he asked Nate for a job. Nate was amazed at the young man's persistence and asked him if he was good with horses. Tom said he could learn. Nate told him not to be fooled by what seemed to be a full-time party–in reality this would be a very tough job.

"Are you any good with that gun you're wearing?" Nate asked.

"Well, not very good, but I can handle a rifle."

"You never know around here–there's bandits, crazy mountain men, and just about everything else that can shoot you, bite you or stick you." Nate paused, considering his next words carefully. "I see you've been taking a fancy to the girls. That could get you in a lot trouble. There are a lot of them here for sure, and most are in their teens. But Cindy–that's Joe Armstrong's wife over there–she keeps a close watch on those girls. Some were captives of Comancheros to the south. That old mountain man you saw skinning that mink rescued most of them. The others just showed up here because they heard about the ranch from travelers. It's become kind of a rescue center and they're learning how to read and write in several language, along with other things."

Tom Sheen listened closely and got a good picture of what to do or not do. He was quickly deciding to stay at the ranch.

As the evening started to slow down, Cindy called the girls and children in. Joe always had Pete pick up the moonshine jugs from the tables one hour after the sun went down. Anyone who got drunk was fired or asked to leave. Joe and Charles ran the ranch with a strong hand, as they had learned from their father.

Joe went to Charles and told him about the deputies. Charles was concerned the problem might be about a recent land purchase. He quickly grabbed his notebook and writing pens and accompanied Joe to the campground. O.C. and Nate were busy talking about the ranch, as Tom Sheen kept glancing toward the cook shack where Yolanda was helping the girls.

As Joe introduced Charles to the deputies, Charles asked about the recent land purchase, and was surprised that they seemed unaware of anything going on in that area. "Well, since you're not here on ranch business, what brings you to our little wolf's den?" Charles smiled.

Douglas Pricer returned the smile. "It's nothing to do with your operation here–everything here looks great. It's a little paradise, if you ask me. What I'm here for is to ask about a man called Wayne Bennis. Do you know such a man?"

Everyone from the ranch at the table exchanged concerned looks.

"Yeah, we know Bennis, but we were thinking he might be dead. Bennis and his brother John stole something from our sacred Indian ground, and we fired them." Joe went on to explain that the brothers had left their wives and families, with plans to send for them as soon as they could get on their feet.

"Well, I don't know anything about John Bennis, but we

have reason to believe Wayne Bennis has been involved in some robberies on the plains near Garden City. We suspect he's the one who has been picking single wagons and taking their gold or cash to gamble with–these people have been stripped of their life savings. It's terribly sad. This Wayne Bennis has been telling everybody his wife and family were killed by the Sioux. Some trail hands that delivered horses to your ranch here told us Bennis came from here. Marshal Tibbs wanted us to find out if Bennis was lying. He is just a suspect at this point, but we need to know."

O.C. exchanged disgusted looks with Joe, and then addressed Deputy Pricer. "Well, his wife was at the table with her two children tonight and she stays with her sister-in-law and kids right over there in that second building. She's a damn good woman, and now we know for sure she's too good for that good-for-nothing Bennis."

"Really," said Doug. "Then that confirms our suspicion. Wonder what happened to his brother? Wayne was in pretty bad shape when he staggered into Garden City."

"Well, we have reason to believe that John is dead. There is part of him hanging on a spear about a half mile from here. You'll have to take our word for it. You can't go there or you might suffer the same fate. It's an ancient burial ground of the Sioux. Bennis and his brother John removed some sacred items. The Sioux chief sentenced them to death for their crime. If we didn't send them away from the ranch, we all would have suffered the same fate. Running Bear means what he says and we are not going to push it."

CHAPTER 13

Garden City

Marshal Tibbs was watching Bennis and also had Jo Bo Hatton watching him from the inside of Eula May's saloon. Jo Bo swept the floors and was in and around the tables every day. He watched the second day as a card shark named Fast Brian Houx drifted into town on the stage line and cleaned out Bennis in about two hours. Bennis accused Fast Brian of cheating, but Eula May stopped the conflict with her ten-gauge shotgun.

Bennis scurried out of the saloon and crossed the street to the Fairview Hotel. Once inside his room, he realized he was totally broke. He fumbled through his clothes looking for money. Mad at himself for losing, he changed into some old cowboy work clothes and went into the street under the cover of darkness.

After Bennis had left the saloon, Jo Bo Hatton had quickly made his way across the street to inform Marshal Tibbs. Tibbs saddled his horse and tied it to the rail in front of the jail. At sundown he mounted and went to a dark part of the street to wait

Bennis walked down the dusty street and into the livery stable where his horse was boarded. He rode at a good pace toward the south end of town. It would be very hard to track Bennis in the dark, so Marshal Tibbs just rode toward the well-worn track used by the wagons that were traveling west. Everybody used the road, from the Mormons to gold prospectors heading to the California gold fields. It was a mixed crowd of families and desperate men in search of easy prey.

The marshal couldn't see Bennis, but he could see the well-used road well. Lightning flickered to the south as a light wind whispered through the sagebrush. He came upon some buffalo hunters camped beside the roadway and stopped at the edge of the camp. He identified himself as a territorial marshal, seeing that one of the hunters had drawn down on him with a buffalo gun.

"No need for anybody to get the jitters," Tibbs assured them. "I'm just traveling down this road. Tell me though, have you seen anybody come through here in the last half hour or so?"

One of the buffalo hunters told him that a man riding by had stopped and asked them for some water. "I gave him some water, and then I noticed a canteen hanging from his saddle," explained the hunter.

"He was probably sizing you boys up. I'm Marshal Tibbs. I think that guy is a road bandit that has been robbing wagons and settlers, families–it doesn't matter to him. If he comes back this way, just let him go on by. I know where he'll be going."

The buffalo hunters agreed, and Marshal Tibbs tipped his hat and rode on down the dusty path. A couple of miles farther he heard two shots coming from south of the trail. He knew settlers would often leave the well-traveled road and camp a quarter mile or so off. They did this to avoid people, and any kind of trouble that might come with them. Tibbs rode to the south until he could see the white cover of a wagon in the distance. Through the darkness, he could hear a woman screaming.

When he arrived at the wagon, Tibbs announced that he was a U.S. Marshal and he was coming in. A young woman ran from the wagon screaming that her husband had been shot. The marshal dismounted and ran to the wagon, where the body of a young man was lying on the ground covered in blood.

"What the hell happened here, girl?"

"A man came out of the brush and pulled a gun on my husband. They wrestled around for a few minutes and my husband was able to best him, but the man shot him!"

As the woman broke down in tears, Marshal Tibbs took a blanket and covered her husband. "I heard two shots–did your husband shoot back?"

Her hands trembling, she explained that she had shot at the man with a shotgun as he was riding away.

"Did you hit him?"

"I think so," she said, crying and hugging her husband's body.

"What's your name, Hon?" he asked gently.

"It's Lisa, sir–Lisa Freeman–and that's my husband Leon."

"Damn," Marshal Tibbs said as he turned and lifted the body into the back of the wagon. "I'm taking you to Garden City, Hon–there's a place you can stay until you decide what to do." He tied his horse to the back of the Prairie Schooner and headed the wagon down the road back into town. When he passed the two buffalo hunters, they told him that the same man they had seen earlier had passed them at a hard run.

All the way back to Garden City the marshal listened to the young lady cry and talk out of her head. It reminded him how much he wanted to quit this job. He did manage to ask her if the man got any money and she told him that, right before the fight, she had handed him their life savings of about two hundred dollars. Tibbs was almost certain that this man was Wayne Bennis. He knew Bennis didn't know he was being followed, and would probably head right back to Garden City.

Tibbs pulled the wagon up to the marshal's office and helped the young woman down. Jo Bo Hatton had seen the commotion and ran across the street.

"What happened?" yelled Jo Bo.

Marshal Tibbs asked Jo Bo to escort the young lady to the saloon and have Pickles take care of her until another place could be found. Lisa resisted, because she had been taught that saloons were immoral. Pickles tried to comfort her, but she was out of her mind with shock. Eventually she fainted, and Pickles and a few of the cowboys took her upstairs.

Marshal Tibbs walked across the dusty street to the livery stable, where he observed that Bennis' horse was back in the stall, still saddled. The saddle was bloody–a sure sign that his man was Bennis. He walked back across the street to the Fairview Hotel. As he walked in, he could see a trail of blood leading toward the stairs.

A caretaker whispered from behind the dimly lit counter that Bennis was upstairs and was hurt. "He said he fell off his horse, Marshal," whispered the caretaker.

"Oh, is that what he told you?" asked Tibbs.

The caretaker kept asking questions as Marshal Tibbs flipped a couple of ten-gauge shells into his shotgun. "Keep out of the way and shut up, Lewis."

Tibbs banged on the door, but no one answered. He kicked the door open to find Bennis lying on the floor in a pool of blood. He yelled to Lewis to come and help him. Together they managed to carry Bennis down the stairs.

"Are we going to take him to Dr. Young's? He looks like he's been hurt kind of bad."

"Now, Lewis, go get a couple of boys from the saloon to help me."

A few minutes later three dusty cowboys walked across the street and helped Marshal Tibbs carry Bennis down the street to the jail.

"Could one of you boys go get Dr. Young? I've got to

watch this one."

They agreed, and soon Dr. Young, cussing and complaining, staggered across the street from the saloon with his whiskey bottle in his hand. "What the hell is going on, Tibbs? A man can't even get drunk in peace anymore."

"Well, I thought you might want to come see your Chicken Man–seems he's not what we thought he was."

Bennis was still unconscious as old Dr. Young turned him over and started cleaning his wounds.

"He's a damn thief, Tibbs–he was stealing from my chicken farm."

"Well, that's not the only thing Mr. Bennis is, Doc. He just killed a young man, and that's his wife that they dragged across the street out of her mind."

"I saw that, Tibbs. Hell, I thought she was just drunk or something."

"Well, it's all true, and from the looks of that shotgun blast, Bennis would have been dead if she had been a little better shot."

Between them they managed to clean Bennis up and place him in one of the old sweat-permeated wooden cells. Marshal Tibbs would have to wait on the Territorial Judge that came after the first Monday of every month. It would be up to the Judge and out of his hands. He told Jo Bo and Dr. Young not to mention to anybody the connection between Bennis and the murder. His plan was to wait until the young woman was well enough and regained her senses so she could identify Bennis as the killer.

CHAPTER 14

At The Ranch

After hearing the story of the Bennis brothers, Doug Pricer had assumed that Bennis was probably the thief they were looking for.

"Well, Mr. Armstrong, if you don't mind, we'd like to stay the night and leave first thing in the morning. But I think young Tom is going to stay here," he went on, grinning.

"Well, if Nate wants to hire him, then that's all right with me."

O.C. then turned and walked to Earl Stockman's cabin. "Hey, Earl, there's some boys here from Garden City you might know."

Sipping on his jug, Earl stepped out of his cabin and looked at the men. "No," he frowned; "I don't know them," he said as he walked over.

"Well, Earl, you don't know us but I know you," smiled Doug Pricer. "You're some kind of legend in our little town."

"How do you know me?" Earl replied.

"I used to sweep the floors at Miss Eula May's. I seen you throw at least ten men out of there one night. They say you skinned two men who killed that little schoolteacher."

"No, that wasn't me–must have been somebody else.

One time, just passing through to see Miss Pickles, I did have a little scuffle there though." Earl just glared at Doug. "That Marshal Tibbs–does he look for me?"

O.C. and Pete looked on, not knowing what Earl would do next if they said somebody was looking for him. They watched as Earl's hand eased down towards his long knife.

"Nah," Doug smiled. "He knew them men were bad and needed just what they got, Earl. We're not here for you. Come to think of it, it was a big half- breed fellow named John Horn or something like that. Sorry–I guess I got a little confused."

With that being said, Earl relaxed and asked, "Pickles, and Miss Eula–are they all right? I'll pay them a visit one day."

"They're fine, Earl. I'll tell them I seen you."

"Tell them I'll come to see them one day." With that, Earl gave the greeting sign from his chest and walked off without saying another word.

"He doesn't talk much, does he?" smiled Doug.

"Well, there for a minute I thought I said the wrong thing when he asked if the marshal was looking for him."

O.C. stared at Pricer with great concern. "If you had not said the right thing you boys would probably be dead about now. He told us about the thought of being locked up in a white man's jail, and, well, he's not too fond of the idea."

"Where'd he get that big scar draping over his shoulder?" asked Tom Sheen. "That's one bad scar if I ever saw one."

Pete looked at Tom and smiled, "Well, he fought a mountain lion up in the Dakotas."

"Did he shoot the lion?" asked Tom, concerned.

"Nah, he didn't have a gun on him at the time–just that big knife."

"Did he kill the lion with that knife?" quizzed Tom incredulously.

O.C. looked at Pete and both of them smiled, "Well,

young Tom," he said, "it was a fair fight and the lion just left after he'd been bested."

"Holy Cow! I never heard of any man ever besting a mountain lion."

O.C. Looked at the young men's faces, as they looked at each other in amazement. "He's no ordinary man, my young friends," O.C. smiled. "Now, if all the story-telling's over, we better turn in. You boys can sleep in the campground tonight by the fire."

O.C. couldn't resist throwing one more thing at the young men and Deputy Pricer.

"Now, if you boys have to pee, better go in a different direction than that rock. Old Tuffy–that big wolf dog of Earls–he's got a really bad habit of biting people's dingles off that go around that rock at night."

"Don't worry, Mr. O.C." Bill said. "No way am I going toward that cabin or that rock!"

O.C., Pete and Nate walked off laughing and the two young deputies stared at each other with wide eyes.

~ ~ ~

The sun was barely a glow in the eastern sky when Doug and the deputies were awakened by Nate and Pete. They had the coffee on and bid Doug Pricer and Bill Larkin farewell.

"Well, it's been nice meeting you fellows," Doug Pricer smiled. He tipped his hat to Nate and Pete and shook their hands. Then the deputies turned their mounts and headed out of the ranch. As they were riding off, Deputy Pricer turned and looked back at the ranch in amazement.

"Boys, I really didn't want to say anything in front of ole Earl, but I really did figure out who he was. That ole boy is known all throughout the territory. Earl Stockman is probably one of the most famous mountain men that ever lived."

"Well, I know one thing, Doug–he sure is a mean-lookin' fellow," smiled Bill Larkin.

~ ~ ~

"You ready to go to work, Mr. Sheen? We'll get you started on those horses! If you hear the bell ring it will be breakfast about nine o'clock."

"You mean we get breakfast?" replied Tom eagerly.

"Breakfast and dinner, and if you want something in between, you can get it from Levi. He's got beef jerky and hard candy, but the old goat will charge you for it."

"Does he have chewing tobacco, Nate?"

"Yeah, he does but only the old Bull Durham. That's what he chews and that's all he keeps handy."

"Wow," said Tom Sheen, "I didn't expect to have breakfast and dinner made for me! I know I'm going to love this place."

"Make no mistake, Tom, I told you the days are long and the work never stops. Joe keeps a steady stream of horses and cattle moving in and out of here."

"I understand, Nate–I hope I do OK for you. I was beginning to hate that Garden City–it's starting to be a rough place."

~ ~ ~

Doug Pricer and Bill Larkin were well on their way back to Garden City when they spotted some rocks with an overhang and decided it would be a good place to camp for the night. As a rain shower passed over, they rode their horses under the rock. As they dismounted, Bill spotted a man's body lying in the sand beside an old fire ring. The remains were mostly skeletal.

"You know, Deputy Pricer, this is probably the body of that John Bennis. I wonder if that weasel Wayne Bennis killed him?"

"Well, this guy happened to have red hair," Doug said with a concerned look on his face as he peered at the corpse. "This man's been scalped; the other hair is still on his skull."

As they looked around, they noticed a pouch of coins and counted out one hundred dollars. Doug remembered Wayne Bennis telling him about the money they had before they were attacked. "I would say this is John Bennis, without a doubt." He sat down, thinking. "You know, Bill, for the life of me, I can't believe that Bennis would make up a story up about his family being killed by the Sioux. He didn't have a reason to. I just think he got to like the girls and fast money."

"Don't forget the whiskey, Doug."

"Yeah, It's pretty certain he's a real snake. Any man that would just leave his family and forget them for a life of gambling and saloon girls is crazy, if you ask me. Don't get me wrong–there ain't nothing wrong with saloon girls. I was just making a point."

"I know–there are a couple of them that I kind of like too. What are we going to do with this body, Doug?"

"Well, I guess we can find a couple of poles and make a drag. This rain has set in but maybe by morning the weather will be better and we'll drag him into town. At least he can get a decent burial."

The next morning the rain had mostly passed, but the wind was howling from the north. It made building the drag very difficult. When they lifted Bennis' body, the leg came off from the decaying carcass. Young Bill Larkin had the dry heaves for several minutes.

Finally, Doug put a hand on his shoulder. "Well, we better get going, son. We've still got a two-day's ride, and it's not going to get any better."

Doug tied the drag to his horse, as Bill Larkin couldn't bear the smell and rode upwind from the rotting body. They could be in Garden City none too soon.

Garden City

As Wayne Bennis began to come around, he started talking to Marshal Tibbs. He could barely sit, and had no idea he was being held for anything. Tibbs just let him talk.

Bennis told Marshal Tibbs that he had been riding down the trail when some buffalo hunters drew down on him. He said that they demanded his horse and money and when he refused and tried to get away, they had shot him with a shotgun. The marshal acted like he was listening to his story and never let on that he knew the truth.

Bennis had a personality that could change in a second. He had begun to play checkers with the other inmates and was a big hit with all of them. In a couple of days, he told Tibbs that he thought he was well enough to get out of his bed, and said if somebody would help him, he would like to go back to the Fairview Hotel.

"Well, Bennis, you're going to have to stay for a while longer. You see, Bennis, I don't believe your story, and there's a little gal over at Eula's that's an emotional mess. She just had her husband killed in cold blood. I find it strange, Bennis, that you had two hundred dollars in your pocket, and that's the same amount they had when they were robbed and her young husband was killed."

Bennis' face turned white as he pretended he couldn't believe what he was hearing. "I won that money playing cards!" he yelled in desperation.

Marshal Tibbs walked to the cell doors. "You mean the day you got shot, Bennis?"

"Yes, I won a lot that day," he said with a trembling voice.

Marshal Tibbs smiled and pointed the next cell. "See that man sleeping underneath that blanket, Bennis? That's a card shark named Fast Brian Houx. He tells a different story than you do, and so do most of the people from Eula May's saloon."

"I don't care what they say!" cried Bennis. "I never killed anybody!"

"You know, Bennis, I followed you that night and I was right behind you when you killed that young fellow. I also talked to them buffalo hunters you say shot you. That poor screaming young lady is going to identify you, and when she does, you're probably going to hang."

Bennis' brash personality changed, and he became a sobbing mess, trying to get sympathy from Tibbs. The old marshal never even looked up as he thumbed through some wanted posters. Three of the other inmates in the cell started beating Bennis. He was on his knees begging for mercy before Marshal Tibbs could back them off with a ten-gauge shotgun. Then he picked Bennis up off the floor and threw him into the cell next door with the gambler Brian Houx.

Houx was awake now and was shaking his head in a water pan trying to sober up. "Shut up, Bennis, you worm," he laughed. "I got all your money right over there in those saddle bags."

Bennis dropped to his knees and begged the marshal not to hang him. Tibbs just looked at him with disgust, slammed the cell door shut behind him, and walked out of the office.

Tibbs breathed in the fresh air and looked down the street. Deputy Doug Pricer and Bill Larkin had just entered town from the north. He walked out into the street to meet them.

"Well it's about time, boys. I thought the Sioux had probably relieved you of that pretty hair. Good God, man, is that what I think it is on that drag?"

"Yes, it is, sir, and he's the one that lost his hair. I have reason to believe this is John Bennis. It all adds up–that's for sure."

The smell was drifting down the street and people were covering their faces.

"Larkin, take this man out to the cemetery, I'll get the undertaker, and fetch Bennis to identify him, if he can." Suddenly Tibbs realized the posse was a man short. "Where's Tom Sheen? Is he all right?"

Smiling and shaking his head, the deputy explained, "Well, he liked that ranch so much he took a job working their horses. He had his eye on a little gal there. She is very pretty." He winked at his associate. "I met an old friend of yours there too, boss. I'll tell you about it later."

Tibbs and Doug Pricer went to the jail, forced Bennis from his knees and half-dragged him from the cell. As they walked to the cemetery, Bennis was still begging them not to hang him. When they arrived at the body and pulled down the blanket, Bennis fainted and had to be carried back to the cell.

Doug Pricer shoved Bennis into the cell and poured a bucket of water on his head. Bennis woke up delirious, calling out his wife's name. Doug turned to Marshal Tibbs, shaking his head.

"Bennis' wife and two children are alive and fine. They're living on that Armstrong Ranch and doing well. He lied to us about what happened to them. She's a fine lady and well respected. It's amazing to me that this worm could have married a lady like her."

Bennis had come to his senses and was listening to Pricer talk. He just kept his head down and cried.

CHAPTER 15

The next morning Marshal Tibbs sent Doug to Eula May's saloon to see if Lisa Freeman was well enough to identify Wayne Bennis. She was still sitting in a room staring at the walls. Doug asked her very nicely if she could help them out. She said she could if he would walk with her. He helped her across the dusty street to the jail.

While Doug was gone Tibbs had put Bennis back in the cell with the four other inmates. His idea was to make absolutely sure that she was in a good enough state of mind to identify Bennis.

Lisa Freeman came in the jail's front door with her head down. She was a shy young lady and very close to tears. Her heart was pounding at the thought of seeing this scum of a man that had killed her love. Marshal Tibbs walked her over to the cell and asked her to take a look at the men inside. She looked right at Bennis and asked Marshal Tibbs if he could have him walk up closer to the cell bars.

Bennis nervously stood up and walked slowly to the bars. Lisa suddenly raised her hand and fired a tiny derringer she pulled from the light jacket she was carrying. The bullet hit Bennis in the cheek and he dropped, cursing and covering up his head. Doug wrestled the derringer away from Lisa.

“My God, man!” yelled Doug Pricer. “I never thought she would do that.”

“Take her back to Eula’s. I’ll get Doc Young to take a look at Bennis.”

Several people on the street had heard the shot and were crowding around the front of the jail. Tibbs yelled for someone to get Doc Young.

Doc Young came in the door, grouchy as usual, carrying his bottle of whiskey.

“You always carry that whiskey bottle around, Doc?” greeted Tibbs.

Doc turned the bottle up and took a big swig of whiskey. “I use it for medicine to ward off infection,” he winked.

Tibbs reached out and took the bottle. “You mind, Doc? After all this I feel kind of infected myself.” He took a drink and shook his head. “I’m gonna quit this damn job pretty soon. I’m getting pretty tired of it.”

“Well, that’s what you’ve been saying for twenty years now, Tibbs. I’m getting tired of hearing it.”

“Just do your job, Doc,” Tibbs said while shaking his head.

As they entered the jail, Bennis was rolling around on the floor screaming in pain.

“Shut up, you damn Weasel! I wish her aim had been a little bit better. Now they’re probably gonna hang you anyway.” Tibbs shoved the whining criminal toward the doctor with his foot.

Bennis fainted when he realized he had a huge hole in his cheek. The men put him on the table and Doc Young inspected his wound. After sewing it up as well as he could, he poured a glass of water in Bennis’s face.

“Stop your whining, Bennis, you little maggot” Doc ordered. “The bullet went clean through both sides of your cheeks. Kind of removed a couple of them teeth too.” He turned to the marshal. “My fee is three dollars, Tibbs. I want to be paid before I leave.”

"Well, the deputies found them brothers' hundred dollars so I've got the money, you old goat." Tibbs counted out three bills from the stack.

"Well, I figure Bennis stole at least ten dollars of my egg money," Doc responded. He pulled the money from Tibbs' hand, counted out ten more dollars, and shoved them in his pocket.

"Why, you old goat, I ought to throw you in one of them cells there." Tibbs laughed to himself as old Doc Young scurried out the door. It was worth ten dollars for him to know the Doc would always be there when he needed him.

"Well, Bennis, get back in the cell. I've had enough excitement for one day. I'm taking the rest of the day off. Doug, you take over–I'm going to Miss Eula May's and have myself several good beers. If anything happens here, just shoot 'em ."

As the marshal left the jail, Bennis was moaning in pain and holding his jaw. "Are they going to hang me?" he whimpered."

"Well, the Territorial Judge will be here in about two weeks, and, yeah, Bennis, I think old Judge Eland will hang you dead. You killed that young man, Bennis, and ruined the life of that little lady over there." Doug pondered as he regarded the sniveling prisoner. "The way I see it, you've got about two weeks to make your peace. I should kill you myself for leaving your family like you did. You see, Bennis, I met that family of yours. Damn nice people and they sure deserve better than you."

Bennis put his hands over his face and cried and prayed for forgiveness.

The Ranch

Carl and his brother Earl sat very quietly as they watched the big flathead catfish swirl with the current in the river. They were fishing for the small perch in the rocks by the river's edge, having acquired several large hooks from Earl Stockman along with some stout woven trotline string. Earl had told the boys that no fish in the river would be able to break the heavy woven line. They first had to catch the perch, but were having a hard time doing it.

"Damn, these perch won't bite," Carl said as he threw his cane pole to the ground. "I've got to figure out how to catch these yellow perch! Something is wrong–we're not doing it right. We need to go and ask Earl how to catch the perch, so we can catch the flatheads."

His brother was disgusted with the whole thing, and just lay back in the warm sand and went to sleep. Carl stomped back toward Earl Stockman's place.

Old Earl was sitting on the stump by his place whittling some bird-shaped objects. He had several other birds he had made from wood sitting around his place.

"Earl," explained Carl, "I can't catch any of those damn perch. You need to help me catch some of those."

Earl winked, teasing, "You're going to get in a lot of trouble if your Mama hears you talk like that, my little friend. If I were you, I would build a trap. I can show you tomorrow if you will gather me a sack of reeds from the river's edge. I will show you how to make such a trap, but you will have to make your own. My father showed me, but I had to make my own, so you will also."

"Fair enough," Carl blurted with excitement. "Are you going to tell us more of the story of the far north tonight, Mr. Earl? I really want to hear more about that mountain lion! And I wish I could have met your friend Little Boy Horse. You think I ever will?"

"It is uncertain in this life that even I will see my brother again, my little friend. If it is meant to be, then it will be. Yes, tonight is a good night to tell the story. Did you ever give that dog a name yet?"

"Yes, I have–I call him Butch. He's a good dog, but he barks too much and scares the fish!"

"Well, he is young, but he'll grow and that will get better–it is written, my little friend."

Saturday night was always a time for the entire ranch to play music and have their great deep pit beef barbecue. As the afternoon was slowing down and the evening shadows slowly crept across the campground, the ranch hands walked their horses down the dusty street. Before it would get too late, Earl would start telling the group the story of the far north and the great journey he had once made. It seemed everyone at the ranch was interested in hearing of this great man's adventures.

Chapter 16

The Story Continues at Rabbit Creek

Several more days brought Kicking Wind closer to her home. She started remembering every hill where she had played and every creek, she had fished in. She rode ahead and stopped at some trees overlooking Rabbit Creek. When Johnny One Horn and Little Boy Horse rode up beside her, she was just staring at the swift little river.

"There," she said, pointing. "That's where BoJack caught me. I was just fishing in my favorite little fishing place." Silently, she dismounted and walked to the edge of the trees.

Little Boy Horse followed. He hugged and comforted her as only he could do. "He's gone now, Wind. He will never hurt you again."

"Will you always stay with me?" she asked.

"Yes, my flower, I'll never leave you."

As they were standing, the roar of the current muffled all other sound until Johnny One Horn whistled. When Horse looked around, he realized they were surrounded by Sioux. It wasn't a war party, though plenty of warriors were in the mix. Two young women ran to Wind and embraced her, stroking her hair and talking very fast. Some of the braves had rifles pointed at Johnny and Horse. One of the women grabbed a rifle and shot at Little Boy Horse. He slid to the side of his horse with his hands away from his weapons. Kicking Wind ran and bear-hugged him to protect him. The rest of the group, upon seeing that, lowered their guns and began inspecting the way the newcomers were dressed.

A medicine man with a fearsome display of war paint kept his gun pointed at Johnny One Horn. Johnny could tell they were suspicious of him, but he jerked the rifle from the man's hands. Several braves drew back down on him until he raised his hands from his weapons and things settled back down. "Poke me with that rifle again and I'll skin you," he warned.

The medicine man became very loud, saying something to Kicking Wind and pointing toward Johnny and Horse. She explained as well as she could, but he kept expressing his dislike for the two. After several more minutes of confusion, things calmed. Johnny could make out some of the words, but they were talking too fast. Kicking Wind kept explaining that these were her friends and had saved her life, but Enapay the medicine man kept jabbing toward Little Boy Horse and chanting something that Horse and Horn couldn't understand.

It was about a mile or two to the village. Enapay kept poking at Little Boy Horse. Kicking Wind could see that Little Boy Horse was getting angry and she tried to calm him. But finally he had had enough. He pulled out his long knife and grabbed Enapay by the hair. The other braves raised their spears as Horse yanked Enapay from his horse.

Johnny One Horn quickly stepped beside his brother.

"We have heard of your journey, little one," said one of the braves. "I am Chatah,"

Kicking Wind didn't remember Chatah at first, then she regained her memory of her childhood friend. As she smiled in recognition, he dismounted, laughing, and hugged his longtime friend.

Chatah glanced at Johnny and Horse, then assured Wind, "Pay no attention to Enapay. He's just overprotective of our people. We have lost a lot of people since you have been gone, my friend."

"It's not old Enapay I'm worried about, Chatah, its Horse! He means what he says and just might skin Enapay here in front of everybody."

Chatah smiled. "Well, we wouldn't want that to happen," He turned and advised Enapay to return to the village. Enapay mounted his horse and tried to wipe the mud from his face and clothing. He was mumbling something under his breath as he rode away. Some of the braves laughed but Chatah quickly hushed them. "Enapay is an elder and we do not laugh at him. It is our custom to be humble in front of our people."

~ ~ ~

As the night fell upon the village the women took Wind to the other side of the camp where they gave her clothing of her tribal design. Chatah told Horse and Horn that they could make camp on the edge of the village. Some of the women were in wonder at the two huge Indians, who were much bigger than the other men in the village. As they whispered among themselves, it made Horse and Horn smile and tease each other.

Johnny and Horse rode to the edge of the village and found a tree to tie their horses. "I think that huge woman wants you, my brother," laughed Horse. "I saw the way she was looking at you. You would have to kill many buffalo to feed her. She might just take you for her own."

"You speak with a fork in the tongue, like those buzz-tail snakes on the prairie. I think she wants you, my brother–after all, I saw you looking at her," laughed Johnny.

"Oh, my brother, you always make up stories. Let's build a fire and see how the night works out."

Cha-cha came out of the tall grass by the tree and sniffed

in the direction of the hills to the north.

"There you are, my friend," Johnny smiled. "You missed all the fun."

The wolf yawned and stretched out under the tree.

The sun was setting to the west in a huge fireball, and the orange glow reflected off the clouds. They gathered a few dried fallen limbs and sticks and built a fire. Suddenly Cha-cha snarled and sprang to his feet. Horse noticed a young woman coming toward them.

"Stand very still!" he warned. "Don't move! The wolf is ours. Let me come to you."

He left the fire and made his way to her in the darkening twilight.

Cha-cha growled a fearsome growl and Johnny quickly went to calm him.

"I am not afraid of him. He just doesn't know me. I have two wolves of my own," smiled the young woman. "You are lucky to have one–they are a blessing."

Johnny walked Cha-cha back to the tree and gave him a piece of leftover rabbit he had cooked.

"My name is Mika, and I brought you some stew," the young woman explained.

Little Boy Horse couldn't help but notice how pretty she was as she handed him the large bowl.

"My sister and I have Wind in our dwelling; she is enjoying her family and says to tell you she will visit you tomorrow. Now I must get back before it is dark." She smiled at Horse, saying, "By the way, I've been told a lot about you."

As she turned and walked back toward the camp, Horse looked at Johnny and smiled. "Did you notice how pretty she is? I think she likes me."

"I see how pretty she is, and I bet half the men in this tribe know how pretty she is. You better not stare too long, my brother–you might get you throat cut."

"Oh, well, they would have a fight on their hands.

because as young Carl used to say, she's damn pretty."

As Horse rambled on, Johnny lay down by the fire and smiled at hearing Carl's name. As he stretched out and looked at the ocean of stars, he wondered what it all meant. Thoughts raced through his mind like swift arrows. For a while he could not get young Carl out of his mind. He lay for hours watching the great wheel in the sky turn above his head. He had never seen so many stars in his life, and the air was crisp and full of distant sounds. His shoulder burned where the bear had torn his flesh. He thought of what Carl would have done if he had seen the mighty grizzly. Fond memories of his little friend lingered in his mind as sleep overcame him.

Two weeks later

Little Boy Horse and Johnny had adapted to the village and its people with a growing bond. Horse had gotten close to Mika and the relationship between the two had not gone unnoticed by the tribe. Chatah had taken a liking to both Johnny and Horse, and welcomed them into the village. Some of the younger braves seemed jealous of Horse, but said nothing.

The weather was slowly changing to fall, and the cold wind whistled through the turning of the trees and the changing of the seasons. The hunting parties were coming back empty-handed and the people were using up their dried meat, fish and other foods.

Chatah had decided to move the people farther west and asked if Little Boy Horse could accompany the braves on a scouting trip. He agreed, and the scouting party left without knowing when they would be back. It was hard for Horse to leave Mika and Kicking Wind, but he was part of the people now and was glad to help.

Chatah asked Johnny One Horn to remain in the village and help with the wood cutting and hunting. Since Johnny had been taught some of the white man's medicine, Chatah thought that his knowledge would be useful.

Enapay never trusted Johnny and was not going to like him no matter how Johnny tried.

One week later

A light crusting of snow had covered the village, and Chatah and the scouting party had not returned. No one was really worried, because they knew Chatah was skilled at avoiding all kinds of danger. Johnny was busy searching for wood with some of the other men when he noticed a familiar face ride up to their work site. One of the younger men said, "Look, it's Sad Hank."

Sad Hank dismounted his horse and gave the younger man a hug. He looked at Johnny and smiled. "Where's the Big Horse?"

"He's on a scouting mission with Chatah and some other members of the village."

"Let's go to the village and talk for a while. I have some news for you, my friend."

As they walked their horses back toward the village, Johnny could tell something was bothering Sad Hank. "Sad Hank, there seems to be something on your mind, my friend. Are there problems with the family?" he asked.

"Well, my friend, a lot of things are happening on the prairie to the south. The Army is digging in for the winter and I won't be needed for a while. I don't think I will return to them. They seem to be catching on that I am leading them away from the villages. I only lead them to the outcast and renegades of our people. I need some different clothes for the winter and then I can get rid of this Army outfit I'm wearing."

"I will tell Mika; she may have something you can wear."

As they sat, the sun was sinking in a huge fireball over

the hills. The air was chill as different tribal members gathered around several fires. Mika brought Sad Hank some furs and tribal dress. He quickly stripped the Army jacket off and threw it into the fire.

As they sat by the fire, Sad Hank began telling Johnny and some of the elders what was happening on the prairie. "Our people of all tribes are blamed for everything the scum of the prairie does. Bands of buffalo hunters and some rotten mountain men have been robbing the helpless settlers and wagon trains as they move across what they call the Oregon Trail. I tried to tell the Army leaders that most of the murders and raids are not done by our people. The Pawnee are fighting back but are quickly being killed off."

"The outlaws are scalping their victims, and using some bows and arrows to shift the blame to us. This village is lucky to be this far north, because there are terrible things going on south along the trails."

"Is there not a sign of the outlaws they can see? Surely there must be something," asked Johnny.

"I showed the tobacco spit on the ground and their rolled smoke papers, but they didn't want to believe me. I told them our people didn't have such paper, but they wouldn't listen. It's happening all across the land there. We are fortunate that the Army will be staying close to their forts and not wandering too far away in the bad of winter."

Sad Hank looked at the elders earnestly. "This village should move farther north before the spring comes. The Army's plan is to move this way in the spring and try to capture or kill any who resist. We cannot convince them that we are innocent of these crimes. This village must move. Their scouts have already scouted this place. I believe you should move now before the winter sets in and the strong winds blow."

Enapay had been getting more and more upset as Sad Hank told the story. "I will use bad medicine against them.

I will talk to the Spirits and repress their army. If we go farther north, we will have to deal with the Crow and they can handle the winter very well. They will try to kill us all and steal our women and young girls."

Sad Hank shook his head. "Try to understand, Enapay. The white man's army can reach across the prairie. There are thousands of them but only a few hundred Crow. We can hold our own with the Crow. We will just have to learn their ways and use these against them."

Sad Hank suddenly remembered something and turned back to Johnny. "There is another thing you must know, Johnny," he shared urgently. "The mountain man Little Boy Horse killed on the prairie was named Red Tom–BoJack still lives! The word that Little Boy Horse killed Red Tom has spread across the prairie. His brother, Mule Tom, has vowed to kill Little Boy Horse. In my opinion, he is as bad a man as BoJack. This man can track anything that walks. He and the Army will be coming after Horse."

"If he comes for my brother, he will die because I will find him first. I will leave at sunrise to find this Mule Tom, and then I will find this BoJack and kill him also." Johnny rose to his feet decisively. "You need to stay with the village, Sad Hank. Teach them the ways of the white man's Army so they can be aware."

Sad Hank shook his head with sorrow and hugged Johnny.

~~~

The next morning the sun glistened over the crusting of light snow. The wind was crisp. Johnny hoped the scouting party would be back; he was torn because he would not get to say goodbye to his brother. Most of the tribe was up except the children, and Johnny quickly readied his horse Coattail for the journey.

Kicking Wind and Mika pleaded for him to stay, but to
~~~

no avail.

Kicking Wind cried and hugged his leg after he mounted Coattail.

Mika looked on with deep concern as the tears streamed down Kicking Wind's face. "Take care, my friend, and may the Great Spirit guide your way."

"I will return, if it is meant to be, but if not, then it is also meant to be, my friends." He looked down one more time, smiled at the young women, and walked Coattail to the top of the hill. With Cha-cha the wolf walking beside him, he turned and waved from the distance, then disappeared over the hill and was on his way.

Kicking Wind was still crying as she turned and ran back to the village.

Mika looked at Sad Hank in disbelief at what had just happened. "You should not have told him, Sad Hank."

"I know that now, Mika, but I didn't think he would go, and I am deeply sorry."

As he looked off in the distance, he knew there was little chance that Johnny One Horn would ever return.

One week later.

Chatah and the hunting party arrived back in the village. All the village ran to greet the worn-out hunting party. Wind was one of the first to run up and hug Chatah. "Where is Little Boy Horse?" she asked with excitement.

"We don't know, Wind–he left chasing some Crow that had stolen a few of our horses and never returned."

Wind screamed, pounding Chatah on the chest. He was finally able to grab her hands and hug her. "Wind, my sweet little flower, it was not our fault! You can't tell Horse anything when he makes up his mind–you know that."

Wind stopped pounding and just sobbed while Mika stood with her hands over her face.

CHAPTER 17

Back at the Ranch

Earl Stockman had taught Carl to construct a trap to catch the Red Eared Perch. The boy was down at the willow trees every day checking the trap to see if he had the perch. He had captured the perch on several occasions, and hooked them very carefully, but the big flatheads would tear them off, and avoid the hook.

That afternoon O.C. and Jack Tunnie were sitting by their favorite fishing hole and watching young Carl as he busily scurried around the willow trees.

"Look, O.C. I believe he's got one!" laughed Jack Tunnie.

"Well, I'll be danged if you're not right, Jack." O.C. stood up and cheered, "Get 'em, Carl! I'll be danged if I don't think that's a big one!"

Carl was struggling with the big fish and the cane pole was bent double. He squeezed himself against the sandy bank, digging his feet into the sand. The big fish surfaced and made a huge splash, swirling the water. Then it surfaced again, and this time the hook came flying back toward Carl and hit him in the foot.

"Damn it, damn it, damn it!" Carl yelled while grabbing his foot.

"Are you OK, Carl?" yelled O.C.

Carl picked up the hook and partially eaten perch from his foot. He was very lucky to have avoided being impaled by the big hook. His face turned a bright red as he hurled his cane pole into the water. “Damn it,” he yelled again.

O.C. and Jack couldn’t keep from laughing and that made Carl even madder.

“Don’t laugh at me!” he shouted. “I don’t see anybody else catching a flathead.”

Earl was pulling on Carl’s shirt.

“Leave me alone or I’ll punch you right in the nose!” Carl growled.

“But your pole, Carl! Look at your pole!”

The pole was floating down the river and it was clear that something else had taken the piece of perch on the hook. The pole slid across the water with tremendous speed and then disappeared into the deep water.

Carl screamed at the top of his voice and then dropped to his knees, then flopped face down in the sand. He lay there for a few minutes and then stomped off back toward the camp.

“Man, that boys got a temper, O.C. You know, he’s just like your son, the first Carl, only, boy, does he got a temper!”

“Yes, he does. I’ve noticed he always stops at Carl’s grave, but he didn’t this time. He must be really mad.”

Just then Carl stopped in his tracks and turned back to the grave site. He stood there a few minutes before he turned and scurried off again.

“Well, he’s got a heart to go along with that temper. He’ll be a fine man someday. It’s too bad the fever got the other Carl–he would have made a hell of a man also.”

“I agree for sure,” smiled Jack Tunnie.

Joe was riding up from the south pasture and had noticed the commotion from the top of the hill. As he rode up, he looked at Carl stomping home and asked what the fracas was.

“Well, he’s just mad because he lost a fish. He’s OK,” smiled O.C.

“Well, OK. I thought I heard him cussing again. I’ll swear I’m going to switch his ass if he don’t stop that. Was he cussing again, Pop?”

“Nah, I didn’t hear him do no cussin’–did you, Jack?”

“No, I didn’t hear no cussing, but of course I was busy baiting my hook.”

Earl started to tell his dad, but O.C. winked at him as he picked him up and sat him on his knee.

“Well, I think he was, but I’ll let it slide this time.” Joe didn’t seem convinced, but he went on. “I wanted to tell you that Nate said the trial of Wayne Bennis will be day after tomorrow. I’m taking his wife, along with some of the boys, to the trial. We’ll be leaving first thing in the morning.” He turned to leave. “Well, I’ve got a few more fences to mend before dark. That dang bull keeps tearing them up.”

“OK, Son. It’s good to see a man work hard. It makes me feel good all over.”

“Yeah, Pop, that fishin’ looks mighty tough. I’m sure glad I don’t have it as rough as you.”

“Here’s to you, Son!” O.C. replied as he waved the whiskey jug toward him.

Joe laughed as he wheeled his horse around and rode off.

“He’s a good man, O.C., damn good man,” smiled Jack Tunnie.

“You bet he is, my friend–the best.”

~ ~ ~

The next morning as the ranch people rustled around getting ready for breakfast at the campground, Nate loaded Judy Bennis and their bags into the wagon. Judy was a shy lady, but very attractive. Nate would escort her in the wagon, and Shorty and two other ranch hands would ride shotgun. Carol Bennis had agreed to take care of the children.

Nate brought breakfast plates from the campground for the travelers before the group left on the dusty camp road toward the trail to Garden City.

Shorty was still chewing on a good biscuit, when he mumbled, "Well, we should be there midafternoon day after tomorrow. I'll ride on ahead and keep a lookout. You men stay with the wagon, I'll check back every hour or so."

"That Shorty's a good man, Nate," Judy smiled, "I think him and Marianna will make a fine couple one day."

"You think so? I don't know–there's a lot of them boys on the ranch that favors her."

"Yeah, Nate, but I see the way she looks at him, and women just know these things."

"Well, you may be right, Miss Judy; I can't figure them out. You know, Miss Judy, I just don't know how you got with Wayne Bennis anyway. Someone as smart and pretty as you. I don't mean to be nosey or anything like that."

"You're not, Nate, and I don't mind you asking. Wayne is a follow-the-leader-type man who will also take advantage of anybody or anything if he can."

"You know, Miss Judy, I heard he killed a young man, and robbed the young couple of their life savings. I hate to say this, but they probably will hang him."

"I know, Nate, I know."

Judy Bennis stared across the prairie and Nate knew he was crossing a thin line. Nate thought he'd better let it go so he got quiet for a while.

Judy stared at a storm to the south. The wind was flowing the prairie grass like waves on the lakes she had seen in the past. Thunder rumbled in the distance, and the prairie grass seemed to give a fresh smell of rain in the air. "Looks like we might get a little storm, Nate. I'm glad we brought a wagon with a cover. I'm afraid your friends there are going to get a little soaked."

"Yeah, but they're a tough bunch, and they've been through many storms. I reckon they'll get through this one."

The storm was very fast-moving and gave everybody a chill with its cold rain. The group traveled until nightfall and made their camp just yards away, unknowingly, from where John Bennis had been killed. The cool wind whipped the canvas on the wagon as the hands and Nate built a fire under the overhanging rocks. Judy Bennis bedded down in the wagon.

"Somebody's been here before," Shorty thought. "I wonder if it was that damned old BoJack. I'll surely kill him if I see him again."

Nate laughed at Shorty's rambling. "Hell, he's dead according to stories I've heard. You men get some sleep–we need to be in Garden City as soon as we can. Don't start telling stories about some booger man–hell, the Sioux will probably scalp all of you by morning."

The two younger hands looked at each other with wide eyes. "You mean there's Indians around here?" blurted one of them.

"Nah, the truth is they all are probably farther north this time of year," Nate explained. "Just get some sleep. I'd sure like to myself, but something sure stinks around here."

Midmorning of the third day

As the morning sun shined down on Garden City, the group from the Triple A Ranch made its way to the front of the city jail. Marshal Tibbs was leaning up against the horse rail in front.

Nate stopped the team and addressed him. "Howdy, Marshal. This is Judy Bennis and I heard you have her husband inside."

The old marshal just tipped his hat back. "You've got to

park that wagon down yonder at the stable. You can just let Miz Bennis out here."

Marshal Tibbs helped Judy Bennis down from the wagon and escorted her into the jail. "Ma'am, he's a mess. I don't think he's cleaned himself up in days. I try to get him to, but he just won't do it."

The jailer opened the door that led to the cells. As Judy entered, the other prisoners started whistling and taunting her.

"You men want ten more days in here?" Tibbs yelled. The prisoners quickly quieted down.

Wayne Bennis ran to the bars and dropped to his knees in front of his wife. Instead of thanking her for coming, he begged her to talk to the judge and ask for forgiveness.

One of the other prisoners yelled, "Hey, Bennis, why don't you tell her about all them whores you been hanging out with?"

Bennis tried to kick the prisoner through the bars. "You shut up, or when I get out, I'll slit your throat, you piece of crap."

The prisoner yelled back. "You ain't getting out, Bennis! You're gonna hang."

"The children are fine, Wayne, and they miss you sometimes," Judy said as she wiped tears from her eyes.

Bennis acted like he never heard her. "Please talk to the judge and convince him that I'm a good man. Did you bring any money? Maybe you could give him money?"

Judy stood there wiping tears out of her eyes as she listened to him grovel. Suddenly she turned and walked from the jail. Bennis kept yelling her name and crawling on his knees in desperation.

As Judy Bennis walked out to the street where Nate and the boys were waiting, she broke down and collapsed into Nate's arms.

Marshal Tibbs looked at her and shook his head. "Ma'am, I don't think that man cares about anybody but himself."

"Let's go, Nate," she said.

"Go where, Miss Judy, to find you a room?"

"No, back to the ranch. I don't want to go through this one more minute."

"But the trial is at one o'clock."

Judy grabbed the reins. "I'm going without you, Nate."

"OK, OK, I'm going. Shorty, take one of the hands and stay for the trial. I'm taking Miss Judy back to the ranch."

Shorty tipped his hat back on his head like he did when he questioned things. "Well, I'll be damned," he said. "You got it, Nate. I'll catch you down the road."

Nate jumped into the driver's seat and slapped the reins. He sat very quietly for a few minutes until the town had faded in the distance. Then, speaking very quietly, he asked Judy why she didn't want to go to the trial.

She just stared across the plains for a minute. "You see, Nate, Wayne doesn't care about anyone. I told him that his children missed him and he didn't even hear that. He just kept begging me to bribe the judge."

"They will hang him, Miss Judy. That territorial Judge Eland, I hear, will hang anybody that has killed someone."

Judy had fixed her eyes on some far-away point across the prairie, but suddenly she turned to Nate and said, "Do you think it's going to rain today, Nate?"

He could tell she was a million miles away and just shook his head.

CHAPTER 18

The Trial

Shorty had sat in the crowded courtroom for about fifteen minutes before Judge Eland entered. He was a stern-looking man and boasted a long white beard. The first man to come before him had stolen a horse and the judge quickly entered a hanging decision. The rough-looking cowboy cursed at the judge as he was escorted from the courtroom. The next man was charged with drunk and disorderly conduct, and was sentenced to thirty days in the city jail and community service.

The last defendant was Bennis. He came into the courtroom dragged by Doug Pricer and another deputy. His eyes were searching the room for Judy, and he pitifully repeated her name.

"Put a gag on that man, Deputy!" ordered Judge Eland.

Bennis was quickly restrained, gagged, and tied to a chair.

"So, you're charged with murder and robbery, Bennis. You're charged with willingly killing a young man, taking his two hundred dollars, and threatening his wife." The judge turned to Marshal Tibbs and asked if there were any witnesses.

"Yes sir," Tibbs answered. "The victim's wife, Lisa Freeman."

Pickles and Eula May had escorted Lisa Freeman into the courtroom. She was still in a very fragile condition, and Eula May helped her stand in front of Judge Eland.

"Are you able to answer my questions, Mrs. Freeman?" the judge asked kindly.

Lisa nodded, and Judge Eland asked if the man that killed her husband was in the courtroom. She quickly turned and pointed to the squirming Bennis strapped to the chair. "It was that bastard right there!" she sobbed. Then she collapsed into Eula May's arms in tears.

"OK. I've heard the witness," stated Judge Eland. "It's about time for lunch. I don't think I need to hear any more." He turned to the defendant. "Bennis, you killed this young lady's husband in cold blood, and what I've already learned from Marshal Tibbs is that you robbed her and left her alone on the prairie without any regard for her life whatsoever. It is my judgement that you be taken to a place of execution and be hanged by the neck until you are dead. Marshal Tibbs, if you will, see that this is taken care of as soon as possible."

Bennis' head dropped and he stopped squirming in the chair.

Lisa Freeman walked by, hanging on to Eula May and Pickles. She stopped in front of Bennis and, before anybody could stop her, grabbed his hair. "Die, you bastard, die," she uttered in a strange, gravelly voice. Eula and Pickles quickly pulled her from the courtroom.

Marshal Tibbs walked out onto the street as the courtroom cleared, and leaned up against the horse rail in his usual way. As the deputies walked by, he beckoned Doug Pricer to come over. "After you get Bennis locked up, I want you to notify the grave digger to go dig a hole. I'm not going to make this some kind of community spectacle."

"You're not going to build a scaffold, Marshal?"

"No, as soon as the hole is dug, let me know, and we'll

take Bennis down to the old oak tree at the end of town and hang 'im."

"Holy crap, man! When?" asked Doug.

"You heard the judge. He said as soon as possible, and that's exactly what we're going to do. Don't tell a soul. I don't want the town to know–they'd lynch him anyway, and I'd have to protect that worthless bastard. Somebody might get hurt, and I don't want that."

"Yes, sir," frowned Doug Pricer. "This just don't seem right."

"Doug," Tibbs ordered, "this is the way it's going to be done, or you can turn that badge in. I'll not have a deputy that can't handle his job."

Doug just frowned, looking concerned at the same time, and said, "Yes, Sir."

Sundown in Garden City

Doug Pricer and Bill Larkin were instructed to take Wayne Bennis out the back door of the jail and load him into a waiting wagon.

As they opened the door to his cell, Bennis nervously asked where they were taking him. He became frantic and started bawling, so the deputies had to gag him. They tied his hands and feet and heaved him into the wagon. Bill Larkin hurriedly covered him up with a blanket.

As they reached the huge oak tree outside of town, Marshal Tibbs was waiting, the rope already strung from a large limb. They wrestled Bennis out of the wagon and sat him on his knees below the limb. When they took the gag from his mouth, Marshal Tibbs asked if he had anything to say.

Bennis looked at the marshal and said, "If you would wait a while, my wife Judy is going to fix everything with the judge."

"Your wife has already left town, Bennis," said Tibbs.

The man begged and cried as they put the noose around his neck. Marshal Tibbs attached the end of the rope to his horse and walked off without looking back. After about thirty feet, Bennis was swinging far from the ground.

Bennis was still kicking as the marshal lit a smoke. "Well, I wish he'd quit that kickin'. I've got a good card game waiting for me at the saloon."

Tibbs got in the wagon and told the deputies to bring his horse back when they were sure Bennis was dead. "See that you take him to the graveyard, boys–the card game's goin' and supper's waiting. Besides, the old hole digger's waiting for you."

"Good God, what a cold-blooded man he is," frowned Bill Larkin. "This just ain't right somehow."

Doug had been thinking, and was beginning to see Marshal Tibb's point. "Well, Bill, who's to say it's wrong? Lisa Freeman's husband is already laying up there dead. That, for sure, wasn't right. Bennis just got what he deserved."

Bill looked at the top of the hill in the distance and could see the gravedigger standing against the skyline. "Yeah, Doug, but still something just doesn't seem right."

~ ~ ~

Shorty and Tom Sheen were just coming out of the saloon as the sun was setting and Marshal Tibbs drove into town and stopped the wagon in front of the livery stable.

"Man, those sure are some fun girls in there, Tom! Why would you ever leave here to move to a dusty old ranch?"

"Well, Shorty, when I saw Yolanda, I knew I had to. She's the most beautiful thing I've ever seen, man!"

"Well," Shorty laughed, "Tom, I think you've gotta be crazy–she flirts with everybody! She's a good girl, but I think you know what I mean."

"Well, I'm still gonna make her my wife if I can, Shorty.

That's it. Let's not talk about it any more."

Shorty just smiled and kept walking towards the livery stable.

"Howdy, Marshal Tibbs," greeted Tom Sheen.

"Well, from a deputy marshal to a cow puncher. I didn't know you had it in you, Sheen."

"I kind of like it so far. I'm working with their horses."

"Saloon girls to horses? Boy, that's a step up for you, eh, Tom?"

Tom grinned.

Shorty asked the marshal if he knew when the hanging was going on and old Tibbs just tipped his hat back and bit down on a block of Bull Durham. "Well, boys, you just missed it. We hung Bennis about a half hour ago. They're burying him as we speak."

"Hung 'im?" asked Shorty. "That's pretty damn quick!"

"Well you were at the trial–you heard what Judge Eland said."

"Yeah, I heard him, but I didn't think it would be today." Shorty was shocked by this and stared at the ground for a second. "Well, I'll be dammed. Justice is quick in this town, huh, Marshal?"

"Yeah, for some it's quicker than others, son. I wasn't about to feed his sorry ass for another week just to hear him piss and moan. He was a murderer and deserved what he got."

"Yeah, I suppose he did," frowned Shorty, "Well, let's go play some cards, Tom. We have to leave at first light."

Chapter 19

Back at the Ranch

O.C. and Pete were tracking down a pack of coyotes when Nate and Judy Bennis returned from Garden City.

"You know, Pete, these damn coyotes are smart. You can't find 'em in the daytime. They use the cover of night to do their dirty work. Might as well wait 'til dark." O.C. took off his hat and squinted up the road. "That's Nate and Judy Bennis and one of the ranch hands. I wonder what happened to the other two? Let's ride over and see–hell, I hope they're OK."

Judy Bennis was still staring across the prairie as the two rode up beside the wagon.

"Miss Judy," O.C. smiled as he tipped his hat. "Nate, how was the trip, and where's the other boys?"

"Well, I left them in town to attend the trial, as Miss Judy here didn't want to stay."

O.C. could tell Judy Bennis wasn't up for talking and just nodded to Nate in an understanding way. "Well, let's just get her back to camp–it was probably kind of rough on her."

"Yes, Sir. I'm sure glad to be home," Nate shook his head, clicking to the mules. "I need a drink of anything cool."

Garden City

Shorty and Tom Sheen were relaxing playing cards, and had told a few card players about Bennis being hanged. The whole saloon was whispering and talking about it.

Eula May glimpsed Lisa Freeman coming down the stairs wearing just a few undergarments. "What the hell," she frowned. Then she called to the young woman, "You don't work here, Lisa! Are you out of your mind or something?"

Lisa was smiling and dancing to the piano music in a trance-like state. Pickles and the rest of the girls began to clap for her as she teased the young cowboys with her moves. She was a beautiful girl and had everybody's attention. This had gone on for several minutes when she pulled a small derringer from her undergarment, placed it to her temple, and fired.

The shot was placed exactly right. Lisa Freeman dropped instantly to the floor, dead.

Doc Young was in the crowd and ran to her, as the cowboys gathered around. He scolded them to get back and let him check her.

But it was just a minute before he stood up and spoke. "Well, that little gun did the job. She's dead."

"She must have found it in one of the dressers upstairs–hell, that's the second one she's found." Eula May was mortified. All of the girls looked like they were in a state of shock.

Shorty and Tom had blood spatters all over them and were stunned at what had just happened.

"My God, I never seen that coming! She was such a pretty girl," stuttered Shorty.

Marshal Tibbs walked through the door and stared at the lifeless body of the beautiful Lisa Freeman lying in a pool of blood. "Well, this is all Wayne Bennis' fault–that's why I hung him this afternoon. Let's get her cleaned up, girls.

We'll bury her tomorrow."

The saloon became very quiet as the marshal left. The crowd thinned out to just a few at the bar shooting shots of Red Eye.

"Damn, Tom, let's just leave! Hell, I'd rather ride than try to sleep tonight after seeing that. Let's just get back to the ranch."

Tom agreed, and the two walked out of the saloon and to the livery stable. They saddled their horses and quickly headed out of town.

"You know, Tom," remarked Shorty, "the ranch has some wild and wooly people, it's true, but towns seem to draw a lot of crazies. There's no reason that pretty girl should have died like that. Hell, she would have probably found another man in no time at all."

"Yeah, Shorty, but it wouldn't have been the man she loved. I guess she just couldn't take the pain of it all." Tom pondered for a minute. "You know, old Bennis was a bad man. He might have killed someone at the ranch if he hadn't been forced to leave."

"Well, Tom, I always thought he was a weak man. Any man at the ranch could best him." He pursed his lips, thinking, before continuing. "Now, BoJack was an evil man. Terrible devil if I ever seen one."

The moon was almost full and blue as the two made their way across the flowing plains toward the ranch.

~ ~ ~

About noon on the third day, Shorty and Tom Sheen made their way back to the ranch. O.C. was helping Rose build another bench for the growing number of people living there. "You boys come on in and have a drink of cool water here in the shade."

Joe and the boys also saw them ride in and came to greet them. "I didn't expect you boys back this soon," said Joe.

"Well, we got tired of Garden City pretty damn quick," Shorty replied, shaking his head. He swung off his mount and plopped down on the bench.

Tom Sheen saw Yolanda standing in front of the school and walked his horse in her direction.

O.C. watched and smiled. "Well, the power of a pretty girl overcomes all obstacles. Ain't that right, Shorty?"

"Yeah, I suppose it does O.C.," Shorty replied. Then his smile turned very serious and he stared down toward the ground.

Joe and the boys dusted themselves off and sat down at the end of the bench. While gulping a cup of water, Joe asked, "What happened at the trial?"

"Well, old Judge Eland found Bennis guilty all right, and that's not all. Old Marshal Tibbs snuck him out of town and hung him that same afternoon. Darndest thing I ever saw."

"Holy Cow," Joe said as he shook his head. "Seems to me that's a might quick."

"Yeah, and that's not all, Joe. That afternoon we were playing cards at Eula Mays place and that pretty little Lisa Freeman started dancing in the saloon half naked and then she whipped out a pistol and just shot herself dead."

"Oh no, is that the truth? My God, man, why would she ever do that?" asked Joe.

"I don't know–I guess she went crazy or something," explained Shorty. "We had her blood splattered all over us. Everybody just felt so bad after they carried her out, they all left, including us."

Joe stood up and held his hat over his heart for a second. "Well, boys, there's a lesson for all of you right there. Don't get out of line when you go to Garden City. Old Marshal Tibbs might hang ya for spittin' on the street." He donned his hat and turned back to his horse. "Well, there's fences to mend and cattle to brand, men. Let's get after it." Joe mounted up, then turned back to Shorty. "Shorty, you take Tom Sheen and ride the section by the river to look for coyotes–them bastards have got several calves in the last couple of days."

"Joe, hell, these boys been riding straight all night and most of the day!" protested O.C.

"Well, Pop, it's not their day off, and they can stop at quitting time. Besides that, I didn't tell them they could stay another day and play cards."

O.C. smiled. "Well, you heard the man, boys, and the boss has spoken. Hell, I didn't know I raised a slave driver."

"I heard that, you old jailbird," laughed Joe. "It wouldn't hurt you to do a little coyote hunting yourself."

"Well, look here, Joe–I got me a real live coyote right here!" he said as he swung Bessie over his knee. He tipped the burlap-wrapped jug at Joe and grinned.

"All the boys laughed at O.C., even Shorty and Tom Sheen, as tired as they were.

O.C. patted Bessie on the back as he rose from the bench. "Darlin', I gotta go over and tell Judy Bennis what happened. I'll be back in a few minutes." Then he walked across the dusty street to the school.

Marianna was nailing a board in the porch of the school and O.C asked if he could help.

"Sure can," she smiled gratefully, and O.C. took the hammer from her hand. He asked Marianna to fetch Judy Bennis for him, and then got busy putting in a few nails. Marianna thanked him for the help and went inside.

In a few minutes, Judy Bennis came out the swinging doors. "O.C., what can I do for you?" she greeted, in good spirits.

O.C. took off his hat and stared off in the distance. "Well, Miss Judy, I have some bad news for you about your husband."

Judy just stood there enjoying the fresh air.

"You see, Miss Judy, that old Judge found him guilty,

and well," he hesitated, then thought he might as well say it. "They hung him the same day."

Judy looked at O.C. without changing her expression. "O.C., if you would, can you get me some seasoning salt from Levi's store and take it to the cook house for me?"

"Yes, ma'am, I sure will." He was having a hard time believing that she had just heard the news and it made no difference to her. It seemed like she hadn't even heard it. He turned, said, "Good day, Miss Judy," and walked away.

~ ~ ~

Later that afternoon, as the ranch hands were all riding up the dusty road and dismounting around the water tower, the women in the cook house were busy with the nightly dinner. There was never a dull moment around the ranch. Today, most of the hands were talking about the hanging of Wayne Bennis and the terrible suicide of Lisa Freeman, even though most had never met her. As the afternoon turned into night, Earl Stockman sat on the old oak tree stump and waited to continue his stories, as requested by most of the people in the camp. He usually would tell stories about old Mexico and sometimes about the fishing. One never knew what it would be next, but the whole ranch seemed to enjoy them.

BoJack and the North Platte River Dwelling

BoJack's leg was healing slowly as he limped through the dusty yard full of chickens. Zack saw that he was awake and hurriedly took Tina and young Sally to the other side of the shed beside the dwelling. "Let's go down to the river, girls. Maybe we can catch a fish."

Tina grabbed Zack's legs, crying, and wouldn't turn him loose.

"It's OK, Tina–he won't see us."

BoJack grabbed a jug of moonshine from the shed and yelled for Wicky. "Wicky, where the hell's them young'uns? I want my back scratched."

Wicky rushed over and scratched his back. "Zack's got the girls and they went down to the river fishing," she said soothingly. "Zack's a good hunter, BoJack, and he takes care of everybody, as far as the food goes."

BoJack just sneered at Wicky and pushed her face down in the dusty yard.

"This is the way you treat your mother, Son? I did nothing to you," she whimpered.

"Cook me something to eat, or I'll do worse than that!" he roared.

BoJack rubbed his leg and his mind drifted back to the night it had happened. He vowed to find the man that had done this and to torture him in the worst way. "He killed old Coon Hawk, the best damn dog I ever had," he howled.

Zack was listening to him rant, and shuddered at the way his father's crazed mind twisted the truth. "Tina, tonight when he passes out from the moonshine, we are going to leave this place. You help little Sally get ready. If we stay, it won't be long before he tries to hurt you both. We'll take that horse and you girls can sit behind me."

Zack knew BoJack's crazed mind would only escalate as he recovered and he would probably kill the two girls, or worse. He had thought to himself many times that he could just sneak up while the man was asleep and cut his throat, but BoJack had an uncanny way of knowing things and would probably catch him and kill him.

As usual, that night BoJack screamed at Wicky until he passed out from the moonshine. Zack would have to be careful–even drunk, BoJack could handle himself well.

It was around midnight when Zack motioned to the girls and made his move. They mounted the horse BoJack had stolen from Red Tom. Zack had taken it to the river's edge earlier, and the sound of the river current would make it easier to slip away. With no horse and a bad leg, Zack knew BoJack could not follow him. He also knew BoJack would find a horse as soon as he could and come after them. They rode hard the rest of the night, north along the river.

The two girls were really worn out when Zack decided it was safe to stop. He picked out a cove along the river's edge. This would be a comfortable place to rest, and Zack knew BoJack was a long way behind them.

CHAPTER 20

Johnny One Horn had traveled several days, coming out of the Dakotas, and had avoided a few hunting parties and small Army patrols. The hunting parties didn't bother him, but the Army might, and that was one thing he didn't want. As he got close to the place where Little Boy Horse had encountered BoJack, he became even more cautious.

Near an overgrown part of the river, Johnny noticed Zack's campfire and stopped to investigate. He dismounted Coattail and quietly slipped through the bushes. The girls were playing in the water and Zack was busy skinning a muskrat to eat.

As Johnny stood up from behind the brush, he smiled at the two girls. They, of course, screamed, and Zack ran at Johnny with the skinning knife. It only took Johnny a second to disarm the young man. Cha-cha Growled viciously at the young man and Zack froze in his tracks. Johnny gave Cha-cha a hand signal and the big Wolf settled down.

"I mean no harm to you," the tall Indian assured the boy. Zack's feet were dangling off the ground and the girls had run off into the brush.

"You speak like me," Zack said. "Please don't kill us."

"I'm not going to kill you," smiled Johnny, "as long as you don't try to stick me with that skinning knife."

"Oh, I was just trying to protect the girls–I didn't know

what you were going to do."

"That is very brave of you, little man. You will make a fine man one day."

Zack called for the girls to come out. They were very cautious, but finally came back to the fire.

After nodding toward the little ones, Johnny turned back to Zack. "My name is Johnny One Horn. I search for a mountain man called BoJack. Have you seen such a man, my friend?"

"Seen him? I'm his son," Zack said shakily. "I'm not proud of it. I know he is a murderer and he is crazier than any man you've ever seen. I took these little girls and ran away just two days ago." After glancing at the terrified children, he lowered his voice and whispered to Johnny that BoJack would have soon grown tired of them and killed them for fun."

"Then he is alive. My brother thought he killed him. If he did not kill him then who did he kill?"

"The horse there used to belong to a mountain man named Red Tom," Zack explained. "BoJack told me Red Tom was killed by the Sioux. BoJack has a bad leg from that fight with the Sioux. He can't get around on it yet–that's the only reason we got away. But his leg is getting better every day, and I know he will come after us."

Johnny remembered the words of Little Boy Horse when he said he had thrown the long knife and hit BoJack. "I intend to kill BoJack." Johnny frowned as he stared at the ground.

Tina and Sally sat huddled together, very shy of this strong-looking man.

Zack stared at Johnny in disbelief. "If you try, please watch every move you make. There's people that say my grandma is a witch. She put a bear claw around BoJack's neck to protect him. They say no man can kill him."

Johnny just kept his eyes on the river as he sharpened his long knife. "Tell me how I can find BoJack. I have dealt with witch doctors before. He will die, or I will die. I made a promise, and it will be done."

BoJack's dwelling

BoJack was walking on his bad leg, as it was getting better with each day that passed. He stood gritting his teeth as he looked down the canyon to the river's edge. A couple of prospectors were downriver panning for gold. The outlaw grabbed his buffalo gun and leaned against a large rock on the edge of the cliff, took careful aim, and dropped the first man dead. The horses spooked and the other prospector ducked into the brush along the river's edge. BoJack limped down the canyon until he got to the horses. The prospector broke from the brush and ran in the sand along the river's edge, firing at BoJack, but to no avail. BoJack took deadly aim and killed him with a roaring bullet from the huge-caliber buffalo gun.

Wicky sat on the top of the cliff, rocking back and forth as if in a trance. BoJack caught the horses and led them back to the dwelling. The prospectors were left where they lay, by the river's edge.

"Make me a poke with some hardtack and bread," BoJack ordered his mother.

Old Wicky rose painfully and limped down from the cliff and into the dirty dwelling.

"I'm gonna kill that boy for stealing my girls, and then I'm gonna find the Indians that stuck me with that knife. First, I'm going to skin 'em," he screeched.

"Don't kill Zack!" pleaded Wicky. "He's your son."

"Shut up, old woman," he retorted callously, "or I'll skin you, too."

When Wicky finished packing the poke, BoJack jerked it out of her hand and walked the horse down the canyon to the river.

Wicky had once placed the bear claw around her son's neck to protect him. After she realized the evil he was capable of, she had tried many times to remove it while he was sleeping, but he would always wake up and beat her for trying. He held on to it even while he slept. She planned to follow him now to see if she could remove it. She knew that BoJack could not travel too far with the bad leg and he would have to rest. She loaded her old pack mule and, about an hour later, she set out to follow him.

From the south the smell of rain was in the air, and Wicky knew all the caves of the river where she had lived all her life. The local tribesmen were frightened of her and left her alone. They would not come close to the dwelling for fear of having a curse placed on them. All the time BoJack was hiding right under their noses without any fear of being captured.

BoJack kept the guns from his mother and Zack, fearing they would try to kill him. This time he had forgotten about Red Tom's buffalo gun. In his pain and delusional state, he had forgotten that he even had it. Old Wicky had removed it from the horse and hidden it. She only had two bullets but she thought she would try to make them count. She knew she had to remove the bear claw before she could kill him. Her dreams told her to remove the bear claw, and she or someone else could kill him. She now regretted ever casting the spell.

This storm could be a perfect time to trap him, as she knew he would take cover in one of the many caves along the river. Wicky eased the old mule along the bluffs beside the river. The rain was pouring down.

BoJack was nipping at thc moonshine and getting quiet drunk. He had reached one of his favorite caves before the downpour and built a fire. Many mountain men knew where the caves were and most of them gathered driftwood and left it stacked along the walls for the next occupant. It was common to build a fire because the grizzly bears liked to shelter in the caves as well.

BoJack stared at the fire and swayed back and forth for a couple of hours, getting more intoxicated as time passed.

He mumbled about skinning Zack to teach him a lesson. As he stared out the cave opening, he became delusional, seeing ghosts of people he had killed. He threw rocks and pieces of firewood at the dead stalking his imagination until he finally became unconscious and fell back into the sand.

Old Wicky could see the fire flickering against the cave walls. She dismounted the mule and quietly untied BoJack's horse at the water's edge. Then, like a stalking animal, she made her way up the jagged cliff to the cave. She could see BoJack, lying unconscious in the sand. She slipped very carefully up to him.

BoJack was moaning as he usually did when intoxicated. Wicky stood over him and very carefully slid her hand under the leather strap that held the bear claw. She deftly cut it with her skinning knife, then hurried to the entrance of the cave. She aimed the buffalo gun and snapped the trigger. But the gun had been saturated with water, causing it to misfire. The woman lost her footing and tumbled down the sharp rocks into the river.

She was bleeding very badly from the fall. The horse and the mule, spooked by the lightning from the storm, had run north up the river and were nowhere to be found. Wicky rose painfully and began to make her way, a little at a time, back south toward her dwelling.

BoJack had never awakened during the removal of the claw. He would never know what happened to it, she thought. Several hours later, bleeding very badly, Wicky became exhausted and sat to rest. She was only about a mile from her dwelling. The rain had continued to pour.

In the lightning, she noticed the cold glaring of eyes through the black night. She could hear the growling of wolves. As she sat, she chanted to the bear claw and threw it into the swift current of the river.

As the rain slowed, little glimmers of light silhouetted the pack surrounding the old woman. The wolves moved in with a vicious hunger, tearing at her already bloody flesh. It was over in minutes as the huge wolves devoured her frail body.

BoJack awoke about sunrise. This was unusual for him unless he drank himself unconscious because his habit was to prowl at night. The first thing he did was reach for the bear claw. When he realized in horror that it was gone, he limped as fast as he could to the entrance of the cave. The North Platte had risen at least four feet and he saw that the horse was gone. Then he saw the buffalo gun lying in the mud. The name "Red" was carved into the stock. A few feet farther, he found Old Wicky's skinning knife. He realized Wicky had taken the bear claw. He used the knife to cut himself a homemade crutch and started back to his home to find the claw and Wicky.

By sunup the rain had stopped and a cold breeze whispered up the river and through the canyon walls. BoJack was completely soaked, but his anger drove him forward. Finally, he came to the last fork leading up to the dwelling. He saw the bloody clothes spread around the trail and recognized them–they belonged to Wicky.

Abruptly, the burning anger changed to pain as BoJack repeatedly called, "Momma." He sat down with the bloody clothes like a little child crying for his mother, his wailing echoing down the canyon walls. After a time, his attention turned to Zack, and he blamed him for the tragedy. He stood and howled, after an hour or so of crying, shrieking Zack's name over and over.

~ ~ ~

BoJack was on his hands and knees looking for the bear claw that he would never find. He was terrified at the thought of being killed by Indians or eaten by a grizzly. But, after several hours of searching, he returned to his dwelling. Zack was forgotten–he had made up his mind to leave the canyon and head north, far away from any other people. He knew mountain men in the far north and he would be safe there. He decided to disguise himself. He found an old picture of his uncle ZebJack, a Methodist preacher. The outlaw shaved his beard and cut his hair. He dressed himself in his uncle's clothes, which his mother had kept in the dwelling.

The next morning the mule returned to the dwelling, and it was a very welcome sight.

BoJack mounted the mule and headed northwest along the North Platte until he saw a wagon train moving west. As he approached the train a scout spotted him and rode to greet him. BoJack remembered how his uncle Zeb had carried himself and did a fine job impersonating him.

The rider asked what his business was, and BoJack acted like he couldn't talk. He was told to join the wagons and he quickly obliged. Being a master of deception, he fit in perfectly with the wagon train.

BoJack was now thankful to be in the company of people he had once scorned. His fear at losing the bear claw had changed him. He had become fearful of anything that seemed hostile. He, in his crazed mind, had transformed into his uncle, Zeb the Preacher. He would point at his throat and frown. The people of the train thought him to be a preacher of some kind, and they gave him a Bible. His uncle had taught him to read when he was growing up, and he got a little better as the days went by. There were people in this train that looked familiar, but he couldn't be sure. Since he looked totally different though, he felt pretty secure.

He didn't realize that he was being watched by young Andy Flint. This group of Mormons had picked up several of the survivors of the hideous killing spree days before. None of the people seemed to recognize BoJack because he had shaved off his beard and was dressed in the black suit of his preacher uncle Zeb. BoJack eventually recognized young Andy because the youngster would stare at the fingers missing from BoJack's hand. BoJack planned to kill young Andy as soon as he had an opportunity. He suspected that Andy knew and would tell the others.

As the days went by, Andy went to the Mormon leader Dell Stuart and told him that this was the bloodthirsty man that had killed his parents and the rest of their party. Stuart just brushed it off, thinking Andy was still in shock from the incident. Andy finally realized nobody was going to believe him, so he slipped up twenty wagons or so under cover of night and stole a ten-gauge shotgun. He knew BoJack would kill him the first chance he got, so he had to make a plan of his own.

Andy noticed BoJack's eyes watching him, so one late afternoon Andy slipped into the trees by the trail and planted the shotgun by a hollow log. Then he planned to act like he was leaving after dark, making sure BoJack was watching him. He would then go to the log and cover himself with brush, so he could shoot BoJack when he came looking for him.

The one thing that Andy didn't realize was that BoJack was a skilled mountain man and tracker. BoJack left the others that were sitting around the wagons, acting like he wasn't feeling good and wanted to turn in early. Nobody in the group suspected anything.

Andy waited for what he thought was about the right time and whistled as he walked by the fire, making sure BoJack could see him. He arrived at the log and started moving brush over and around him. Just as planned, he could see the evil man sneaking through that bright moonlight, coming right towards him. A strong smell was coming from a deer carcass just a few feet away from the log. Andy could see the reflection sparkling off the huge knife BoJack was holding. Fear of dying rushed through his veins. He backed the hammer on the old ten-gauge. Just then, he glimpsed what looked like a small dog snuffling around.

BoJack got closer and closer. He stopped a few feet from the log and his eyes scanned the ground. He looked at the log and instantly knew where Andy was. "Well, there you are. I'm gonna have your gizzard for my dinner tonight," he laughed.

Andy took careful aim and pulled the trigger, but the old gun misfired. BoJack dragged him from the brush by the feet and raised the knife to slash his throat. But he paused as he heard the brush rustle and strained to see what it was. As his eyes focused, BoJack realized a huge grizzly was just a couple of feet away, standing on its hind legs. The rustling they were hearing was a bear cub. In a split second, the mother bear lunged at BoJack, taking his head and half his shoulder in her giant mouth. BoJack screamed as the giant bear ripped at his flesh. The mountain man fought back until he was like a limp rag being tossed through the air. The people from the wagons came running to the direction of the screams. The bear ran and her cub followed through the thick brush.

BoJack was finally dead. When Dell Stuart arrived, yelling "What happened?" Andy, still shaking from the horrid sight, just told him that a mama bear killed the preacher.

Andy went back to his wagon while the men from the party moved what was left of the body. Dell Stuart gave instructions about giving the preacher a righteous burial the next morning. They never would believe this man was the same satanic man that had murdered the Flint party, so Andy kept quiet.

The next morning as the sun was rising, they had the body of BoJack wrapped in a white sheet and were digging the grave, when, out of the trees came about thirty Sioux warriors. The Stuart men froze as the women screamed, grabbed the children, and ran for the cover of the wagons. The war party tied the body of BoJack to one of the horses and dragged it back into the woods. It seemed a scout had seen BoJack and had been following him all along. When they had dragged his body away from the wagon train, they decapitated it.

As they disappeared into the trees, Andy Flint raised his hands to the sky and thanked God. A peaceful smile came over his face.

That night, when everybody was asleep, Andy slipped from the wagon train and headed back down the heavily used wagon ruts in the direction they had come. He had taken BoJack's mule and was slowly walking to the southwest, not really knowing where he would go. The half-moon was bright, and he traveled most of the night before stopping and curling up beside the trail.

As he woke up to the sound of horses, Andy was terrified to see the entire scouting party encircling him, staring down on his makeshift campsite.

The braves all knew who he was and were friendly. One of them was a former scout that spoke broken English. "You not hide very well, little man. You not live long in this land if you not learn better."

"I don't really know where to go," Andy trembled. "I have no home."

"We take you east to River. There we meet with grizzly fighter One Horn. We see he has other children with him. You be OK."

"Grizzly fighter?" Andy asked, his voice shaking. "Maybe I should just go on by myself."

Several of the braves laughed but the scout gave them a stern warning. Then he turned back to the boy. "You try stay this country alone, little man, you die for sure."

Andy slowly nodded and got up and mounted his mule. As he traveled with the party, he gradually began to talk more and more. His confidence in the braves grew and he felt welcome. They told him they would be at the river by sunset as they cautiously crossed the prairie hills.

CHAPTER 21

Back at the North Platte River

Johnny One Horn hid Zack and the two girls in the thick brush along the river and instructed them not to build any fires until he returned. He told them if he didn't return before the next moon, they should travel south and he would find them.

He traveled south along the river's edge, just keeping far enough into the trees that he couldn't be seen easily. He found the clothing from Wicky and, not knowing who or what it was from, offered prayer to the Great Spirit.

At the edge of the creek he noticed the bear claw with the cut leather strap attached. "A witch's bear claw," he smiled. He reached the dwelling a few minutes later and searched the area. Inside he could see that BoJack had been there recently. Cha-cha sniffed the air as his keen eyes scanned the area.

Johnny noticed as he circled the dwelling that a lone horse or mule had left the area. He followed the tracks for hours until they reached one of the well-traveled trails. The trail disappeared there. In his mind, he perceived that the sly mountain man had joined a wagon train going west. He noticed more wagons coming from the east and decided, after much thought, that he would have to abandon his search. In this dangerous land, Indians didn't dare approach a wagon train. He thought to himself, "If I had my white man's clothes, it would be easy, but dressed like an Indian it would be suicide."

On his way back to where Zack and the girls were hiding, Johnny stopped on a hilltop and gazed west across the great country. It was time to ask the Great Spirit to protect the people of the wagons from the devil that had just joined them.

Three Days Later

The scouting party had reached the river. Johnny met the party with the usual greeting sign and gave a sign to Cha-cha to settle down. The huge Wolf did so resentfully.

"I bring you young Andy, from the wagon train," explained the scout. "I have told him of the other children and that you will take him to a safe place. The devil is dead, killed by a mighty bear. This boy has suffered and must heal."

"You got here just in time. We are leaving to the place called Ranch at first light."

Johnny welcomed Andy to the group and thought again that he would have another hard task getting the children all the way back to ranch.

But the scouting party had brought in a deer. The evening was full of cheer as the group celebrated the death of BoJack.

The Scouting Party of Little Boy Horse

The snow still lightly covered the rolling hills as Little Boy Horse and the scouting party moved quietly through Crow country. They had not seen any Crow, but the deer were a little more plentiful along some of the creeks. Chatah was leading the way as the others kept watch.

A group of buffalo hunters took a few shots at them the following morning, and they watched closely as they moved through the trees.

"These white men are thinking us to be as the stories they have heard," frowned Chatah. "They shoot at everyone. They probably think we are Crow."

The late afternoon sun was partially dimmed as the shadows of clouds moved endlessly across the hills.

"We will camp in that group of thick trees there. There's good water in the creek, and I've been here before."

Little Boy Horse scanned the skyline. "There's something about this place–like I've been here before too. I know I never have, but it seems that I have."

"Maybe it's the future you see," suggested Chatah. "I do it often. Sometimes it means something and sometimes nothing. I don't like it–it's too strange."

"I've seen visions in dreams mostly," smiled Horse, "but not quite like this."

Chatah slid off his mount and tied it to some brush. "It's dry here, so this will be fine. This chill tells me of a snow in the air."

Everyone helped set up camp, stretching the buffalo hides between the trees to make a temporary shelter.

As the midnight moon reflected off the shimmering snow, Little Boy Horse, lying in his buffalo hide, realized how cold the night had become. Light snow was softly falling and the north wind whistled through the tree tops. He heard the horses rustling and knew how cold they must be. The custom was to drape buffalo hides across them to keep them warm.

A couple hours had passed, and sleep would not come for him. He noticed there was nothing but silence and thought to himself that the horses had finally become quiet. Not a sound, he thought as he lay there. All at once it dawned on him that things were too quiet, and he sprang to his feet. "The horses!" he thought as he ran to the trees they had been tied to. His intuition was right–the horses and most of their supplies were gone. He quickly woke the others, and they searched the area trying to find the animals.

"This is the work of the Crow," Chatah said as he shook his head. "I should have known better than to let our guard down. In this country, one can die very quickly, either from the weather or from the Crow."

The young men quickly gathered around, worried about the situation they were in.

A young warrior by the name of Lone Bird asked, "What are we going to do?"

"We will do what we always have done–try to survive like the men we are," Chatah responded firmly. "Are we not warriors of the Sioux? We will go to sleep, and when the morning comes, we will make our way back to the safety of our numbers."

Little Boy Horse took Chatah aside and told him that he was going after the horses. Chatah ordered him to stay and return to the camp with them in the morning.

"I am not of your tribe. With no disrespect, I am going to do it my way."

Chatah thought about this for a second and then hugged Little Boy Horse. "We will travel along the ridge and tree line. If you find our horses, my friend, you will know where to find us."

Little Boy Horse walked away, following the tracks that led to the northwest. The snow was scattered now, and the moon was breaking through the clouds, creating large shadows that moved eerily across the ground. He walked a couple of hours and, as the sun was rising, he sighted the Crow camp. He could see his own horse among the others. He moved silently until he came to his own horse. He knew that if he took his own horse he could survive, but he had to try to take as many as he could. The horses spooked, which alerted a young Crow brave that was sleeping near them. He yelled to alert the others and attacked Little Boy Horse. They rolled around in the snow but Little Boy Horse quickly got the advantage and knocked the young warrior out with his fist.

Eight other braves swarmed around Little Boy Horse and were finally able to hold him down and tie him. He knew from what he had heard that he was probably going to be killed.

The leader of the war party walked him with his knife drawn and grabbed him by the hair. “This is a prize,” he told the others. “Our leaders will give us much praise for this one. This is one of the two from the far south our scouts have told us about. We will not kill him, but will return to our village to let our chief decide his fate.”

Some of the other men wanted to kill him, but the leader, a fierce-looking warrior named Black Tree, argued against it. After several minutes of quarreling, they settled down and agreed to take him back to their village.

As they tried to lift him from the ground, Horse head-butted one young warrior and knocked him unconscious. The young man dropped like a stone in the soft snow.

“I told you,” scolded Black Tree, “This is the legend from the far south swamp.” He laughed at the young warrior stumbling to his feet. “Keep the rawhide tight and keep your eye on him all the time. I hope this is a lesson to all of you.”

The warriors looked with fright upon the fearsome Little Boy Horse. They remembered they had been tossed around like feathers before all eight could get the advantage.

~ ~ ~

They traveled hard the first day to the northwest. Little Boy Horse was amazed by the beauty of this land. He watched as they killed a deer, which seemed to be a lot more plentiful here. The mountains were like those he had only seen in a dream. He watched as the eagles soared through the beautiful canyons and trees. The sounds of the birds and crows of the area seemed to carry for miles.

The Crow gave Horse no water or food in hopes they could weaken him. When nightfall came, they dragged him from the horse and double-tied his feet and arms so he could not even move a hand. Black Tree was taking no chances. He posted two warriors and changed them every couple of hours. He was not going to let his prize get away. Little Boy Horse lay in pain from being tied so tightly. He was beginning to realize what years of war had done to these people. They were cruel and eager to kill, and had no respect for the Sioux. He pleaded to the two warriors that were guarding him for water, but they just sat and stared at him. There were just two of them and they dared not to get too close.

~ ~ ~

For three days, they tied him behind one of their horses and dragged him behind. Being so weak from no food, Horse began to lapse in and out of consciousness. His hands were bleeding and most of his clothes were torn off. At the end of the third day they reached the Crow village. The people gathered around and stared. The chief of the village made his way through the crowd and stood over the unconscious body of Little Boy Horse.

"This will please you, my chief. This is one of the men our scouts have told us about–one that lives with white men from the far south." Black Tree motioned to the women and a few of the younger men. "Take him and give him water and food, but not much. He is a warrior that could kill any of us if he were strong."

Chief Ten Killer was anything but happy. He scolded Black Tree for bringing the prisoner to their camp. "This man is known throughout our land, and the Sioux will be searching for him. I hear he is the son of Grey Wolf who was banned from their tribe years ago, but he had many followers. This is a warrior of great substance and yet you have treated him like a snake in the woods. When we break our village, we will leave him here. It looks like he will die anyway, and I don't want this known to the Sioux. This is a disgrace," Ten Killer yelled angrily as he walked away.

As the night closed in, several of the women gave Little Boy Horse bits of deer meat. He could barely sit up, and he choked from exhaustion as he tried to eat the meat. They had tied him to a broken tree in the center of the tepee. He took a few bites and fell back, unconscious.

One of the women shook her head. "This man is hurt very bad," she said. Tears ran down her face as she looked, horrified, at the bloody body. "Black Tree is worse than any snake for doing this. Killing him would have been better. At least he would not have suffered in this way." She said a prayer and the women left the tepee.

~ ~ ~

As the sun was rising, the Crow started breaking down the village. Black Tree presented Chief Ten Killer with the seven horses he had stolen from Little Boy Horse's scouting party.

The chief was pleased with the horses, and told Black Tree he was proud. Still, he asked why he had disgraced a great warrior. "He is yours to do what you want, Black Tree, but give him respect."

Black Tree had watched as the tepee was taken down around Little Boy Horse. He ordered that he be left tied to the post. As he walked over to Horse, he grabbed his hair and lifted his head. "This is your destiny, my friend, to freeze to a post."

One of the women screamed at him to stop.

"He's going to die anyway. Why do you yell at me? I conquered him, and I am the best man." Then he shoved the woman down in the snow, hurting her leg. Several young girls helped her to her feet as Black Tree mounted his horse.

As Black Tree rode away, one of the younger girls pushed some dried deer meat beneath the snow next to Little Boy Horse. Then they left hurriedly and joined the others as the camp was very quickly disassembled.

Chief Ten Killer walked to the post and spoke in a quiet voice. "I wash my hands of this, and it is not of my doing. I was privileged to meet a great warrior. I wish things were different. I'm sorry this is to be." He mounted his horse and joined the women who were dismantling the village. Horse saw him speak quietly to some of the women.

After the warriors and most of the tribe had departed, several women furtively came back and placed a buffalo hide, along with his precious long knife, in front of Horse, quickly covering them with snow.

Little Boy Horse was barely conscious as he said in a weak voice, "Thank you."

As the women hurried away, some turned and looked back at the lonely, slumped figure, easily seen in the white sea of snow.

Chief Ten Killer, too, stopped at the top of the hill and surveyed the pitiful sight.

"He doesn't look so big and mean now," scoffed one of the young braves.

Ten Killer scolded the young man with strong words. "He could probably whip five of you. It is a shame that a great warrior should die like this, as food for wolves instead of in a battle."

Ten Killer shook his head with disapproval as they turned and continued northward.

As the last of the tribe disappeared out of sight, Little Boy Horse drifted into unconsciousness. The exhausting turn of events was too much for his body.

Hours later as the sun was setting, Little Boy Horse awoke to the sound of wolves tearing at his clothing. As their teeth tore into his flesh, he screamed out in pain. The sound echoed down the canyon.

Horse thought he heard the sound of a buffalo gun thunder in the distance, and a wolf fell dead by his face. Little Boy Horse quickly lapsed back into unconsciousness.

The shot came from an old mountain man named Shagging Jim. He rode his mule up beside the post and dismounted. "Well," he said in an easy-going way, "aren't you a mess? What the hell did you do to make somebody this mad?"

Jim looked around and could see where the village had been, and realized Little Boy Horse must be a Sioux, judging by the way he was dressed. He checked to make sure he was still alive, and cut some poles from the nearby trees to make a drag. "I better hurry, son," he frowned as he loaded Little Boy Horse on the drag.

Shagging Jim had a cabin three miles away in a rockbound canyon.

"You're about the luckiest damn Sioux I've ever seen. I never come this way. I was just checking to see if the Crow had moved yet." He really didn't know if Little Boy Horse could hear him or not, but he was just talking to entertain himself.

As he rode to the front of the cabin, a woman opened the front door and ran to the injured Boy Horse lying on the drag. "I figure he's a Sioux. I found him tied to a pine snag–left for dead, I guess."

"Well, stop yakking and help me get him inside! He's cut up pretty bad."

"Damn it, Cookie, you're always griping. I'm moving as fast as I can."

Once inside, Cookie undressed Boy Horse and started stitching the wolf bites with thread. Little Boy Horse was moaning in pain, but still unconscious.

CHAPTER 22

The next two days were difficult for Little Boy Horse, as he kept going in and out of consciousness. His hands and feet had a slight case of frostbite and Cookie was treating them. By the third day he was awake and wondering how he wound up in the small cabin with a woman sitting over him singing some kind of chant.

Cookie jumped with amazement as Little Boy Horse reached and grabbed her hand.

"How did I get here?" he whispered, his weak voice trembling.

"Aww, you speak the tongue of the white man," she smiled, nodding her head. "How does a Sioux, the way you are dressed tells me that you are, get yourself tied to a pine snag and left to die?" Cookie was speaking in the Sioux language and didn't know what to expect next.

Little Boy Horse sat up and rubbed his forehead. "I was raised by an outcast far to the south, across the great river."

"Well, aren't you something. You must be the son of Grey Wolf."

With that statement, Little Boy Horse's eyes widened. "Did you know my father?" he asked.

"No, I didn't, but Shagging Jim knew him. I've heard a lot of stories, but you will just have to ask him. He's the one who brought you here. I am his woman, or he is my man. Whatever," she laughed.

"Where can I find this Shagging Jim? I would like very much to talk to him."

"Well, he's running around trying to tame the world, but he should be back about sunset. In this country, you have to stay busy to stay alive. You are lucky to be alive, my friend. Black Tree is a cutthroat, hungry for power. I believe he would kill Ten Killer if he could get away with it." Seeing that the mention of these names brought pain, Cookie thought it best to change the subject. "Tell me, did you see the Sioux village a little south of here? They are my people. They will be coming this way soon."

"Yes, I did. I was in a hunting party with Chatah when we were robbed of our horses in the night. Black Tree and his people stole them very quickly. They are very silent."

"Oh, Chatah. I guess he's finally growing up. He is my brother's son. I would have thought he would be better at watching his horses. My brother would have never let his horse be stolen by a Crow.

It wasn't long before Shagging Jim burst through the door. He placed the buffalo gun in his rack and stared at Little Boy Horse. "Well now, I see you're still alive. You wouldn't be if I had not come along. I'm curious to know what you did to get yourself tied to that pine snag!"

Little Boy Horse started to speak, but was quickly interrupted by Cookie.

"He's from the far south and Grey Wolf is his father–or was, anyway."

"Grey Wolf is dead? I never thought anything could kill him! Tell me, son, what happened to him?"

"It's a long story, Jim, but I'll make it short."

"You speak pretty fair English, my friend," smiled Jim. "Where did you learn that?"

"Well, most of us in the swamp where we lived could speak a little English, but we have very close friends that speak it well." Little Boy Horse grinned, thinking of the

Armstrong family. Then, bringing his thoughts back to the other question, he continued. "You asked what happened to Grey Wolf. Well, he was killed by a great cat of some kind. We never saw it, but no one who sees the cat could live. He is a mighty Spirit that roams the swamp."

"That's kind of interesting, but your mighty cat would be a snack for the grizzlies we have here. Have you seen a grizzly, my friend?"

"I have seen them from a distance, but my brother Johnny One Horn had a fierce fight with a grizzly."

Shagging Jim looked at him with a concerned expression. "Well, I'm sorry for your loss, Boy Horse."

"No," grinned Little Boy Horse. "My brother defeated the great bear."

"Whipped a damned grizzly, son?" Jim laughed. He laughed so loud that it echoed from the cabin down the canyon walls. "Now just how in the hell did he do that?"

Little Boy Horse slid the long knife from his side and stuck it deep in the ground in front of him. With this he smiled.

"My God," Jim said as he stared at the knife.

"My brother let him go free, but the great bear is going to have a sore foot for a long time. He said the bear was a Great Spirit and he refused to kill him."

"Well, son, I never heard of anybody whipping a grizzly. I'd sure like to meet this brother of yours someday." Jim shook his head in admiration. "Tell me another thing, Horse–what brings you here?"

"We returned a little girl that was stolen from your woman's village. Her name is Wind. She was stolen by a crazy mountain man named BoJack."

Shagging Jim's eyes narrowed as he looked at Boy Horse. "I know BoJack. He's about as bad as they come. He's a cold-blooded killer. I almost got the drop on him one time down by the North Platte River, but he managed to kill my horse. I escaped through the brush at night. He followed me for days, but he finally turned back after he had a run-in with some Comanche."

Little Boy Horse slid the knife back into its holder. "You don't have to worry about him any more. I killed him down by the North Platte and hung his body on a tree for all to see."

As the night went on, they told many more stories about the old days when Grey Wolf was a young man in the north. At last, Horse leaned back from exhaustion and fell fast asleep.

Cookie looked at Little Boy Horse and smiled. "He's quite a young man, isn't he, Jim?"

"Yes, he damn sure is. But as much as I would like to believe it, I don't believe that devil BoJack is dead."

~ ~ ~

As the days went by, Little Boy Horse grew stronger and stronger. He offered to stay and help Shagging Jim and Cookie finish building their cabin, and hunt and store food for the winter. He had really grown to like the pair and was enjoying his stay with them. They laughed and joked and became close. Then winter closed in on the canyon and hunting became difficult. Little Boy Horse would stand on the canyon ridge and take in the dangerous beauty of the place that in some ways brought him peace. He missed Wind and Mika, but he would see them in the spring and the thought of that made him feel warm even on the coldest day.

The Ranch

Winter had set in at the small community, and driftwood and dried firewood were beginning to run a little low. O.C. and Joe organized wood cutting crews to travel down the Arkansas River in search of dry wood.

Charles had sent Pete and five hands with wagons to Abilene to pick up coal he had ordered from the Union Pacific Railroad. They had purchased pot-bellied coal stoves in the fall and installed them in the buildings. Coal was his best option, but competing with cattle for the train cars was getting expensive.

Johnny One Horn had arrived with the children, and was settling them in with the clan at the ranch. The girls were loving the ranch, and the boys were quickly catching on to a better life than they were used to, especially Zack, who was a young man but had lived a lifetime of misery with BoJack.

Johnny had developed blood poisoning in his leg from a thorn along the way. His horse riding had become very limited, so he could not travel back to the north. He planned to stay the winter before trying it again. He knew the trip was long and torturous, and he spent many days trying to recuperate from the journey. Even Cha-cha the wolf was weary and grouchy from the ordeal, but he had grown very fond of all the children. Johnny spent a lot of time thinking about Little Boy Horse and wondering if he would ever see him and Wind again.

~ ~ ~

Joe decided to take some of the swamp gold, even though it was against his better judgement, and sell it in Abilene. He would take Nate and Shorty with him.

It was early morning and Joe was saying goodbye to Cindy and the boys. "We will be back in about seven or eight days if the weather doesn't slow us down too much," Joe promised, surveying his assembled family.

"Just stay out of that saloon, cowboy, or I'll come gunning for you." Cindy teased him, but he could see the tear glistening in the corner of her eye.

Joe just grinned and threw the saddlebag over his horse,

Old Red. "Now get in out of this cold," he scolded lovingly. "I'll see you in about a week or so."

The boys were waving out the front window of the house. Joe yelled for them to take care of their mother as he mounted and rode down the snow-covered street, heading toward the morning sun.

"I hope Pete's picked up that coal by now. If all goes well, we should meet them on the way back," Joe remarked as he joined his men.

"Well, Pete can take care of himself," Shorty said.

"I'm sure he'll take care of the boys and the wagons," Nate agreed as he poked some chew into the side of his mouth.

"How in the world can you chew that stuff?" frowned Shorty. "I'd rather chew a buffalo patty!"

"Well, you chew your buffalo patty, Shorty, and I'll chew this tobacco," grinned Nate.

The first day of traveling through the light snowpack had gone well. The men picked the shelter of some rocky bluffs in a creek bed to shield their horses and themselves from the wind, and set up camp for the night. As they sat around the fire, they were glad they brought dry wood from their woodshed. They talked about the abandoned wagons and things they'd seen along the trail.

Nate was shaking his head as he recalled seeing all the remains of desperate people's belongings. "You know, Joe, it almost seems unreal that all those people either just died or abandoned all those things. I guess hunger and outlaws got most of them. I bet there are a lot of bodies beneath this snow."

Joe looked up as he stirred the coals. "Yeah, it's damn sure a sad thing. It's sure not safe to use this trail in warm weather. Speaking of being safe, I'm going to bury this gold over there away from the campfire. I'm sure there are some yahoos still out here digging through the leftovers."

A couple of hours after the three fell asleep, Nate was

suddenly awakened by the rustling of the horses. He sprang to his feet, straining his eyes to see through the light snow falling. He slipped through the brush until he reached Joe. "Joe," he whispered, "someone is messing with the horses!"

Joe sat up. Something was definitely rustling in the brush. Nate went on ahead, motioning for Joe to circle around. Joe saw the gesture and nodded.

Then, as Joe slipped through the brush, he heard Nate fighting with someone. By this time Shorty had heard the commotion and came running through the snow.

Nate and a stranger were rolling around through the snow. Joe pulled his .44 and yelled for the stranger to stand down. He repeated the order, but it made no difference. The intruder was getting the best of Nate and fists were flying.

"Ow! You bit me? You son of a bitch!" yelled Nate. Joe and Shorty both grabbed the intruder and wrestled until they had him secured on the ground.

Nate finally got to his feet and pulled his .44, placing it firmly between the stranger's eyes. "Now walk that way or I'll blow your head off," he ordered.

They wrestled the would-be thief back to the camp, tied him up, and slammed him into the rocks with his hands tied behind him.

"Damn!" Nate suddenly bellowed. "I ought to just shoot this bastard! Look where he bit me!"

He had a vicious bite on the side of his neck, and Joe could see that it was giving him much pain. Joe pointed his .44 at the stranger and asked what he was doing there. "Were you trying to steal our horses? We'll hang you on that dead oak tree right now."

The stranger reached up, pulled the buffalo hood off his head, and blurted out, "Shoot me. I've be shot and hanged before."

"Oh, my God, boys, it's a woman!" laughed Shorty.

"Yeah, I'm a woman. Have you ever seen one?" The

woman went on, "I know the next question, and it's going to be, 'What are you doing out here in the middle of nowhere?' Well, it's a long story. I wasn't trying to steal your horses, but my mule, Sally, is just a little skittish around people and I was going to tie her up with the horses before I came into camp. I camped out on the hill but I've been watching your fire for about an hour now–it looks awful inviting. Can I have a swig of that moonshine? I haven't had a drink since I was a bouncer in Eula's Bar over in Garden City."

"You were a bouncer over at Eula's saloon?" Joe asked, grinning. "I guess that's why you almost got the best of my foreman Nate, here."

"She didn't get the best of me, by God! She bit the hell out of me!" Nate protested.

"I'm sorry about that, Nate, but I didn't know if you were going to try to kill me or not. My name's Retha. I think my last name used to be Miller, before I got kicked by a buffalo bull. It got me right above this ear. That was about five years ago and I don't remember anything before that. I don't know if my name is really Retha–it's just a name that Pickles and Eula May called me. Old Eula fired me–said I got too rough with the customers. I've been out here hunting coyotes. The hides bring three dollars in Abilene."

"Coyotes, huh? Well, we got plenty of them stealing our calves at the ranch," Joe mused.

"Yeah, I used to hunt buffalo, but they're gone now. I'm on my way to Abilene to sell my hides. That's how I ran into you fellows."

"Well, maybe we can all get some sleep now. You can travel with us if you like. That is, if you don't bite me again," offered Nate teasingly.

"You know, Retha, you're mighty pretty for a big gal," smiled Shorty.

Retha laughed while she was making her bed. "You

keep thinking that, Mr. Shorty, but I may have a husband somewhere, and just may run across him one of these days. I know I don't have any young'uns–that's something a woman just knows!"

Chapter 23

Abilene Kansas

Joe's group arrived in Abilene a few days later and Retha disappeared to cash in her furs. Joe met Pete and the five ranch hands at the train depot, still waiting for the coal cars to be unloaded.

"Hey, Joe!" Pete greeted as he walked out of the depot.

"I thought we would meet you coming back, Pete. What's the holdup?"

"Well, they say we're going to have to wait. Seems water got in the coal cars and is froze solid. It won't run out of the chutes at the bottom."

"Hell, we could wait all winter for that! We need that coal! Let me go talk to them and see what we can work out."

"Good luck. I've tried everything I could and nothing has worked," Pete replied, shaking his head.

Joe walked into the crowded depot office and was amazed at the number of people standing in line. He started to stand in the line, but the man at the desk yelled, "Hey, buddy, you have to set down and wait your turn!"

"I thought this was the line."

The man yelled back, "Sign in and then you'll get called to stand in line."

"Damn, this don't make sense," Joe argued.

"Don't raise any hell in here," the man shouted, "or that deputy outside will remove you from the property."

Joe saw right away that the place was in chaos. He just signed the tablet and sat down on the floor beside the door.

Four Hours Later

Joe's name was finally called and he could see everybody in the room had run out of patience. He finally was able to sit down at the desk where a grouchy bald man sat stamping papers.

"Make it quick, fella, I get off in five minutes," the man barked.

"My name is Armstrong and we have thirty tons of coal sitting in those boxcars on the side rail."

The man kept fumbling through his papers. "Yeah, and it's froze in the chutes, and unless you unload it yourselves it's going to sit there until we can dump it. You only have four days left to unload it or we ship it back to St. Louis. Inside a foundry they can thaw it out and unload it."

"Well, we will try to unload it, if we can. We'll start first thing in the morning. Thanks for making this such an enjoyable day, Mister. I can't remember when I've had such a good time."

"Well, just get the hell out! The boxcars still leave in four days whether you get your coal or not, cowboy. You see, I don't give a damn one way or another," snarled the man.

Joe just shook his head and walked out to where Nate was waiting.

"Damn, I couldn't keep from hearing that ass yelling at you. Why didn't you knock his head off? That's what I would have done!"

Joe just shook his head. "We start unloading coal first light in the morning. That butthead said we got four days or we lose what we don't have unloaded." Joe strode away from the depot building. “That’s what we get for shipping this time of year, I guess, but they won’t even talk to you in the warm months. The cattle come first then.” He stopped, thinking, then turned to Nate. “I’ll run down to that hotel and get us some rooms. I’ll meet you boys at the saloon as soon as I can get over there. Tell everyone what’s up and remind them we won’t be drinking too much tonight.”

~ ~ ~

The saloon was alive with piano and banjo music, and Pete had all five Mexican boys sitting at the same table. He was watching over them as they laughed and flirted with the young saloon girls. Nate was involved in a card game, so Joe just sat down and enjoyed watching all the dancing girls twirl around the place.

It wasn’t very long until two Deputy Marshals walked in and came to Joe’s table. “It’s against the law to carry guns or weapons in here, boys, so if you have any, you need to give them to us now.”

Pete and the boys had been there a week and already knew the rules, and Nate had turned in his gun on the way to the saloon.

“Most of us know the rules from being here before, sir,” Joe explained politely.

“OK, but if any of you get caught with one, it’s three days in the poke.” The lawmen turned, and one slapped one of the girls on the behind as they left the building.

“I don’t like those two. They were the same ones that were here the last time we were here, remember, Joe? Nate growled.

“Yeah, I remember. A couple of real buttheads.”

“Hey, Joe, there’s Retha over there playing cards.”

Retha sat at a table playing cards with four scruffy-looking cowhands. She had just cleaned them out of their wages, and the cowhands were mad and yelling at the top of their voices. One called her a cheat, and she promptly whipped out a ten-inch skinning knife and held it firmly against his neck.

He was a big man, but quickly started yelling, "OK, I'm sorry!"

Retha slammed him back into the chair and slipped the skinning knife back into its holster. "You better be, Donkey Humper!" she retorted.

The commotion had gotten the attention of the two deputies outside, who quickly burst through the door and drew their guns. Retha immediately raised her hands and spit on the deputy.

The two deputies wrestled her down and tied her hands behind her back with a piece of rawhide. "Well, if it ain't Retha Miller," one of them sneered. "You can't stay out of trouble, can you, heifer! Come on, let's just see how you like spending three days with me and big Bob Foster here. You see, before he became my deputy and I became the marshal, he used to skin buffalo for a living."

Retha kept on fighting so they had to put a gag in her mouth.

"How did all this start?" asked Deputy Foster.

The bartender pointed at the big cowhand. "It was Slick Harry over there–he accused her of cheating."

"Slick Harry? Well, I'll be damned–Slick Harry Vigil. He's wanted over in Dodge for stealing a preacher's mule. Boy, today's full of surprises."

Joe and the boys looked on in near disbelief as the circus seem to grow crazier and crazier. Finally, Joe pushed back his chair, stood, and ordered the group to head to the hotel. "Let's get the hell out of here, boys, before anything else happens," He shook his head, smiling. "Damn, it's been a long day."

Deputies Swartz and Foster wrestled Retha and Slick Harry Vigil to the jail. It was quite a job, and they could barely get them there even tied up. At last a couple of cowboys saw the action and helped the two deputies succeed.

"Damn, I've never seen a tougher woman," moaned Swartz.

"Yeah, she bit the hell out of me," snarled Bob Foster. "You know, though, she's kind of pretty to be a big woman."

Slick Harry was still busy calling Retha names, and she was busy calling them back.

"I catch you out on the prairie one of these days, you witch, and I'll whip you with these two big dirty fists, until you call me daddy and follow me like a good little bitch dog that you are," swore Slick Harry.

"I would love that, you ass licker–just tell me where and when. I'll turn you into a woman with my Bowie knife!"

After about two hours of name-calling, Swartz and Foster finally had enough. They called in two cowboys off the street and had them help gag them both.

~ ~ ~

Foster had spent the night at the jail guarding the prisoners. The next morning, he was sitting by the coal stove trying to wake up when Swartz arrived back at the jail.

"I'll take them gags out of your mouths and give you coffee if you'll shut the hell up," Swartz snarled.

Since both were suffering from hangovers, the prisoners who had been so vocal the night before had calmed down. They both nodded.

"I never seen two people hate each other so much," laughed Foster. "I'd like to see that fight you two were talking about."

"I'll be damned if I wouldn't give a five-dollar bill to see it," agreed Swartz.

The five cells in the jail were full, with most of the

prisoners due to be released by noon. As the crowd thinned out, Retha noticed Fast Brian Houx sitting in the cell next to her.

"Dear Lord," she said, "anybody except Fast Brian Houx."

"Howdy, Retha. I see you don't love me anymore. I'm heartbroken. I remember the last time I saw you–you didn't love me then either. I just can't bear the thought of it."

"I'll never love you, you card-cheatin' son of a bitch!"

"Well, thank you, honey. You're so sweet."

~ ~ ~

Joe and the boys were busy lining up the wagons and loading the coal, using hand picks. The rain and snow had frozen the coal into a solid block. It was a hell of a job, but once they got the top off, it could be shoveled into the wagons.

"Well, Joe, it will take about three days to get this done, and that's a little better than I thought," Nate remarked toward the end of the first day. "But, Joe, I kind of feel a little bad about Retha being down there in that jail. If it's OK with you, I think I'll go down there and see if I can get her out."

"Yeah, this is going OK here. I'd like to find out what's up with her anyway."

Meanwhile, Fast Brian Houx was busy stirring things up at the jail. He was talking to Swartz and Foster about having a public fight. They would get half the take and the winner would get the other half, plus he would get out of jail without a fine.

"You know, Brian, you might be smarter than I thought you were," laughed Swartz. "What about it, you two? Will you agree to fight in the street with the winner getting half the take, and getting out of jail free?"

Retha and Slick Harry stared at each other for a few

moments, then both yelled at about the same time, "Hell, yeah!"

Swartz and Foster laughed and slapped hands together.

"OK, Fast Brian, you go set it all up in the saloon for the day after tomorrow." Swartz opened the cell door and set Fast Brian free.

As he left, he had a request. "Damn, this is going to be fun, but my rent is due at the hotel and you boys took all my winnings. Could you give me a little advance? I smell like a polecat."

"You think we didn't notice?" Foster retorted, frowning. "Here's ten dollars–we'll take it out of the proceeds. Now go clean up, but I think you always smell like a polecat. And, you know you cheated those cowboys."

Fast Brian had no comment as he raced out the door and across the street. He rented a tub and put on some of his fancy gambler's duds. Then he was on his way to the Abilene newspaper office. He spent three dollars to have fifty flyers printed, and sat and waited until they were done. The flyer read:

NEVER BEFORE IN THE HISTORY OF ABILENE HAS THERE BEEN A PUBLIC FIGHT OF A MAN AND A WOMAN. FOR ONLY FIVE DOLLARS YOU CAN SEE THE WILD COYOTE WOMAN RETHA MILLER TAKE ON THE DREADED SLICK HARRY VIGIL. BUY THE FLYER AND THIS WILL BE YOUR TICKET.

When Fast Brian first walked in the swinging doors of the saloon, the bartender yelled for him to get out. But after several minutes of explaining, the bartender, who was also the owner, agreed for a cut of fifty cents a ticket.

Fast Brian was thrilled to see the flyers almost sell out. The saloon set up betting tables and started taking bets. Fast Brian ran back across the street and ordered one hundred more flyers to be printed.

The newspaper demanded cash. Everybody knew not to

trust Fast Brian Houx. Fast Brian told them he would be back as soon as he got out of the marshal's office, and dashed down the street.

He burst through the office door yelling, "I sold all the tickets in forty-five minutes!"

"Well, you better have all the money or them ticket holders will get to see a hanging to go along with the fight!" teased Big Bob Foster.

Fast Brian very carefully counted out the money. "Now here's the receipt for the flyers, so I can get one hundred more in the morning, and I'll bet I sell them all by noon."

"Good, good," laughed Marshal Swartz. "In the meantime, you just get right in that cell there. I'm not going to take a chance with a no-good like you."

"Cell? I thought you said I could go free if I got all this going for you!"

"Well, when this is over you can go free, but in the meantime, I don't trust you."

"Well, a man can't sleep listening to Slick Harry and that coyote woman yelling at each other all night long!"

"Shut up!" hollered Slick Harry as he tried to spit on Fast Brian though the cell bars. "After I win this and this woman is turned into the laughingstock of the whole town, I aim to skin you, Fast Brian!"

"Laughingstock?" shrieked Retha. "You're gonna look real funny with your marbles hanging on that saloon wall. I think I'll hang 'em on that goat's head in there for everyone to laugh at!"

"See what you got started, you jackass? Now none of us will be able to sleep," groaned the deputy. "Sometimes I hate this job. You know, that's why Hickok quit. It was driving him crazy."

Otto Swartz laughed. "Well, he damn sure didn't better himself. He was shot in the back of the head by a drifter up in Deadwood."

"Killed? I didn't know that," Big Bob said, shaking his

head in disbelief.

"Yep, deader than a doornail," laughed Swartz. "You know, I never did like that horse's ass; you never could tell what he was thinking. He sure was good at dealing off the bottom of the deck though. I watched him, hoping I could see him cheat, but I never could."

CHAPTER 24

Nate and Shorty had left the ranch hands at the hotel and walked to the jail to see Retha. Nate was determined to offer her a job at the ranch hunting varmints. As they walked in, Swartz warned them not to take much time because he was locking up soon.

Retha stomped to the bars. "Well, howdy, boys," she said, smiling. "I didn't think you would remember me after two long days."

The boys shook hands with her in a manly fashion and she leaned into the bars. "Shorty," she whispered, "get me some Croatian oil."

"Croatian oil?" he snickered. "Are you…, well, you know?"

"No," she said. "Just get it and bring it to me early tomorrow morning."

"What's all that whispering about? I'll havc nonc of that, you hear?" yelled Foster.

"I'll just tell him so he won't arrest me when I do," Shorty whispered. "Surely, he knows that when somebody can't go, they can't function right."

Shorty walked over to the deputy with his back to the cells and whispered, "Marshal Foster, Miss Retha can't go. She needs some Croatian oil."

"Can't go where?"

“Not that–she can’t go do her business.”

“Well, here–she can use this bottle. It’s still got plenty in it! Just don’t stink up the cell.”

Shorty walked back over and handed it to Retha.

“Retha, maybe you should call this fight off,” Shorty advised. “Hell, you know you can’t win with the drizzles, and that’s exactly what that Croatian Oil will do to you.”

Retha never answered, except to say, “Well, thank you, Shorty. I’ll see you later.”

Shorty shrugged his shoulders. “Well, OK, Miss Retha.” As he walked away, he had a bewildered look on his face.

Back on the street after the visit, he turned to his friend. “Well, Nate, you didn’t say much. You know, I’ve seen cowhands take that stuff and in twenty minutes they were running for the bushes.”

“Yeah, it’s bad news all right,” Nate nodded, grinning. “I hope I never have to use that stuff.”

Back in the jail, Retha stuck the bottle underneath her bunk and carried on arguing with Fast Brian Houx.

Every morning Deputy Bob Foster would set their coffee on a table between the cells, and the inmates would reach through the bars and grab their coffee. Retha had noticed Slick Harry would always grab the largest cup and it had given her an idea. She would grab the big cup first and put the Croatian Oil in it, and then when he complained she would give the cup back. She figured it would take effect just about fight time.

Slick Harry Vigil took a shot of laudanum every night before he tired of arguing, and it put him fast asleep. Deputy Foster didn’t mind because it was very common and could be bought at the local dry goods store.

The night when on with Retha and Slick Harry bickering back and forth, and Fast Brian yelling at them both. When the lanterns were turned out and everybody settled down, the piano could be heard playing across the street at the saloon.

Slick Harry took a big swig of laudanum. "Just wanted you both to know," he said quietly, so as not to alert Deputy Foster who was snoring like a train rumbling, "I think you two are the sorriest polecats I've ever known."

"Oh no," whined Fast Brian, "not again." He turned over and covered his head with the blanket.

"Well, thank you," laughed Retha. I'll take that as a compliment, coming from you, Harry." She paused a minute. "Harry, I'll make you a bet. If I beat you, you have to work for me for three months skinning hides. If I lose, I'll work for you doing cooking and everything except being your whore."

"I'll take that bet," laughed Slick Harry. "I'm really going to enjoy having you wash my feet, and some other things too."

"I told you, Harry–it's work only."

Retha was making her plan all along, and Slick Harry was playing right into her hands.

"You know, Harry, it's too bad you don't like me much because if we didn't fight all the time, I would kind of fancy you."

Harry's eyes lit up and he sat straight up on the bench. "You do?" he asked, swallowing really hard. His whole attitude changed. "You mean you could be my woman?" he asked wonderingly. Harry had been moonstruck, and he moved to the bench closest to Retha's cell so he could look at her in the moonlight shining through the large, barred window.

She knew what he was doing and stood up to pull her buckskins off, then stood in the moonlight looking the other way. Retha acted like she didn't know he was watching, but she had to hold back the laughter.

At last, Retha lay back down, covered herself with the blanket, and stuck one leg right in the moonbeam for Slick Harry to see. She didn't know that Bob Foster was secretly watching from his bunk across the room.

Retha lay there moaning and putting on a show for Slick Harry, and his eyes grew bigger than a cow's eyes soaking up the scenery. Retha fell asleep knowing that Slick Harry would be up most of the night and be worn out come morning.

The Next Morning at the Merchant's Hotel

While Joe and the ranch hands were having breakfast at the hotel, Joe asked Shorty how the visit with Retha went.

"Well, I guess it went all right. But she can't go poop, I guess, so I got some Croatian Oil from old Deputy Foster and I guess she took it. Hell, I don't know what happened after that."

"Croatian Oil?" laughed Joe. "Man, I heard about the fight she's going to have today. That gal has something up her sleeve–you can bet on that."

They all laughed and made jokes for several minutes.

"Well, you boys about done? We got them wagons to load," Joe groaned, stretching.

"Joe, there's another thing," Shorty remembered. "Joe, you remember that Marshal Hickok that used to be here?"

"Yeah, I remember him all right. He was a dangerous man, I heard. I know he didn't like us much."

"Well, he's dead. He got shot in the back up in Deadwood, wherever that's at. They said he was playing cards, and after he fell over dead, the hand he was holding was a full house of aces and eights. Ain't that something?" Shorty was shaking his head.

"Well, I'll be damned. That's why. I wondered why I hadn't seen him lately. Well, let's go, boys. If we get them two wagons loaded by ten o'clock, we can all come back and see the fight."

The hands all cheered to show their approval, and they headed down the muddy street toward the train depot. As they stomped through the mud, they could see the men roping off a round circle in front of the Alamo Saloon.

The hands were all talking about the fight and who they thought would win. “Joe, who do you think will win?” asked Carlos, one of the young Mexican hands.

“Well, boys, I’d put my money on Retha anytime. Like I said, she’s got something up her sleeve and I would almost bet it’s going to be good.” Joe winked, then bent to the task of unloading coal.

The Jail

Deputy Foster was heating up the coffee and had boiled some eggs for the inmates. He would always set the cups on the table, but this time he set the whole pot and the cups there. Retha was quick to grab the largest tin cup because she knew Slick Harry would do that exact thing. Slick Harry was just waking up and rubbing his eyes after a long night of watching Retha. She noticed that Deputy Foster was also moving kind of slow.

When Slick Harry realized someone had taken the big cup, he started yelling. Retha had already poured the Croatian Oil into the cup, but calmly put it back on the table. “I’m sorry, darling,” she said as she pushed it toward him across the table.

Slick Harry was moonstruck from the night before, and tried to put his hand on Retha’s hand, but she quickly moved it.

“Did you mean what you said last night, my darling?” he stammered. “I don’t think I want to fight you now that you love me,” he drooled.

“I didn’t say I loved you–why, how could I love someone that wants to beat me up? I feel sad that you’re that kind of a scoundrel!”

“Hey, Marshal,” he yelled, “I don’t want to fight Retha any more–ya see, I aim to marry her.”

Deputy Foster slammed his cup down on the table. "You're gonna fight or you'll stay in here till you're old and gray. I might just talk Marshal Swartz into hangin' ya."

"Hanging me? For being drunk?" he moaned. "I ain't never heard of that."

"Well, there's always a first time, son. I'm sure, with all the money that's at stake, he would hang ya. I don't want to hear anything else–people came from all over to see a fight, and by golly, they're gonna see a fight. If you don't give your best, you will be stretched by the neck for sure."

Marshal Swartz walked into the jail after kicking the mud off his boots. "What in tarnation is all the racket?" he boomed. "I can hear it all the way down the street."

"Well, Slick Harry all of a sudden fell in love with the coyote woman, and now he wants to marry her. I told him that if he shirks the fight, we'll hang him for sure."

"Damn right we'll hang 'im! I swear, I never heard of anything like this before."

"Let me out! I've got a hundred tickets to sell!" yelled Fast Brian. "That damn coyote woman is playing him on, Marshal–I heard her do it. She also undressed and shook it at him all night long."

"How do you know, Brian? Were your eyes bugging out too?"

"Don't you talk about my woman like that! I'll skin ya when I get out of here," threatened Slick Harry.

CHAPTER 25

As Joe and the hands were busy loading the wagons, they watched the crowd gather in front of the Alamo Saloon. Finally, most of the coal was loaded with only one wagon left.

"Boys, let's knock it off and get ready to watch the fight," yelled Nate.

"You gonna make any bets, Joe?" someone asked as the group headed for the saloon.

"Well, I don't know," Joe smiled. "I sure don't want to see Retha get hurt–that's a big old boy!"

They could see the marshals leading the prisoners out of the jail and toward the muddy roped-off ring. As Retha and Slick Harry were untied, the crowd cheered. Women and children lined the wooden sidewalks as the festival was getting underway.

Retha's long blonde hair was tied up in braids as she faced Slick Harry. Slick Harry's mohawk was sticking straight up as the marshal untied the two.

There was a makeshift announcer stand on a wagon next to the rope ring. Some women from the local Women's Club were protesting loudly as they waved signs.

Fast Brian, who was acting as referee, was ringing a bell that he got from the town blacksmith. Immediately, Retha ran across the ring and kicked Slick Harry between the legs.

He screamed, “But darling, I don’t wanna fight ya! I wanna marry ya!”

The crowd laughed and booed. Retha threw him face down in the mud and kicked his behind.

Finally, Slick Harry began to realize that he had been suckered and started trying to fight back. As he tried, the Croatian Oil began to rumble in his stomach. Retha punched him in the belly and the condition worsened. A strange look came over Slick Harry’s face, and he jumped the rope and, somewhat wobbly, ran down the street holding his behind.

The crowd started booing and jeering, calling him a coward. The Women’s Club was even more appalled at what was taking place. Slick Harry headed for the outhouse beside the jail. As he ran into the outhouse, there was a cowhand sitting on the stool and Slick Harry threw him off like a rag doll. The cowhand had his pants around his knees and began kicking the door cursing Slick Harry. Slick yelled, “Oh my God!” as the Croatian Oil rumbled from his fat belly. Nate and Pete were standing in the crowd not too far away, and heard the mighty flapping and growling sounds coming from the outhouse.

Some of the Women’s Club ran from the area holding their hands over their faces. People were laughing everywhere.

“My God, man, did you hear that?” Nate laughed. “It sounded like two big dogs fighting.”

Pete smiled and shook his head. “Man, I don’t think I ever heard anything like it.”

When it was over and Slick Harry finally stumbled out of the outhouse, the offended cowhand was waiting by the side with a shovel, and knocked Slick out cold. The cowhand ran down the street, mounted his horse, and quickly rode out of town.

Retha walked down the street wiping the mud from her

face and laughing at the same time. She grabbed a bottle of whiskey from a bystander and took a big slug. Then she stood over Slick Harry and poured the rest in his face. "Get up, you mangy rat. You got work to do, remember? You lost, so you skin my coyotes for six months."

Slick Harry sat up. "What happened?" he moaned. "Who hit me?"

"Well, some cowpoke that you threw out of the outhouse didn't really appreciate that," she answered, smiling sweetly.

"I'll skin that varmint! Where the hell is he?"

"I don't know, Slick. He rode out of town."

People were still laughing and jeering as they passed by on the muddy street.

"Well, get up, Slick, you idiot! The boys from that Armstrong Ranch will be leaving as soon as they get them wagons loaded, and they gave me, and now you, a coyote hunting job. So get cleaned up and I'll meet you at the depot."

Slick Harry staggered to his feet, still wobbling, and walked over to a partially frozen horse trough, breaking the ice so he could wash the mud from his face and eyes.

Down the street, Joe and the hands were finished loading the last wagon and were packing up the food and supplies. Joe entered the depot and signed the receiving papers. Then he headed back to the wagons and made sure they were ready to go.

"You men, all but Pete, head on back to thc ranch. I'vc got to do some business. Wait on the trail until Pete catches up with you–it won't take long."

Joe and Pete walked to the Abilene Bank and cashed in a handful of the gold coins, receiving a little over a thousand dollars cash. They would order provisions from the dry goods store and purchase another wagon and horse team from the local stables. Pete would drive the wagon, and Joe would ride alone with the rest of the cash. He planned to ride with the group until dark, and then ride on ahead under the cover of night to the ranch.

After Joe and Pete caught up, the group traveled the rest of the afternoon, but stopped and made camp before the dark winter night set in. Joe gave a few instructions to the hands before riding off into the night. He traveled for hours in the cold clear night, the bright moon shimmering off the snow. The wind was whistling, and blowing snow created blind spots along the trail. Ahead, Joe spotted the overhanging rocks that travelers often used to shelter themselves. His thoughts ran back to the Bennis brothers. Joe knew not to stop, and rode on through the freezing night. He came upon a tree line and a frozen creek bed and thought of stopping until dawn, but his instincts told him to keep going. He was weary as the relentless cold wind pounded his face; he could only pull the scarf up to his eyes and urge his horse on.

In the distance he could see several sets of eyes reflecting the bright moonlight. At first, he thought they were coyotes, but as he got closer fear jolted through him as he realized the eyes belonged to wolves. As they came closer into view, they started circling. Joe fired his .44 in the direction of one of them. They retreated, but soon came back. Some lunged at the back legs of his horse. The horse spooked and fell backwards, throwing Joe several feet behind him. As wolves lunged at the horse's legs, his faithful horse Buck ran to get away.

Joe knew they would methodically chase the horse until he collapsed, and then devour him. He was left alone with his dried beef. The cash, along with matches and rifle, were on his horse. He had hurt his shoulder during the fall and the pain was relentless. He walked about a hundred yards or so and crawled under some sagebrush. He noticed blood soaking through his shirt before he passed out in the snow.

When the sun started to rise, Joe regained consciousness, severely shaking and trembling. He got to his feet and stumbled through the snow. It occurred to him that he should go back to the rock overhang. He thought, "If I can make it back there, somebody might find me." He slowly dragged his bruised body back in that direction.

An hour or so later, he reached the overhang. There was nobody there, but at least he was out of the wind. He was thinking that Pete and the hands would come by the rocks, but would have no reason to stop. Joe was in severe pain and still bleeding. He tried desperately to stay conscious. He sat, shivering and staring across the plains toward the trail back in the distance. He passed out several times and didn't realize that the wagons and ranch hands had passed within fifty yards of the overhang. Since they didn't realize anyone was there, they just kept heading toward the ranch. Night was fast approaching and again Joe was sick and weak. He finally collapsed in a cramped position and passed out once more.

The cold night set in with a fury, and whirling snow drifted in, covering part of Joe's body.

Later that night, his eyes slowly opened and he could feel warmth coming over his body. He thought for a few minutes that he was dreaming. Then his eyes slowly focused on the flickering of a warm fire. He could see two figures sitting by the fire roasting a rabbit. Then he recognized the coyote woman Retha Miller.

"I wish them wolves would come a little closer! I'd like to see what them hides would bring at the market," she laughed. Every once in a while, she would take a pot shot and the .44 would sound like a cannon echoing around the overhang.

Joe struggled to sit up and Slick Harry Vigil came to help. "For a while there, my friend, we thought you were dead," smiled Harry.

"I thought I was too. Thank the Lord for you two."

"Well, we were tracking the wolves and ran across your horse with your belongings still in the saddlebags, even the money. We figured you would probably find the nearest shelter, and here you were."

Joe hung his head. "Buck was the best horse I ever had. Did he suffer much?" he mumbled.

"Well–doesn't look like it. He's tied over there with the rest of the horses," grinned Retha. "Oh, he's got a few small bites that we doctored, but other than that he's fine."

"Oh, Buck!" Joe said, trying to stand up.

"Don't try to get up so soon! We will probably need to leave at sunup–by now everyone at the ranch knows you didn't show up, and people will be looking for you. If I know Nate, he's already coming," Retha assured him.

~ ~ ~

After eating a small piece of the rabbit, Joe leaned back on the buffalo hide Retha gave him and fell fast asleep. Slick Harry and Retha finished out the cold night shooting at the wolves to keep them away from the horses.

The next morning Retha found Joe huddled next to the warm coals of the dying fire. She quickly wrapped another buffalo hide around his shaking body. Blood had seeped into the snow beside him, and she quickly put pressure on the torn arm and shoulder.

"He's got the fever with this wound, Harry. We're going to have to take him back to town and find a doctor," she said nervously.

Harry quickly helped her load him into the wagon and tied his horse Buck behind. They headed back toward Abilene as fast as they dared without tearing the wagon apart on the hard-frozen ground.

CHAPTER 26

The Triple A Ranch

O.C., along with Earl Stockman and Jack Tunnie, was busy carrying wood to the cabins. The wagons had been late coming in–the night before had been so bitter with the blowing snow that it had made traveling impossible. Nate and Pete were the first to ride up as O.C. brought a bundle to Cindy's door, and Nate asked immediately if Joe was there.

O.C., surprised, asked why he wasn't with the group. "We haven't seen him, Nate." O.C. dropped the sticks and yelled to the ranch hands to saddle his horse.

Cindy came to the door. When she saw that Joe wasn't with the men, she cried hysterically. "Where's Joe?"

"Bring me a fresh horse!" Nate ordered the hands. "Shorty, this time you stay here. We can't all be gone with just the hired hands to protect the place. Hell, half of them can't even shoot."

Marianna brought the men a pot of hot coffee from the cook house. O.C. stuffed some beef jerky in his saddlebags and mounted. He, Nate, and Pete drank the rest of their coffee and were ready to go.

"Jack, you, Earl, and Shorty can take care of the place. We'll be back with Joe as soon as we can," O.C. instructed as the men rode into the direction of Abilene.

The wicked prairie wind whistled as the men rode toward the morning sun. Blowing snow was almost blinding as the burn of the cold beat against their faces.

"We need to spread out, boys," O.C. yelled over the howling of the wind. "Let's get a ways from each other, and remember to try to notice every little thing. Joe's life may depend on it. We already know something has gone wrong. Fire your gun if you find anything. Let's keep going along both sides of the trail. Places where it disappears, just use your best judgment."

Nate and Pete nodded in determined agreement and spurred their horses into the bleakness.

They traveled for hours before Nate fired his .44 and O.C. and Pete joined him.

"What did you find, Nate?" O.C. asked anxiously.

"Blood in the snow, O.C. It's all over the place."

"Wolf tracks!" yelled Pete. "But here's some boot tracks leading to the east. Man, that's a lot of blood–he must have fought them off."

O.C. was looking pretty upset, so Nate quickly put in, "You know, all that blood might have been coming from the horse."

O.C. shook off his worry and once more took charge. "Maybe, but let's get on the tracks."

O.C. was quieter than usual as his eyes followed the blood trail. Then he realized that the only shelter for miles would be the rock overhang. By now the place had gained the name Dead Man's Hole. He spurred his horse in the direction of the hole at a fast pace. Rather than following the blood-stained trail, he focused on getting to the rocks.

"What the hell?" gasped Nate as he watched him ride off in a hurry.

"He's right, Nate–he realized that Joe would be trying to find shelter, and that's the only one around for miles."

They rode for almost an hour before they reached Dead Man's Hole. O.C. quickly dismounted and moved into the opening of the cave. He had seen smoke coming from the west side of the overhang, and he felt a relief come over him. Nate and Pete rode up behind him and started to dismount.

As O.C. scanned the overhang with careful eyes, he gestured to them to go on. "You boys ride around and circle the area to see if you can see anything."

O.C. realized Joe had been there from the blood in the snow and all the tracks–but where was he now?

Then he heard Pete yell from the west side, "There's wagon tracks over here!"

O.C. mounted his horse. "They've headed back toward Abilene. Let's ride–maybe we can catch up to them."

Abilene Kansas

Retha drove her mules as fast as she could, almost running over some cowhands crossing the street.

Marshal Swartz shook his head. "What the hell is going on?" he yelled. "You lookin' to get locked up again?"

Slick Harry jumped from the wagon, picked up Joe, and carried him inside the jail.

Marshal Swartz realized what was going on and started to help. "What the hell happened to him?" he demanded.

Slick Harry was taking the bloody rags from Joe's shoulder. "Get Doc Puckett fast!" he yelled.

Retha had already run to Doc Puckett's place and told him the story. The doctor hastily followed her across the street.

After examining Joe and stitching for about a half hour, the doctor helped them dress him in a warm gown and carry him across the street to Doc Puckett's building. It was a good size for the town, as many of the cowboys got injured. There were seven bunks, two nurses, and a warm fire.

Joe was fading in and out of consciousness and talking

out of his head. Doc Puckett continued to examine his shoulder with concern as Slick Harry and Retha looked on.

"What about it, Doc? Do you think he's going to make it?" Retha asked hesitantly.

Puckett turned with a serious look on his face. "Well, he's lost a lot of blood, and that shoulder's infected." He pursed his lips and shook his head. "Only time will tell. The thing he needs now is rest, so you two get on out of here." He reached for the whisky bottle and took a big swallow as he pointed toward the door.

Though Retha obeyed, she kind of smiled. "You know, that old man is about the grouchiest old man I ever saw."

"Yeah, but he's all we got," frowned Slick Harry. He reached into his pocket and then bit off a big hunk of chew.

"My God, Slick, I don't know how you chew that stuff! Why, I just as soon chew a damn buffalo patty."

"Well, it's a free country, I guess," smiled Slick Harry. "Anyway, we have to get somewhere warm tonight, so let's start looking."

A few hours later it had begun to snow, and strong winds swirled the snow through the streets of Abilene. O.C. and his friends had arrived in town and got the story from Marshal Swartz. They sat at the bedside and talked to Joe for a minute and then went to the Merchant's Hotel.

They were exhausted from the day, but O.C. went back to Joe's bedside and remained there the rest of the night. Doc Puckett's nurse would visit about every half hour and urge O.C. to go to the Hotel and rest, but he refused. He sat for hours and thought about all the events of his lifetime. He knew it would probably be many more days before he could take Joe home. The following morning, he would send Pete back to the ranch to tell Cindy of the news about Joe. He knew she would be sitting up day and night not knowing whether her husband was dead or alive.

Two days later

Pete arrived at the ranch and was greeted by almost everyone there. He explained to Cindy and the boys what had happened. She quickly asked Levi to ready the wagon, but Pete explained that would not be necessary because O.C. would probably already be on the way back with Joe by the time she got there.

"He'll be OK, Miss Cindy. He just needs some good rest and old Doc Puckett said he'll be fine."

It was very hard to talk Cindy out of it, as she was almost frantic. The other women gathered around and tried to comfort her.

Levi called Pete aside and quietly asked how Joe really was.

Pete kind of dropped his head and quietly explained, "I don't really know, Levi. He lost a lot of blood, but the old Doc thinks he'll make it."

"Well, I hope to hell so," Levi frowned. "Things seem to come in threes around here."

"How's Johnny One Horn's leg doing, and those kids?" asked Pete.

"Well, all those kids went through a hell of an ordeal with that devil–it's a wonder they can hold on without going crazy. You should hear some of the stories those kids can tell! It will just about put you in shock. I think they'll always be affected in some way. I hope they can forget it in time, though–it's really bad." Old Levi clicked his tongue as he shook his head in sympathy. "As for Johnny, he's doing a little better, but he still can't ride or even walk very well."

"Well, I hate to hear that. He surely is one of our leaders and I hope he gets back to himself soon. There's a lot of people around here that need him."

CHAPTER 27

One Week Later

O.C. and the hands had returned to the ranch with Joe, who, even though he was not very mobile, was healing quite fast.

Johnny One Horn was walking a little better and was spending a lot of time with the small girls he had rescued from the insane BoJack. Tina and Sally were beautiful little blonde girls that were quickly learning the ways of the ranch. Still, they were scared of most men and were very cautious when any man even spoke to them. Tom Flint and Zack were attending Cindy Armstrong's school and loving the ranch. They were grateful to cut wood, haul coal to the buildings, and become part of a functioning community.

Every morning inside the cook house all the ranch hands would gather to drink coffee and discuss the day's work.

"You know, O.C., young Zack told me that Johnny One Horn was going to leave and go back to the river country," Pete mentioned one day. "I'm just wondering if he was telling another story, or is it for real?"

"I don't know, but he usually doesn't make things like that up. I'll ask Johnny today when this damn cold wind stops blowing."

The sun was just coming up and swirls of snow were blowing in a circular motion down the street of what seemed like a small town. Nate walked up to the table where Pete and O.C. were talking. “You know, there was a fellow rode in last night asking for you, O.C. He’s a young fellow named Sam Carter; he says he knows you.”

O.C. frowned. “I don’t know no Sam Carter. He must be looking for someone else.”

“Well, he was pretty set on talking to you, so I let him stay in the bunk house.”

“Well, you boys might as well go get him. I want to see what he’s got to say.” O.C. smiled amiably.

The cook house was bustling with ranch hands and girls preparing breakfast. O.C. kept busy chatting with the girls, but his mind was on the man that was looking for him. He reached under the table and readied his .44 when he heard the door swing open and a man arguing with Pete.

Pete and Nate wrestled the man up to the table and O.C. motioned the girls to leave the room. He laid his .44 on the table. “Why is it, Mister, that you should want to talk to an old codger like me?” he asked, smiling.

The man reached up and pulled the scarf off his face.

“Oh, this gets interesting. What in the world ever brought a black man to this place, and what in the world could you want with me?”

By this time O.C.’s demeanor had calmed the mood down. O.C. invited the man to sit down at the table. “Pete, you want to get our guest a cup of coffee?” he asked.

“Mr. Armstrong, you knew my grandfather, Neil Carter. He said you was a close friend and just like family. Well, he died several years ago, but before he did, he told me a story. I think you know what it is.” The young man leaned back in his chair, sipping his hot coffee.

O.C.’s expression changed. “Yeah, I know that story, but I can’t talk about it here. You’re welcome to stay here in the bunk house, and we can have a long talk about this later when we can talk in private.” With that, O.C. stood up and left the building.

Pete had given the hands the day off because the weather was fearsome. Wind whistled down the street, with freezing temperatures dropping lower as the day went on.

O.C. got the news from Amy that Jack Tunnie was very sick, and he hurried to their cabin. When he walked into the cabin he found his longtime friend in his bed, with his eyes closed. Amy was sitting beside him while two of the girls from the ranch supported her.

"What happened?" O.C. asked. "Has he got a cold or something?" O.C. fervently hoped that was all it was.

"No, I just found him like this when I woke up. I couldn't wake him up so I sent for you."

O.C. rubbed Jack's forehead as tears trickled down his face. "Oh, my," he said sadly. "This is what's the matter with this place, as beautiful as it is–we don't have a doctor. I'll send a couple of the boys into Garden City to fetch old Doc Young."

As O.C. reflected for a few moments, though, he realized that old Dr. Young would never make the trip in the bitter weather. "Marianna, go get Nate and Shorty from the cook house."

In a few minutes the men hustled through the door.

"Something's wrong with Jack, boys. He's going to need a doctor. Can you boys rig two of the wagons–one to put Jack in, and the other for a spare with plenty of bedrolls? I'll ride in the wagon with Jack. You can get the hands out of the cook house to help."

It took about an hour to get the wagons ready for the trip. "Get some of the buffalo hides to drape the horses," Nate instructed, reacting to the blustering wind chill.

As they bundled Jack up for the trip, O.C. turned to Tunnie's wife. "Amy, I hate to tell you this, but you need to stay here. In this weather it is far too dangerous for you to go."

Amy touched her husband's face, then put her hands to her face, sat down, and whispered a prayer. The men carried Jack out to the wagon and were soon on their way.

Later the next afternoon

The cold wind was whistling but the storm was slowly passing. O.C. kept talking to Jack, but there was no response. It was extremely cold, and ice had formed in O.C.'s beard as he sat beside his longtime friend. Jack was wrapped in hides and O.C. was sure he was safe and warm, but Shorty and Nate were shivering from the bitter cold.

"Thank God!" Shorty yelled as the main street of the city appeared out of the blowing snow. "We're here!"

Nate went to the back of the wagon and found O.C. asleep sitting up. "O.C., we're here!" he said as he brushed the snow off O.C.'s face. "I'll go get old Doc."

Bus as he rushed across the frozen street, Nate noticed the doors were boarded up on the building. He could see a few people through the frozen windows across the street a Eula May's saloon, so he turned and ran there. When he rustled trough the almost frozen door, he saw Eula May sitting at a table having a drink with some of the other girls.

Eula jumped up in surprise. "Well, if it ain't Nate! My goodness, man, what are you doing out here in this weather?"

"I need Doc Young, Eula, but the doors are all boarded up. Where is he?"

"Well, he's dead, Nate, but we have a new doctor staying here in the boarding house."

"Well, we've got a real sick man with us." Nate turned and ran back toward the wagons.

They carried Jack in and, with the help of the girls and Jo Bo Hatton, they got him into a room upstairs.

Eula was trying to wake the new doctor, and finally he opened the door after what had seemed an eternity. "What the hell's this all about? slurred the half-drunk young man.

O.C. grabbed the young doctor by the collar and yelled,

"Get some coffee in this yahoo!"

Pickles and the girls quickly brought the coffee pot upstairs.

O.C. slapped the doctor. "Wake up, you idiot! I have a friend here that may be dying!"

After a half hour or so, the young doctor had begun to come around.

"What's your name, son?" asked O.C.

"It's Mike Dunn, sir. Who's the S.O.B. that slapped me?" he blurted, touching his stinging face.

"That don't make any difference at this minute, boy. Just look at our friend here."

"You make a habit of slapping somebody you don't know, Mister?" the doctor asked.

O.C. pulled his .44 jammed it to the Mike Dunn's cheek. "Mister, if you don't stop talking and do something, I'll blow that smart head of yours to somewhere in Arkansas! Get busy!"

"Yes, sir," the doctor replied nervously. He studied Jack Tunnie silently for several minutes. "I think this man has had a stroke, and a bad one. I don't know how to treat these. I'm not a surgeon so all we can do is to wait and see what happens. Sometimes they get better with time and sometimes they don't. I do know this: he will lose a lot of mobility if he makes it."

"What sort of mobility are you talking about?" O.C. asked worriedly.

"Well, like walking, hand and arm movements, and speech. We never know ahead of time, but it takes time and a lot of it. All we can do now is keep him warm and as comfortable as we can. I'll stay with him tonight and keep watch."

O.C.'s eyes slowly dropped, and he stared at the floor.

Nate stepped forward and put his hand on his shoulder. "There's nothing we can do now, O.C. You need to get some rest."

O.C. walked to the window and contemplated the frozen street below. "I'm staying here, Nate. You boys go and take care of the horses. See if Eula has a room for you. I'm staying with Jack." He sat down in the old wooden rocker beside the bed and softy began talking to Jack. Every now and then he would walk to the window and stare out at the swirling ice show below.

The night seemed to drag on forever as O.C. sat with his hands over his face. He finally drifted into a heavy sleep. He awoke with the doctor's hand on his weary shoulder.

"Mister, I'm afraid your friend is gone. He passed on about an hour ago. I'm sorry."

"Oh my," O.C. shakily said. "Old Jack is gone." Tears streamed down his face as he stood over his old friend. "It's all right now, Jack. We're taking you home."

Later that day Nate and some cowboys from the saloon loaded Jack's body in the casket obtained from the town undertaker into their wagon, and the group headed back to the ranch. The weather had broken, and the sun was melting the bitter snow.

As they made their way back, O.C. was wondering what to say to poor Amy. He knew how much she loved Jack. His mind flashed back to the many years they had spent together. He wondered when it would be his time. He tried very hard to dismiss the thought, but it just would not let go.

The Ranch

The trip back to the ranch was a difficult one with slushy mud and high creeks that were normally dry at this time of year.

It was difficult to tell Amy about Jack, but O.C. made it through. He thought he was having a heart attack a couple of times, but he fought to hide his emotions. Life would go on at the sprawling ranch, but without his old friend. He would bury Jack in the little cemetery by the river alongside his son Carl. He smiled when he thought of that, and it eased the hurt for a while.

This was not the only bad news O.C. would have to deal with that day. While he was away, Cha-cha, Johnny One Horn's beloved wolf, had died suddenly. Johnny was devasted by the loss. He buried him by the river not far from the little cemetery.

The Return of Little Boy Horse to the Sioux Village

Little Boy Horse had weathered most of the winter helping Shagging Jim and Cookie. Now that the weather was calming, he decided he should return to the Sioux village. Shagging Jim offered to let him use his favorite pack mule. "Take care of old Pole Cat Horse, now. See that you bring him back."

Horse smiled. "I sure will, Jim. It's been a hard winter and I know I would not have survived without you and that loving wife of yours–you're a lucky man, my friend."

Shagging Jim had been told the direction of the village from some fellow mountain men, and he passed that on to Little Boy Horse. The trip was long and difficult. Little Boy Horse had to use all his skills to survive. He was thankful for all he had learned from Shagging Jim, for that knowledge served him well on his journey.

He arrived at the village two weeks later and was reunited with Mika and Wind. The whole village celebrated his return. Around the campfires, he repeated his story many times, and heard many conversations about his brother, Johnny One Horn. He was told that news had come from the southern tribes that Johnny had brought some orphaned children to the Armstrong ranch. He was told of the great bear and the death of the crazed mountain man BoJack.

The northern spring slowly approached with an April visit from Sad Hank. He brought news that Johnny One Horn planned a return to the southern swamp. Horse wondered about the dangers there, since they had been gone so long. He wondered if his people could ever be found.

There was a secret place on top of the highest cliff where Horse spent many days with Wind and Mika. But Horse's thoughts often drifted to his brother. He questioned whether or not he would ever see him again.

Chapter 28

Spring at the Ranch

It was the middle of April and the plains had warmed considerably. Johnny One Horn walked to the river every day to visit the grave of his beloved wolf Cha-cha. Sometimes one of the children would walk with him. The walks were helping both his heart and his leg to heal.

He had also developed a strong relationship with newcomer Sam Carter. One day on the river Sam asked Johnny about the gold in the swamp. Sam really didn't know what the response would be, but he held his breath and hoped Johnny would not cut his throat.

Johnny had to take a deep breath. "I know of this evil yellow rock," he finally answered. "You will be better off if you just leave things alone."

Sam trembled as he asked if the boys had found the gold from the swamp.

"We found some, but there is probably a lot more still there. It was under water and it was hard to get." Johnny looked squarely at his friend. "I knew your grandfather Neil. My brother used to tease him a lot about his curly hair." Johnny laughed at the memory.

"He mentioned both of you in the stories he told," explained Sam. "I didn't think you were real until I saw you in person. Tell me, where is your brother, Little Boy

Horse?"

Johnny smiled and looked to the north. "Somewhere up there chasing his dreams. I think he's happy there."

As they walked back to the campground, they could see O.C. at one of the tables.

"Tell me, Johnny, was my grandfather with you when the gold was found?"

Johnny stared at him for a moment, then simply said, "No, he wasn't there. He knew it was there. But I tell you, Sam, that stuff is evil and you best leave it there or bad things will happen."

Sam knew it was time to shut up. Johnny turned to go to his dwelling and several women walked in behind him.

O.C. motioned for Sam Carter to come and sit by him. Sam sat down but didn't know what to expect for a few minutes, as O.C. was perusing some papers in his hand.

Finally, O.C. spoke. "You know, I never knew Neil Carter had a grandson until now. I believe I know why you are here." O.C. paused, considering his words carefully. He needed to assess the sincerity of the young man. "Sam, is your grandfather still alive? How about Minnie? Neil is a good man and a great friend."

Sam, looking down at the ground in front of him, slowly shook his head. "No. It's been about ten years, I guess. Grandpa Neil died from pneumonia and Grandma Minnie died pretty soon after that. I guess she died of loneliness–we just don't know. But before he died, Grandpa told me that he, along with you and another man, found a fortunc of gold. I asked Johnny One Horn and he said Grandpa Neil wasn't with you when you found it." Sam lifted his eyes hopefully to search O.C.'s face for some answers.

O.C. smiled and said, "Well, he wasn't there when the boys found it. You see, your grandfather, me, and Bud Whitaker found the treasure and buried it a long time ago. Then the swamp rose suddenly and covered it with twenty or thirty feet of water. I was gone and your grandparents had moved away when my boys, along with Johnny and Horse, decided to dive down into that leech-infested water. I think maybe they found about a third of the gold. It was enough to last us all our lifetimes. It was very hard to get it, and I still don't know how they done it." He bit his lip and contemplated for a while as Sam sat nervously beside him.

Cupping his chin in his hand, O.C. sighed and at last turned to face the young man. "If you came here to claim Neil's share, I guess you have that right. I'll have Charles set up a bank account in the bank at Abilene. It will include your share of the ranch as well, son."

Sam Carter's eyes were watering and he lost the ability to speak for a minute. Then he slowly stood and hugged O.C.'s neck. Choking on his words, he told O.C. about how poor his family was, and that some were barely surviving. "That old Armstrong swamp place is for sale, O.C., and I intend to buy it," he declared. "With this money I can find the rest of the gold. If I can get the rest of it, I will split it with you and everybody else that has a share, I promise."

"Well, that will be great, Sam, but there are always bad things that come along with finding a treasure. You have to be careful when you're dealing with gold or you will end up dead."

"Do you think I can get the boys to come with me–and you? You could show me where it is!"

"No, Sam, we have enough to last several lifetimes. But you can look for it if you want. I can't even tell you where it is because too many years have passed. I know things would all be different now."

~~~

Sam Carter didn't know how to handle his new-found riches, but quickly made plans to return to Mississippi and find the rest of the bounty. He had several long conversations with Johnny One Horn about joining him on
~~~

the perilous journey. He tried to convince Johnny that they could take the train and river steamboat, and the trip would be very fast compared to the long, seemingly never-ending cattle drive that had brought Johnny to the ranch. It took a while, but Johnny finally agreed to accompany him. It had long been his dream to return to the swamp and find his tribe. He anticipated teaching them how to survive in a world full of change.

Johnny had become very attached to the children he had brought from the far north. Zack and young Tom Flint were coming along very well. He thought they would make fine ranch hands one day. Tina and Sally had been welcomed whole-heartedly into the ranch community, and had become especially close to Joe's wife Cindy. They enjoyed the little school and were slowly becoming more like normal children. As he watched them play with the other children, sometimes the big man would find tears trickling down his cheeks. They would be OK. He felt it was safe now for him to leave them and return to his home in the swamp. He had long wondered if any of his people were still alive.

In the following days, they told O.C. and the rest of the ranch family about their plans. Joe and the men of the ranch planned a going-away feast for the two. They held a big cookout, and all said their goodbyes. Everybody took Johnny's leaving very hard, especially young Carl.

The pair planned to leave in the early morning before anybody was stirring. Johnny truly didn't like goodbyes, and wanted to avoid any more hurting inside. Levi had the wagon ready and had volunteered to drive them to Abilene. Everything was lightly packed for the trip, and Joe, Nate, and Pete, along with O.C., met them at sunrise. Young Carl couldn't sleep all night, and watched through the window with tears streaming down his cheeks.

Johnny and Sam shook all the men's hands. Joe had to wipe his eyes and turn away.

"Goodbye, my good friend," O.C. smiled sadly. "Do me a favor, Johnny, and put some roses from time to time on my Martha's grave."

Johnny, a lump in his throat, just nodded his head.

"I don't have the words, my friend. I'm going to miss you." Nate frowned to keep from crying.

Pete and Shorty sat on their horses nearby and gave the sign from their chests. Johnny returned it as the wagon began to move.

O.C. and the boys stood for a while watching as the wagon traveled to the hilltop east of the ranch.

"Damn, old Horn is gone!" lamented Joe. "I can't believe it." He scuffed his feet in the dirt a minute, looking down to hide his emotions. Finally, he looked up and nodded to the others. "Well, let's get on with our work. Nate, you and Pete check them west fences before breakfast. It's not a holiday, you know."

"Boy, you're getting to be quite bossy in your young age," remarked O.C. as they rode out.

"Well, I had a good teacher," returned Joe as he headed back to his cabin.

At the top of the hill Johnny asked Levi to stop for a minute. He stepped out of the wagon and walked away from the company of the other men.

"What is he doing, Levi?" asked Sam Carter.

"He's not leaving–let's just be quiet and let him say goodbye in his way," Levi assured him.

Johnny walked fifty feet or so from the wagon, got to his knees, and surveyed the ranch and surrounding area. He chanted a few native chants and continued to stare for a few minutes. Then he returned and boarded the wagon without saying a word. He just motioned to Levi that he was ready to go. Sam Carter was at a loss for words as the three rode into the sunrise amid somewhat cloudy skies.

Mississippi Bound

After stopping at the bank, Levi let Johnny and Sam off at the railroad depot where they managed to get their tickets to St Louis. There they would take a steamboat down the Mississippi. The trip was rather uneventful since the two avoided the other passengers.

The river trip seemed like the longest he'd ever endured, as Johnny was still trying to get over the train ride and the white man's clothing he hated. He was fascinated with the steamboat though. He wondered how man could build such an enormous beast.

When they arrived in Vicksburg, Sam went to the local livery stable and managed to buy a couple of horses and gear. Even though they were exhausted from the long journey, they left rather quickly to avoid suspicion. They traveled most of the night down the same old dirt and rocky road toward the old Armstrong home place.

Once there, they camped out below the burial mound. Johnny could see lights in the distance north of the mound. The night was full of familiar sounds that filled the heavy air.

"Sam, the water never went down. Where your folks' old place was is now under water."

"Yeah, I knew it was. I thought you knew I was here once before. We have to be careful here, Johnny. Things have really changed since you left. There are a lot of people looking for that gold."

"But how did they know?" asked Johnny. "There weren't too many people that even knew about it."

"My Grandfather Neil was going to come back and find it. He organized a work party, but he died before he got it started. He promised them all a cut of the profits in exchange for work and equipment, so a lot of people knew."

"My people–did they ever say anything about my

people?" Johnny seemed concerned.

Sam dropped his head and answered slowly. "Just that they seemed to disappear deeper into the swamp."

Johnny turned slowly and faced Sam. "I will show you the place as the sun rises, but then I am leaving. I want nothing to do with this cursed yellow devil iron."

When the sun finally rose, Johnny was shocked to see that most of the burial ground had been destroyed. Huge piles of dirt had been dug from the area. It was clear that the place had been the victim of gold-hungry men with the fever. The crosses were gone from the top of the mound, and pieces of the wooden casket were scattered to the sides. Tears ran down Johnny's face as he inwardly screamed in pain.

"Sam," he said, his voice shaking, "I will show you where the yellow iron is only if you promise to find any remains and take them to the ranch. There she will be with her family."

Sam stared across the swamp for a few seconds and then extended his hand. "It will be my honor, my friend. But what are you going to do, Johnny? Don't you ever plan on going back?"

"I may not, since my plans are to find my people and help them if I can. Now, come with me to the edge of the water and I will show you where the yellow iron is hidden. The old cypress thicket is still there but I see the money tree is gone. It probably fell–it had been struck by lightning." Johnny pointed toward the cypress trees. "Northeast of those trees, about six hundred steps. That's all I can tell you. It's very dangerous to swim in there with cottonmouths, leeches, and alligators."

"Oh, I'm not going to swim, Johnny–I'm planning to buy a steam dredge. It's like the iron horse but it floats on water. It has a huge bucket that reaches into the water and brings up everything it can grab." Sam reached into his jacket and pulled out a picture. "This is what it looks like,

Johnny."

Johnny wasn't very interested in the picture and quickly handed it back. "Things like this will one day destroy this beautiful land, my friend, and I warn you again that the yellow iron has a curse upon it. Be careful and pray to your God to spare you from its wrath."

Johnny put his hand on Sam's shoulder. Goodbye, my friend. Just remember what I told you."

After Johnny had walked some distance away, he turned and watched as Sam scrambled to his horse. The Indian shook his head in sorrow. He knew another friend had succumbed to the lure of gold.

CHAPTER 29

Finding the Tribe

At the edge of the swamp, Johnny One Horn turned to see Sam Carter riding as fast as the poor horse could carry him down the muddy trail. Then, along the edge of the trees, he noticed a trail leading to the water's edge. He got a little excited at the thought that his family tribe might still visit this area. He wondered how many were left, and if any would remember him.

With new vigor, he followed the trail into the swamp. Soon it became clear that it was used quite frequently. He came to a four-way split deep in the swamp and knew immediately which trail to take. It was a rule that the correct trail was always the second one from the left. Many trails split and ran in different directions to confuse anybody that might be trying to track them. The wrong trails usually led to traps and dangerous things that could kill a person in a split second.

Johnny traveled most of the day before stopping to build a camp for the night. He gathered vines to make a sort of hammock. This would keep him off the ground and away from the damp, almost muddy, ground. He constructed a small fire stack a little downwind from his hammock with dry bark peeled from the trees. The smoke would help with the early evening mosquitoes. Usually these would vanish as the night passed. He ate a little dried beef he had brought from the ranch, and got into his self-made cocoon. For an hour or so, he lay there, listening to the sweet sounds of the swamp. It had been so long and it brought him an easy feeling.

Early in the morning, he awoke to the sounds of small children talking and laughing. He quickly moved the leaves and vines away from his head and shoulders. The little ones looked shocked, as they had thought the familiar cocoon-style hammock would contain someone they knew. He smiled at them, but they quickly scurried down the trail and vanished into the dense undergrowth of the swamp. Johnny just smiled, elated that his tribe had survived. He quickly tore down the hammock and spread the remains throughout the undergrowth. He wanted to hide any evidence of his ever being there. Then he followed the trail until he was suddenly surrounded by five young braves with arrows pointed toward him.

In their language they were chattering among themselves, and to their surprise Johnny began answering them. Confused, they looked at each other in amazement.

"What are you doing here?" a boy asked at last.

"This is my home," Johnny smiled. "And who are you, my friends?"

Some of the young men began telling him a little about themselves, but one with an angry voice yelled, "Why have we never seen you if you live here?"

"It is a long story, my young friends, but I am the son of the great chief Gray Wolf."

"Are you a spirit?" one asked.

"No, I am not a spirit, but I am blood-related to a lot of you."

"How did you get so big? None of us are that big!"

Johnny made a fierce-looking face and growled, "It's from eating live alligators!" Then he laughed.

He was quickly accepted by the young warriors, and

asked them how far their camp was. They explained that they were on a hunting mission and were a couple of miles from their camp. They told him they move around a lot to follow the game, and because men with firesticks also hunted in the swamp and sometime killed members of the tribe.

"The white men are mostly by the edge of the water, though, and most of them don't venture this far into the swamp," one young brave explained. "It seems the mosquitoes like them a lot and they can't handle them!"

"Can I ask your name?" a young man asked.

"Sure can. I am Johnny One Horn. What is yours, my friend?"

"They call me Sleeping Tree. I'm the leader of this hunting party. We have to hunt most of the time because there is not enough food any more to feed us all. We rely on our lines in the big water for fish, and we hunt the geese that come from the far north this time of year."

It seemed so strange that there was not enough food. Johnny remembered that game used to be plentiful. As they moved along the trail, he wondered how many there were left. He had thought most would be dead by now.

They arrived at the village about sundown and, to Johnny's surprise, several members of the tribe came running to greet him. Several that he could not even remember even hugged him. A lot of them called him by name, and he felt very much at home. He noticed that this had not changed a lot since he had left. There were also a lot of questions about Little Boy Horse. He explained the best he could and promised to go farther into the story later. There were not many old members of the village left. It was said that a fever had spread through the village a few years before that had taken most of the aging members. This was really sad because Johnny had known most of them. The tribe hustled him down through the village, laughing and touching him, until they arrived at the chief's small stick hut.

"This is our Chief!" one of the young men announced. "Meet Emot."

Chief Emot gave him the peace sign from the chest and Johnny returned it. "I remember you, my friend. You were younger, but I remember how you and your brother Little Boy Horse protected us from the bad and the evil. Tell me, are you still a medicine man? If so, we have a lot of sickness here in our village. It comes and goes and makes many very sick. Come into my hut and we shall talk of this, and of your journey."

They sat by a small fire in the center, which was intended just to create smoke for healing.

"Tell me, One Horn, where you have been for so long, and what you have seen."

"I have seen many amazing things, my friend. I will tell all of you, but first let us talk about this sickness that spreads through the people."

"Well, it causes bad cramps and fever, and sometimes it lasts a long time. Some of our older members have even died from it."

Johnny was listening very closely to Emot and remembered something from the cattle drive. "Tell me, Emot, where do you get your water?"

"There is a creek that runs not far from here that has clear water, and all our drinking water comes from there," replied Emot.

"Have you ever been to where this creek starts?" quizzed Johnny.

"Yes, it is several miles to the west through some rocky hills."

"Are there animals or people there?" Johnny pressed.

"Yes, the white men have cut the trees and they have their cattle there."

"OK. I learned this from being around the white man's cattle. They boil their drinking water, and the heat kills the sickness. I do not know what makes this, but I do know they boil the water from creeks and rivers, and that keeps the sickness away."

"But we drank this water for many years and there was no sickness. I really don't understand," frowned the chief.

"I know, Emot, but the land has changed with the coming of the white man's cattle. But there is a good thing I have learned. We must trade or buy some of these cattle and raise them for milk and meat to feed our little ones. From now on, everyone must boil the drinking water. I will go to the white men and see if they will bargain for a few of these cattle."

Emot looked uneasy. "Johnny, these men are not easy to deal with. Sometimes they shoot at us just to laugh. You might be killed. We stay very far from them."

"Emot, I have come to know the white man's ways. Most of them are good, but some, like any other people, are bad. I will take my chances."

As days passed, Johnny became lovingly attached to the tribe. It was as if he had never left. Several of the young women began to gather around, amazed at how he towered over the rest of the tribesmen.

Those in the village had begun to boil all their drinking water, and the everyday sickness slowly disappeared. The tribe believed Johnny was a true medicine man sent by the Great Spirit.

At night the tribe would gather around a large fire pit and Johnny would tell them stories from the cattle drive and the great rivers he had crossed. The children sat in wonder as he told of the things and animals he had seen on the great prairie to the west. He told them of the large tribe at war with the white men, and the hunting of the buffalo. They loved hearing of the far north and the endless snow and bitter cold. They asked many questions about the ranch and all the people there. They were amazed by the true tale of the great grizzly, and the friendship of the wolf Cha-cha.

Many stories were told for several days, and Johnny enjoyed the kindness and love of his people.

At last Johnny decided it was time to act on his feelings. The tribe was extremely poor, and survived on very little. The weather was mostly warm, but the people needed many things and he was determined to make sure they would have a better way of life. The children needed the knowledge of what was changing in the world outside of their small existence. They would someday have to move on and learn the ways of the changing world, or they would perish.

One night, he explained that he would have to leave for several days to see if he could bargain with the white men that owned the cattle. "I have a friend I need to see. He made the journey from the west with me. He should be back to the old Armstrong place when I return there. If not, I plan to seek out the owners of the land that holds the cattle."

The people were saddened that he was leaving so he comforted them by telling some funny stories of the white man's town in the west called Garden City. The stories of the huge city of St. Louis seemed unreal as they listened in amazement. As the night grew late and most were asleep, he gathered his things and slipped off through the darkness.

On his way back through the swamp, Johnny wondered if Sam Carter had made it back with the huge steam dredge. He was surprised to find many men working and roaming around the remains of the Armstrong farm. He came upon a young black man tending a few horses. At first sight of the huge Indian, the young man reached for a pitchfork lying nearby.

"Whoa, young fellow, Johnny smiled, "I'm not going to hurt you. I'm just looking for my friend Sam Carter."

"Oh," the young man sighed in relief, "You must be Johnny One Horn. Sam has told us a lot about you–he said that one time you fought a grizzly bear and won!"

"Well, I did fight him, but my limp was caused by a little ol' thorn that grows on the prairie. The old bear got his licks in though–he tore my shoulder. It was a long time before that healed."

"Did you kill him?" the teen asked excitedly.

"No–he was just protecting his home, so Cha-cha and I decided to let him go in peace."

"Who's Cha-cha?" the boy wondered.

"Well, Cha-cha was my pet wolf. He recently died of old age. He was my brother."

The young man just stood for a few seconds with his mouth open in disbelief. But he had heard many stories from Sam about the honesty and feats of this great man. He finally remembered that Johnny had been looking for Sam, and responded, "Sam's out on the barge working, getting the steam shovel ready to dig. He says he's looking for an old ship or something."

Johnny realized from the conversation that the men working for Sam had not been told much.

The young man sprang into action. "Here, we will take the canoe and I will go with you, Mr. Horn!"

"That is good," Johnny agreed.

"By the way, Mr. Horn, my name is Neil, and I'm Sam's son. I was named after my grandfather."

"I knew your grandfather, Neil Carter. He was a great man. My brother used to have fun with him." Johnny laughed a little as he remembered Little Boy Horse rubbing Neil's curly hair, and that Neil was scared to death of him.

At young Neil's questioning glance, Johnny explained. "I was just thinking back, my young friend, of a good time a long time ago."

CHAPTER 30

Getting that old steam shovel loaded onto the barge had been a difficult task, but the hardest part was putting it all together. Sam had found the shovel after it had been used to complete a huge rock dike in Clermont Harbor. The owner had been glad to sell it for a fair price. The only problem was navigating it forty miles through the Saint Louis Bay, then north to reach the old Armstrong place. It had been an exhausting trip. Most of the crew were worn out by the time they reached their destination, but out of loyalty they all stuck with Sam.

Johnny and young Neil boarded the canoe and arrived at the barge in several minutes. As they drew near, Sam stood on the edge of the deck. He had seen Johnny arrive and noticed him talking to the boy.

As they stepped out of the canoe onto the deck, Sam hugged Johnny and smiled. "Did you find your people, Johnny?" he asked. "I've been kind of worried about you."

Sam looked worn and tired. "Johnny, you wouldn't believe how hard this last month has been. It's a long story. One day when we have all day," smiled Sam, "I will tell you about it."

"My people are ok, but they are suffering. The swamp will not provide the things it used to. Most of the beaver and muskrats that they use to make their blankets are gone, and only a few deer remain. It's very hard for them. I don't think they can survive much longer this way. Only about seventy are left and they are dying off very fast." Johnny turned away and stared across the still waters of the swamp. "It really bothers me to think I left them and stayed gone for so long."

Sam put his hand on Johnny's shoulder. "My friend, I've got the best news for you and your people. Their hurting will soon be over. You see, I bought the old Armstrong place from Buck Plumber's granddaughter. It extends from the land there at the old Armstrong house to the rolling hills in the west. Three thousand acres, and that includes the swamp all the way to the white farmer's land to the west."

Johnny was surprised to hear this. Tears ran down his cheeks. "But how does that affect my people? That is your land, Sam."

"Johnny, you never claimed your share of the gold even though you and your brother Little Boy Horse were the ones who dove down in this mud hole and found it. You showed me where the rest of it was here. If you don't want your share of the gold, then I give you the land, all three thousand acres of it. The Armstrong boys at the ranch will be proud of what I've done. I was making the deal on the land before I even went to Kansas. Swamp land is not worth much, and I managed to get it cheap."

"But this all comes from the yellow iron, and will bring bad things with it," worried Johnny. "I really can't accept this."

"Johnny," Sam explained, "I was buying this land before I had any gold. I had talked to the Plumbers and we settled on a price long before I talked to O.C., so this land does not come from the gold. In fact, if it will make you feel better, you can buy it from me."

Johnny considered that for a few seconds and then smiled. "Ok, Sam, you've got a deal." He grasped Sam's hand to seal the bargain.

"Good," Sam grinned, "I'll have the legal papers drawn up in Vicksburg and then it will be legally yours and that's that." Then Sam turned away, hesitating. "Johnny, I haven't told you the latest I heard from the ranch. It's not good. The latest wire I got in Vicksburg said that O.C. is very sick. I don't know the details–all the wire said was that O.C. was very bad."

Johnny's heart sank. "I need to go, but I feel I must stay and help my people. This is hard for me and I hurt inside. Please send another one of these wires and get more information for me, Sam."

It was a bad day for this worrisome news. Conflicting thoughts raced through Johnny's mind. He also believed that his great friend O.C. would want him to stay and take care of the problems of his people. Still, he ached to be with his friends at the ranch during their time of need.

Present Day at The Ranch

Joe, with his wife Cindy, stood at the bedside as Dr. Ray examined O.C. "Thanks for coming here, Sir. I know it's a long trip."

"Well, ever since I came to Garden City, it seems every trip I make is a hard one."

"Sorry to hear about Dr. Young, Sir. He was quite a character."

Dr. Ray glanced up at them for a second and shook his head. "I knew Dr. Young, and I warned him about staying drunk all the time, but he finally drank himself to death."

Joe didn't really say anything–he just nodded his head a little. "What's wrong with Pop though? He was fine that morning, and the next thing I knew, Nate was carrying him into the house. He said he found him unconscious by the river. Sometimes he becomes conscious for a few minutes, but then he fades back out. He hasn't said a word."

"Well, son, your father has had a heart attack, and I don't think he will get much better. Nobody knows how long he lay there before your ranch hand found him. All you can do is give it some time and see what happens. I've seen this before and some get better. But some don't. Just keep him quiet and calm, and I'll be back in about three days to check on him. See if he will take food or water–that is a critical thing that might determine the outcome."

Most of the ranch crew was standing outside waiting for Joe and Cindy to come out and tell them any good news that would make them feel better. Everybody on the ranch loved O.C., and each one felt heavy in the heart. Bessie sat beside the cabin praying, and Charles and his family were anxious to hear what Dr. Ray had said.

As Dr. Ray drove away in his carriage, Joe explained to the people what the doctor had said. It was very difficult to speak, and he had to stop to regain his composure several times. He asked everyone to go home and let O.C. rest. They agreed and slowly turned away.

"Someone will have to stay with him night and day," Cindy said when only the family remained. "He might need us at any time."

Charles and Joe offered to trade off with Cindy and Rosie so someone would always be near.

~ ~ ~

Three days later, O.C. took his first water and a little food and finally opened his eyes. He couldn't talk, but would try, though no one knew what he was saying. The group that had been watching over him was completely exhausted, so Nate would sometimes take a turn.

After a week or so, O.C. was able to sit up. Although he couldn't talk yet, he was able to draw with his right hand. He drew a sketch of the river and the chair. Nate was the first to see it and asked if he wanted to sit by the river. He nodded his head yes.

Nate showed the sketch to Joe, and Joe said he thought it might do him good. So, for a few days, Nate and Joe took O.C. to the riverside. He would sit by Carl's and Jack Tunnie's graves and stare at the river. Someone would always keep him company. Though his grandchildren would talk to him, he couldn't reply. He would just smile.

As O.C. watched the children fish, tears would trickle down his cheeks. It was very difficult for him to be so helpless, as he had been a strong man and a leader throughout his life.

Nate was on watch for a few hours one afternoon and walked to O.C.'s chair. "Are you all right, O.C.?" he asked. O.C. nodded his head and then pointed to his mouth.

"Are you hungry, Boss?" Nate guessed. "Would you like me to run down to the cook house and grab a sandwich or something–maybe a good cup of coffee?"

O.C. smiled and nodded.

Nate mounted his horse. "OK, Boss, don't go away! I'll be back in a few minutes."

O.C. watched him for a few minutes, then turned back to stare at the swirling river. His mind drifted to times and people of the past. He saw his son Carl laughing and complaining. His loving Martha filled his memory. Everything in his past rapidly flashed through his mind like the pages of a book flipping in a wind. Tears streamed down his face as he started rocking the chair at the river's edge. Then he rocked with more urgency until the chair, with him in it, tumbled into the fast-swirling water. As the current carried him away, O.C. smiled and relaxed as he and his chair slowly disappeared beneath the water.

Joe saw Nate coming out of the cook house and called, "Nate, did you leave Pop alone?"

"Yeah, he was hungry. I've only been gone a few minutes."

Joe, looking toward the river in alarm, quickly mounted

his horse and raced to the cemetery. When he arrived, there was nothing. "Oh, God!" he prayed as his eyes scanned the river. He galloped his horse downriver, watching the current for any sign. His heart was pounding, there was nothing to be seen. He knew his father was most likely gone. Nate soon joined him, and they searched until the sun had set.

"It's not your fault, Nate. Pop had been trying to get Cindy to give him his pistol for a few days. We thought he may have wanted to kill himself. Pop was a man that couldn't live in a bed or chair the rest of his life, no matter how long that might be."

Eventually, they were joined by all the ranch hands, and the search continued the rest of the night and all the next day. No one saw anything, and Joe knew that O.C. could be miles down the rain-swollen river.

Finally, at sunset on the second day, Joe sent the hands back to the ranch with Pete to get a little rest, but asked them to go back to work in the morning. He and Nate would continue the search downriver.

Five Days Later

Joe and Nate were camped on a sandbar, exhausted from so often investigating things in the river, only to find they were branches or other debris. Still there was no O.C. Joe had decided the search was over. He placed his saddle on the ground beside the small driftwood fire.

"Hey, Joe, this might help you sleep." Nate handed Joe a bottle of moonshine.

Joe quickly gulped about a third of it. "Thanks, Nate. Hey–I want you to know I hold no hard feelings. This is what he wanted, old friend."

"Thanks, Joe, but I just can't get it out of my mind."

"I know, Nate, I know."

As Joe lay there that evening, his mind meandered

through many memories. As he drifted between dreams and reality, he saw a figure walking across the glimmering water toward him. He knew this was his father. O.C. had a strange glow about him and seemed to be gliding across the surface of the water, smiling as he approached.

"It's OK, Son. I'm going to meet Carl and your mother. You take care of the kids and Cindy because you have many more years of happiness ahead of you. Sorry to leave all of you this way, but it was time, Son." The figure turned, then looked back and smiled again before slowly fading into the reflection of the moonlight on the water.

"Joe, you OK? You were talking to yourself or something." Nate had a strange look on his face. "Did you hear that, Joe? That whippoorwill keeps squawking. I've never heard any of them here. There were some where I used to live in Southeast Missouri, but not here."

Joe turned his head to look at the shimmering river. "That's no whippoorwill, Nate. Get some sleep."

The Next Morning

Joe and Nate returned to the ranch and everyone ran to meet them, desperate to hear some good news.

Joe couldn't bear to face these eager faces, but he knew they needed to hear something from him. Finally, tears streaming down his cheeks, he choked, "The river's too high–we can't search anymore." At their shocked silence, he shook his head. "The truth is, folks, Pop is gone. We all just have to accept this. He's gone." Then, head down, he disappeared into his cabin.

Many sobbed as the crowd slowly dispersed.

"My God," Earl Stockman said to himself, frowning, "O.C. is gone."

As the days dragged by, everything at the ranch seemed to move in slow motion as the small community tried to pull things back together. The air held a silent emptiness.

Chapter 31

Back in the Swamp

"Well, Johnny, I better get back to work, but tell me–am I sitting in the right place with the steam dredge?" Sam turned to survey the barge, which was tied to a tree. "I did find one gold piece in the shovel, but I only made a couple of dips so far."

Johnny considered the surroundings. "It looks like you are very close to the spot, but it's been a long time," he finally acknowledged. "I can't say I'm sure, though."

Sam nodded. "Well, we'll just have to wait and see what I come up with." He smiled, looking at something behind his tall friend. "It looks like we have some company. Anyone you know?"

Johnny turned to see Emot and several of the young boys approaching from the tree line alongside the swamp. One boy ran ahead of the others and was quickly at Johnny's side. He grabbed Johnny's hand and held on tight.

"These are people from my tribe–Chief Emot and some of the children." To the boy, he smiled. "You're a fast runner! What's your name?" Johnny thought it was strange that he had not seen this particular boy in all the days he had spent in the village. The child certainly wasn't shy–he just looked up at him with a huge smile.

When Chief Emot and the other boys got nearer, they hesitated, walking very cautiously, spears drawn. They had never seen men of color.

Emot, eyes wide, asked Johnny, do these men wear war paint?"

Johnny laughed as Emot quickly grabbed a piece of deer hide from his waist, wet if with some water, and reached for young Neil Carter's hand.

At first, Neil felt threatened and resisted, but hearing Johnny's laughter, he gradually smiled and relaxed. Emot tried to wash off the color, and then realized it was, without a doubt, the real thing. Neil laughed, and new friendships were created. When the village boys saw that Johnny's, friends were not a threat, they circled Neil and looked with wonder at his curly hair. Neil good-naturedly allowed them to touch his hair, patting their shiny hair in return.

In the native tongue of his people, Emot told Johnny, "I see you have met Keena. He cannot hear or talk, but he smiles all the time. It is very strange, but he was born that way. He does get into a little mischief, and he does things that all boys do, but he is a good boy, and we all love him very much." The chief fondly tousled the boy's smooth black hair, and Keena turned his smile upwards toward him. Then Emot turned back to Johnny. "We wanted to see if your journey here was safe, and if you are well."

Meanwhile, Sam took out the coin that he found and showed it to the boys. "My name is Sam, and I'm Johnny's friend. Tell me, boys, have you seen any of these coins?"

They didn't understand what he was saying, but they knew what the coins were, and each boy seemed to point in a different direction. This confused Sam and he just laughed it off.

Keena tugged at Johnny's arm and pointed toward the woods.

"Yes, my little friend, we will go home now." Johnny figured Keena was tired and wanted to leave. He knew that it would be getting dark soon. He waved to Sam. "I will be back in a few days, Sam; we have a lot of work to do in the village, and I have some sick people to take care of."

After learning that the land now belonged to the tribe, Johnny was eager to return to the village and tell his people. He knew he would be able to explain it a little better than Emot could, because in Emot's eyes, the land was already theirs.

Several times on the way back to the village, Keena tugged on Johnny's hand, pointing in the opposite direction. How cute and pure this little spirit was, Johnny reflected, as Keena quickly captured his heart.

Sam pondered the way the boys had pointed in so many directions. Could it be that they had found these coins all around the place? His excitement grew as he hurriedly rowed across to the barge.

Sam worked long and hard for the next couple of weeks, but, to his disappointment, he never found the huge treasure he was looking for. The steam shovel was plagued with breakdowns, and his five crew members were getting on each other's nerves. The long hot and humid days were getting to them. Even though it was still early spring, the weather was brutal. The men complained about everything and some talked about leaving.

Sam often doubted that the gold was still there, wondering if it had already been taken. Keeping the nature of the operation quiet was another thing–it seemed the occasional trappers and fishermen he encountered were getting more and more curious.

~ ~ ~

Johnny had become friends with one of the trappers, and paid him to bring a load of garden seed to him. He knew the survival of the village people would soon depend on their planting and raising their food. Wild game was fast disappearing and soon would be hunted to extinction.

The best place to raise crops would be on the rich soil of the old Plummer place where the Armstrongs had farmed. It had become largely grown over, but could easily be cleared. In his mind's eye, Johnny drifted back to a time when he could see the old house and barn. He remembered young Carl running through the fields, happy and healthy. He missed his young friend, but Johnny was grateful that the land would now give health and happiness to another family he loved.

Johnny and his escorts arrived at the village just about sundown. The children ran to greet them, but Keena would not leave Johnny's side. Emot had explained that Keena's mother had died while giving birth to him. Emot believed the child was about six seasons old, but he was not quite sure. Johnny asked no more questions about Keena; he was happy to be a part of his life.

Around the fire that night, Johnny explained to the village people about the garden seeds and his plan to farm the old Armstrong place. He revealed that it was theirs now, and they would never have to leave.

Emot looked bewildered when Johnny spoke. "We have lived here for many seasons, but you are now telling us that we just now own our land?" he frowned. "I do not understand this. How can this be?"

"My Chief, in this new world of the white man, many things have changed. If we do not change, our people will soon perish. All that will remain will be the memories of a few that survive," Johnny explained patiently as Emot shook his head in disbelief.

Johnny nodded solemnly. "It is so. But now, according to the white man's ways, our people own this land. There is enough land to give our people a better life. We have the swamp and the farmland–if we work hard, our people will prosper. Many things have changed, Emot, and we must change or we and our ways will be swallowed in time."

It seemed like hours went by, but Emot was beginning to believe Johnny and trust his words. The village people, as well, gradually warmed up to his ideas, and were excited to embark upon this new way of life.

Secretly, Johnny sometimes wondered if he was right about their ability to change their way of life, but he also knew nothing could stop the change that was bound to come one way or another.

Mid-Spring, at the Ranch

Joe Armstrong stood near the cemetery and gazed across the dwindling river. The wind was hot and dry, and dust swirled as it reached the river. It hadn't rained in a month, and things were getting dangerously dry. The vegetable garden was the only green spot on the entire ranch, because Cindy and the girls faithfully carried pails of water from the river each day to water the plants. The pastures, though, were parched brown, and the threat of fire was dangerously high. Joe mounted his horse and rode back to the ranch.

Before heading back to the ranch, Joe paused beside the gravestone they had placed for his father. He and his boys had searched the surrounding cliffs for a fitting stone, and he thought they had chosen well. The red sandstone seemed to glow in the late afternoon light, reminding those who had known O.C. of his light-hearted spirit.

Joe flicked a teardrop from the corner of his eye. He must get back to work–though he now had one more reason to visit this cemetery on a daily basis, memories of the loved ones who had gone before him would spur him on to maintaining their vision for the Armstrong family well into the future.

Levi was leaning against the corral gate as he arrived. "Joe, the water tank in the tower is going dry pretty damn fast. If we don't get rain soon, we're in some big trouble."

Joe didn't know what to say–he just squeezed Levi's shoulder and slowly nodded his head.

Levi knew that Joe was having a hard time coping with his father's death, especially when it came to making important decisions without being able to consult with O.C. But he also knew that Joe appreciated having him there to share his years of experience and advice. It eased Joe's job as leader of the large ranch just a little.

No one was in the picnic grounds, which at one time would have been filled with music and cheer. The dust was so thick that even scarves didn't seem to help much. Cindy had placed a bucket of water on one of the benches in the gathering area, along with a few towels. Joe filled his hand with a little water and rinsed his face and eyes.

Nate and Pete appeared from the street like ghosts from a mist. Though Nate tried to keep his mount calm, the animal was restless and eager for water. He rushed to the water trough.

"We're going to have to start watering our horses with the cattle at the river, Nate."

"Yeah, I know. I'll tell the rest of the boys not to draw any more water from the tower."

"Joe, the pastures are all parched–the cattle are just eating dry stubble, and it won't be long until that's gone," Pete reported. "I've never seen a year when it didn't rain by now–it's kind of crazy."

"I hear they had some rain north of here, but it's just hearsay–it may not be true," Nate offered.

As the days passed by, the cattle were shaving the stubble smooth in the pastures. But Nate and Pete learned that there were plenty of untouched pastures to the north around Cheyenne Wells.

"Good country up there," Pete told Joe. "I was there about ten years ago. Drove some cattle up there to Wyoming. Seems to me I remember it all belonged to an old boy named Ron "The Whip" Bolivar. They called him that because he carried a bull whip on his side and was quick to use it. I think he just had the land homesteaded. He let us pass through, but that was all. He said he was always having trouble with the Indians–probably the Sioux. But I don't recall seeing any when we passed through the territory. I'm sure they were watching us, but we made sure not to shoot at any buffalo, and they left us alone." That was a long monolog for Pete, but he could see Joe wasn't quite convinced yet. "There's lot of grass there, Joe; we've got to graze these cattle north if they're going to eat! And if we don't start in a few days, we're going to start losing them."

Joe knew they had no choice. "I agree, Pete. We've worked pretty damn hard for what we've got. We can't just stand around here and let them starve. Is there water along the way? How far is Cheyenne Wells?"

"I reckon it's about a hundred miles–you know, give or take a few," Pete responded.

"You know, Joe, we can just let them graze as we go," Nate put in. "Just let them kind of show us the way. Hell, I bet there's not twenty people between here and Cheyenne Wells! Most of 'em are scared of old Running Bear, but I don't think he'll bother us, do you?"

"Well, we haven't seen him in a long time. It would be bad if it turned out he died and some young brave that will want to take our hair took his place," Joe quipped as he walked toward his cabin.

Joe spent a quiet night with Cindy and the three boys. He explained to them what they would have to do to save the cattle, and maybe to save the whole ranch. Carl urgently begged to go along, causing quite a ruckus, but eventually backed down when his father explained the perils of the venture.

The family played checkers all evening as Joe talked matter-of-factly with the boys, trying to settle everyone's minds about this huge gamble. Even though young Carl still tried to talk his dad into letting him go on the cattle drive, this easy-going atmosphere served to calm him down.

As usual, Joe had placed Nate and Pete in charge. Most of the ranch hands would be needed on the cattle drive. But Joe planned to keep at least five of the hands, along with Levi, Earl, and the women, who could help keep things running smoothly at the ranch. The men would leave after Joe met with Nate and Pete the next morning.

The following morning, Nate placed the twenty-three cowboys at intervals around the herd, instructing them to let the livestock graze their way north. He planned that it would probably be a slow journey. As an added precaution, Joe had devised a plan to bring two water wagons along; they would alternate back and forth from the ranch or the nearest river to the herd.

CHAPTER 32

Tagah

Within a couple of weeks, Johnny had taught the tribe many things about the changing times. Sam had also delivered several wagonloads of supplies to the tribe.

One of the first things Johnny taught them was fishing using modern fishing techniques. He enjoyed his trips with Keena to run the lines in the bayou. He had acquired real fishhooks from the crew at Sam's barge, and things were looking better for the small village.

One day as Johnny and Keena were preparing to run their lines, Emot hurried over, looking very concerned. "Johnny," he said, "I believe Tagah has shown up again."

"Who is this Tagah?"

"He was once a member of the village, until his evil ways caused us to drive him away. He is a murderer. He and his band of renegades try to steal our young women. He is very evil."

"Where can I find this Tagah?" Johnny furrowed his brows in determination. "I will deal with him. I may not be as strong as I once was, but still I fear no man."

"We can not know for sure, but one of the girls said she was being watched as she drew water from the creek."

Johnny assured Emot, "I will watch for this Tagah, and

if I find him, he will bother you no more." He touched Keena on the shoulder. "Come now, young Keena, let us run our lines. The day grows short."

~ ~ ~

Tagah had watched through the thick undergrowth as the two men were talking. His party of five crouched behind him. "So, that is the great Johnny One Horn," he snorted as he glared through the brush. "I have heard much about him, but he is older now and will be no problem to me."

An older warrior behind him shook his head cautiously. "Tagah, do not underestimate this One Horn, for he is deadly with a knife. I remember him from the old days. He was feared by many. He has been known to appear and disappear out of nowhere. Some said he and his brother were part spirit. His legend is even known by the white man. They have said he whipped a bear in the far north, one on one. He has also been known to skin people. He mixes well with the white eyes, and even they seem to favor him."

Disgusted, Tagah whirled and declared fiercely, "No one can defeat me one on one! I will show the tribe this is so, and then I will take my choice of the women. This One Horn will be ridiculed, and I will be feared."

"Do as you will, Tagah," said the old warrior. "Just remember–I am with you and not against you."

"Then speak no more about him. My arrow will find him before this day is through. Go away from me now, and take these braves with you. I want no one to say I could not defeat him alone."

As his braves faded back into the shadows, Tagah covered his body with mud and followed Johnny and Keena through the dense growth. He slithered though the mossy water, silent as a snake, not taking his eyes off his prey. The swamp became dense, and a menacing fog began to block his vision.

Johnny and Keena reached the edge of the bayou and the boy ran to check the first line. He turned and smiled, raising his finger to signal that he had a fish. Though Johnny motioned for him to put down the line, Keena didn't understand and continued to point at the line.

Tagah thought for sure that he had Johnny now. He sighted his arrow.

Johnny, emotionless, stared across the swamp. Then, like lightning strikes, he wheeled around and sailed his blade toward the underbrush. It hit Tagah in the cheek, slicing through the back of his jaw. He painfully jerked the long blade from his face and threw it into the mud. As Johnny started a methodical walk toward the location, Tagah struggled to get to his feet, and dove into the thick underbrush.

Johnny bent to retrieve the long knife from the mud. His first thought as he walked stealthily through the swamp was to finish Tagah. But the reality that little Keena with him suddenly overcame his revenge instinct. "Let us finish our lines, Keena. It is late in the day."

Keena looked at Johnny in bewilderment and formed his hand into a questioning gesture.

Johnny motioned back to tell him it was a deer. Many sign phrases were made while hunting in silence, and Keena was satisfied. They ran their lines and caught what they could carry back to the village.

Meanwhile, Tagah moved as fast as he could through the muddy soup toward the camp of his small group of braves. The pain was almost unbearable as blood flowed from the wound. The words of the old man ran wildly through his thoughts. "He's deadly with a knife" echoed insanely through his brain.

It was late in the day when Tagah collapsed inside the camp. The young braves quickly ran to wash the mud from the wound. He had lost quite a bit of blood and was very weak. As the young men cleaned him and chanted prayers to their Spirit, the old warrior stood shaking his head.

Several days went by before Tagah began to recover. The long knife of Johnny One Horn had cut part of his tongue completely off and knocked out several of his teeth. The bloody scar reached from his ear all the way into his mouth. He looked deformed, and was not recognizable anymore. He didn't argue with the group when they decided to take him back to their home in the south.

"I will return and kill this One Horn one day, he mumbled as the group left the swamp. "It will be my life's quest."

The old warrior looked at him with amazement. "Why do you not just settle down and live out the rest of your life in peace, Tagah? Things are changing, and so should you. You should not be ashamed. Johnny One Horn let you live, and you should be glad."

"I am going to come back to this place and kill him," the bitter warrior insisted. "I still fear no man."

"I believe that to be true, Tagah," reasoned the old warrior, "but One Horn is no ordinary man."

~ ~ ~

When Johnny and Keena reached the village at last, the people were excited about the nice catfish. Many offered to prepare the fish, and Johnny gratefully gave up that job as he must talk to Emot.

Emot was patiently communicating with Keena and Johnny realized the boy was telling him about the encounter with Tagah. Emot looked concerned as he walked to Johnny's side. "Keena tells me you hit something with your long knife. He said it was a deer with man footprints–he noticed them in the sand."

"Yes, I told him I hit a deer, but I think it must have been this Tagah you talk about. I knew he was following us for a long way. He was covered with mud and carried a long bow. I watched as he slid like a snake behind us, but he never knew I saw him. I hit him square in the face with the long knife, so I don't believe he got far. There was a bloody trail, and I would have tracked him if it had not been for Keena. I did not want to take a chance of Keena getting hurt."

"If he is not dead, Johnny, he will return for vengeance–this I know. Maybe he is, and this would be great news.

The whole village celebrated the bounty of fish that night. But Emot placed several guards around the perimeter of the village, not wanting to take any chances.

The Barge

Sam Carter and his crew, in their search for coins, struggled to wash the mud with homemade sifters. After many fruitless days, Sam shook his head in frustration over the few coins that were found. "I know I'm in the right place," he thought, "or we would not have found any at all." Still, even a few were worth a lot of money.

The days were beginning to get hotter and the swamp mosquitoes were at their peak. Most of the crew were netted down at night and confined to their tents. Sam wondered why the Indians were not bothered by the irritating madness of the blood-sucking insects. He decided to ask the tribe for advice and seek something for relief. Two of his crew had already left without telling him, and the three that were left were at their limit of tolerance.

Sam sent a message to Johnny when he saw the tribesmen checking their fishing lines the following day, explaining his situation with the gold and the relentless mosquitoes. One of the fishermen told Sam of a plant that was plentiful by the edge of the creeks that would repel mosquitoes. Sam and his crew harvested some that afternoon. It smelled good, like strong perfume. They mashed the leaves into a paste and rubbed it on their skin.

The paste was white in color, and lightened their dark skin as though they had been painted. Nevertheless, the mosquitoes hated it. The tribesman hadn't told them they were supposed to eat the plant, but the paste did the job.

The next day the white tradesmen that had been bringing their supplies arrived. They were startled when Neil Carter walked up silently. One of the men screamed and ran off into the undergrowth. Neil and the other young black men laughed until tears streamed down their cheeks. The other tradesman just stood there with his mouth open.

"It's OK, Seth–it's just mosquito medicine," yelled Sam Carter.

"Well, I never seen any damn mosquito medicine like that," Seth quivered. "There's all kinds of stories of things like voodoo people in this damn swamp."

"Well, there's no voodoo people here–just us and these dang 'skeeters! If we look like voodoo people, then I guess we'll scare off the 'skeeters, along with you," grinned Sam. "I'm sorry, but it's worth it!"

After Seth returned from rounding up his partner from the underbrush and calming him down, he handed Sam a wire from Charles Armstrong at the ranch. As Sam read it, his head dropped and he walked away from the others.

He sat that night and stared at the moonlit swamp for hours, thinking about his meetings with O.C. He would always remember those meetings, and would hold that man in high esteem–almost like his own grandfather.

It was early morning when Johnny arrived at the barge. Sam approached him so hesitantly that Johnny realized something was very wrong. "What's wrong, my friend?" Johnny asked. "You're showing your emotions on your face."

Sam had to choke down a huge lump that had formed in his throat before he could answer. "Well, Johnny, I just got a wire from Charles at the ranch. O.C. is gone." He had to look away quickly.

"Gone! You mean gone, Sam–or dead?"

"Charles said he drowned in the river after he had a terrible stroke or heart attack or something."

"What is this stroke, Sam? I do not understand this."

"I think it's a sickness of the brain, Johnny. I really don't know. They said he became so sick he couldn't talk any more."

Johnny turned and walked away. Should he quickly return to the ranch? No, he must stay with the tribe. They needed him more than the Armstrong boys did, didn't they?

He paced through the swamp until he came to a secret place where he and Little Boy Horse used to hide when they were kids. Now Johnny disappeared from the others as only he could do. As he gathered dry driftwood, he marveled at this magical place he once enjoyed as a child. The place was full of memories. Ghost-like visions melted through his mind.

Night fell, and the fire cast mesmerizing, glimmering sparks toward the stars. Johnny painted his face in ceremonial paint made from the black mud and colored plants he found beside a small creek. His heart was heavy, and his mind raced for hours with recollections of his friend.

Finally, as the sun rose, he walked out from the underbrush to the bayou and began washing the ceremonial colors from his face.

Not too far away, Sam Carter was making coffee by the bank of the bayou. He saw Johnny and, relieved, walked slowly toward him. Johnny's knife was deadly, and he sure didn't want to feel its wrath.

But before Sam got within fifty feet of him, Johnny spoke. "You know, I know the way you sound when you walk, Sam, or you would be dead by now."

Sam swallowed really hard. "Yes, I know I would. I wasn't trying to slip up on you–I was trying not to startle you for that very reason!"

Johnny had washed and was ready to start his day. He decided to get back to the business he knew Sam had called him here for. "I was told you are not having luck finding the gold. It is strange because I believe you are searching in the right place."

"Some of your tribe members were worried about you, Johnny, and they showed up here last night. Keena walked the shoreline for hours. He wanted to look for you, but Emot would not let him."

Sam turned to retrieve the few coins he had found just as Keena walked up and grabbed Johnny's hand.

"I can't believe that's all you found with that big digging machine, Sam! There were many, many still down there when we left.

Keena tugged on Johnny's hand and pointed toward the bluffs in the distance above the trees.

"What is it you see, Keena?" asked Johnny. "We will leave soon and return home–is that what you want?"

Keena was shaking his head no and kept pointing toward the bluffs.

"What do you suppose he sees, Johnny? Maybe it's about the bats that come out at night, or is he just being funny?"

Johnny studied the strange rock formations along the bluffs. "I don't know, but he always seems to point in the same direction. If he keeps it up, I will go there and see for myself. It does seem strange that he always points in that direction."

Sam sighed. "I don't know how long I can keep looking, Johnny. I'm not finding enough to keep going, and I sure don't want to spend it all."

"I'm sure you would be welcome back at the ranch with your family, Sam, you are part of the family there now."

"What about you, Johnny? Will you ever go back there?"

"No, I will not leave my people again. They need me

here, and now that the land is ours, I think we can live a better life." Johnny took Keena's hand and said goodbye to Sam with a gesture from the chest.

Sam thoughtfully nodded and slowly walked back to the canoe and returned to the heaping stack of mud the hands were sifting on the barge.

A strange feeling came over Johnny as he and Keena walked away. He turned and stared at the barge for a minute or so. Something was wrong. "Follow me, Keena. I have something to do." His mind drifted back in time as he climbed the ancient burial mound beside the old Armstrong farmstead. Martha Armstrong's old cross was still standing, but had been propped up with rocks. The WIT cross where Joe Armstrong had left the gold for O.C. had rotted off at the base, and slid down the hill several yards. Johnny could tell right away that greedy people had desecrated the grave looking for gold. It infuriated him. He turned his head toward the sky and screamed to the heavens. This frightened Keena, who ran down from the mound. Johnny decided he would return with the men from the tribe and restore what bad people had destroyed. He followed the boy down the mound and comforted him. He attempted to explain with hand signals, but Keena only knew the tribal language signs. They weren't sufficient to convey the deep feelings Johnny was dealing with.

It was nightfall before they returned to the village and he could explain to Emot and the elders his plans for the mound and the people. There were so many things to do, and it would take a lot of the white man's money. He was determined, and asked the medicine man to remove the curse from the gold.

The medicine man, Lawa, was one of the oldest members of the tribe. Johnny estimated that he was around sixty seasons old. He listened to Johnny's plan for the gold, and at first refused. But he traveled in the night to the secret mound and prayed to the spirits for hours. In his visions he saw the tribe prosper with the white man's money, but it came at a terrible price: he would have to give his own life and the life of one more unknown member of the tribe would be sacrificed. Not knowing who the other was, he returned to the village the following morning with a heavy heart. He would wait until the sun was high and the tribe's fishermen had left the village before he would discuss the vision with Johnny One Horn.

CHAPTER 33

The Cattle Drive

The first couple of days of the drive were accompanied by a howling south wind and almost no visibility. Dry lightning would sometimes spook the herd. The hands had to wet their bandanas frequently so they could breathe.

It was the morning of the third day when the stiffening torment of dust at last slowed down. The morning was pleasant and had a relieving cool touch that both the hands and the animals enjoyed.

Nate had sent Pete ahead to scout for the best route. He returned with the news that better grass and conditions waited only about twenty miles ahead. They pushed on to reach them as soon as possible, establish a camp, and settle in for a few days. Nate knew the herd would soon exhaust the grass and they would have to move on.

As the grass dwindled on the third day, the herd started moving on its own. It was a very pleasant day with a slight south wind, unlike the terrible onslaught of the preceding days. Prairie dogs were everywhere, and so were rattlesnakes. Nate's experience told him that the snakes would be around the prairie dog towns. Several of the cattle were bitten, and the hands stayed busy searching for them and treating them.

Pete, with a few of the ranch hands, approached Nate. "There are a couple of dead steers beyond that hill Nate."

"Rattlesnakes?" Nate asked.

"No–these were butchered. Looks like a crude job. If it were the Sioux, it would have been clean, but this was whacked and wasted. Who ever did this was not Indian. I'll take these guys and search those trees by the bluffs."

Nate followed determinedly as the men rode out. Through the afternoon they searched the area until they spotted smoke from the backside of the bluffs. They dismounted and cautiously approached on foot. Two men were staggering around a campfire. They had built a tri-pod and were attempting to cook a large piece of beef. Pete and the hands slipped through the brush until they were within twenty feet of the men.

"Hell, man, they're drunk!" laughed one of the ranch hands.

Pete fired his rifle in the air and the men scattered like a couple of rabbits. Jose, the oldest ranch hand, mounted his horse and within a minute threw a bolo around a fleeing man's legs, dropping him to the ground. The other walked from the brush with his hands in the air.

Nate sliced a piece of the roasted beef from the tri-pod. "Hey–that's good!" he smiled. "Bring those two boys over here and tie them to that tree. We'll hang 'em after we eat."

"Hang us? We're just starvin', Mister! We'll work for free and pay the damages! But please don't hang us!" The tallest rustler begged. "My name's Lee Cross, and this here is my brother Darrel."

"What are you two boys doing way out here anyway?" questioned Pete.

"Well, we kind of got in some trouble down in Garden City."

"What kind of trouble, kid? Looks like you got yourselves into a lot of trouble here, too. We hang people in this country for killing our cattle," Nate barked gruffly.

"Well, we were playing some cards at the saloon when this card shark drew down on us. My brother shot him. We don't know if we killed him or not, but we weren't going to hang around to find out. We heard that old Marshal Tibbs just as soon hang you as look at you. We been riding day and night, and those two calves would have died from them rattlesnake bites anyway. They were real bad, sir."

"That so? Well, you're probably right," acknowledged Nate, "but you boys will have to work a spell to pay for this."

Lee Cross turned and looked toward the hands that were carving up the roasted calves. "How long, sir? It looks to me like we just cooked you boys a pretty good supper."

"Nate," yelled Pete, "let's just go ahead and hang these two ungrateful rats! Hell, no one's gonna see us do it out here!"

A couple of the hands grabbed the two brothers and held them.

"Whoa, wait a minute! We were just foolin' around! We'll work as long as you want us to, won't we, Lee?" wailed Darrel Cross.

"All right, boys, let 'em loose," Pete finally relented. "Now, you boys better keep your mouths shut and do as you're told, unless you want your neck stretched after all. Now, Jose, why don't you find these boys a bedroll, and after they eat, put 'em to work."

Jose gave the boys some beef and escorted them over to the wagons. "You'll find some bedrolls in there, gringos–don't take too long."

"Jose," asked Darrel Cross, "do you think he really would have hung us? We're not bad people."

"Well, yeah, but I think he would have skinned you first." Jose turned away and walked back to the camp, laughing out loud along with the rest of the hands.

Lee Cross looked at Darrel. "Hell, man, they were just kidding all the time, and here I peed my pants, I was so scared. I guess these are good people. I think we found us a job and that's a damn good deal."

During the following week, the Cross brothers blended in unexpectedly well. Everybody liked the boys, and they were keeping the hands' morale up with their antics. They played tricks and made everybody laugh. They had truly found a spot where they belonged. They planned to work for a couple of months and then try to make it to the California gold fields. What they didn't know was that the gambler had died in Garden City, and old Marshal Tibbs had formed a posse and was looking to hang them.

CHAPTER 34

The Vision

Lawa met with Johnny in the afternoon to discuss the troubling vision he had seen. It was as though it was real, but not real. In the vision, the tribe would indeed prosper, but not without the development of greed which would cause tribal members to fight among themselves. The money would bring the love of evil things, dividing family loyalties. The vision's messages had alternated from one thing to another, as though the future could unfold in one of two ways.

Johnny considered what he had just heard. Finally, he spoke. "Well, we will just use what we need and no more," he reasoned. "That way the people in the village won't have anything to fight about. I think I will take a few boys over to the barge tomorrow and give Sam a hand. I don't see how it could anger the spirits if we just take what we need to live."

Johnny paused, thinking about Sam's troubles. "Sam must be digging in the wrong place. He has only found a few coins. Maybe with more workers, we can help him find them."

Lawa turned away, ignoring Johnny's words, which made Johnny suspicious. "Lawa, why do you never speak of the gold? I am concerned that you always turn away."

"Oh, it is not you, my friend. It is the curse of that yellow iron. You know it brings evil, but now you wish to seek it? All I ask is that you beware the temptations it brings. With my own eyes, I have seen it take away what it gives. Last night as I was on the mound, I saw the Wisp sliding across the water. It looked toward the barge in anger. It has been several years since anyone in the village has seen the Wisp. We must always be aware of its presence."

"I haven't seen that old ghost in years, but I would have liked to," Johnny teased.

As the early morning sun was rising above the swamp, Johnny, with the five young braves, approached the barge. In horror, he recognized the bodies of two of Sam's crew in the muddy water at the edge of the swamp. The young braves panicked and ran into the undergrowth. Johnny dragged the bodies from the swamp. Though he was a strong man, with heartfelt emotion he chanted to the Great Spirit as tears welled in his eyes. Each of the young men had died of multiple stab wounds. Johnny could see another body lying on the side of the barge. It was another of the crew members. Inside the barge, tied to the seat, Johnny found Sam's body. He had apparently been tortured and killed slowly.

Johnny's heart plummeted, and he bellowed in rage as he slid the long knife from belt. His keen eyes scanned the edge of the swamp for clues. After a moment, he realized that only Sam's son, Neil, was missing.

One of the young braves ran to the village to alert Emot. Johnny spent some time regrouping his thoughts, and then carried Sam Carter's body to the shore. His young friends helped him lay the bodies of the crew and Sam on some dry sand next to the swamp. Johnny instructed the boys to gather wood and prepare the bodies for his return. "Then find young Neil, or his body, boys. I will return as soon as I make these devils pay for this."

A couple of hours later, Emot arrived at the barge and the young braves told him the details. Emot knew that Johnny One Horn was in a relentless pursuit of Tagah and the men responsible for this terrible deed.

Late Afternoon

Tagah had left several members of his band with instructions to kill Johnny and the young braves. When they heard Johnny's war cry, though, they cowered and slid back into the swamp in fear, scattering in many directions to keep from being tracked. They had heard many stories of Johnny One Horn and they were terrified.

Now, Johnny moved through the thick vines and underbrush like a ghost in the darkest night. His plan was not to kill the murderers, but to tie them with their own clothes until he captured every single one of them. Rage fueled by grief consumed the mighty Indian, and as he tied them to trees one at a time, he threw them around like rag dolls. Some screamed like they were dying, for they were sure Johnny would kill them. After seven were found and tied, the night was beginning to turn into morning. At last, Johnny returned to the barge where Emot and the young braves were waiting.

"We were worried, my friend," said Emot gently. "Did you find the madmen that did this terrible thing?"

Johnny's eyes were still glittering with rage as he turned to Emot. "Yes, I found seven and I think these were the only ones involved. I tied them to trees. They will be easy to find because I marked the trees. I want you to gather them and take them to the village. Keep them there until I return."

"Why did you not kill them as I would have done?"

Johnny turned slowly. "Emot, they were just kids–just kids doing what they were told. They know no better. I am going to continue my search for Tagah, for he is to blame for this. Burn the bodies of these poor men tonight, and pray to the Great Spirit for them."

Emot sent the young braves to search for the prisoners. Tagah's young men were spread out, so it would take most of the morning to find them. Rain was moving in, and looked like it was going to stay a while as it pounded the swamp and the undergrowth.

Johnny moved quickly through the swamp toward Tagah's village. He hoped to overtake him before he arrived, because he would have allies there.

Tagah had been moving through the swamp at a very slow pace. Sam Carter had been able to wound him in his left leg. He groaned in great pain as he struggled to keep moving. He knew that, at this pace, Johnny One Horn would track and catch him before the night was over. The night was lit by flashes of lightning, and the sound of thunder echoed through the humid air. Storm winds howled through the trees, and the rain beat down with more force by the minute. Tagah's pain was worsening as he chanted to the spirits. He collapsed beside a giant Cypress tree, moaning at the excruciating pain. Suddenly, in a great flash of lightning, he saw the face of Johnny One Horn staring directly at him from about fifty feet away. His face seemed to glow from the war paint. Tagah knew his death was imminent. He slid his knife from its sheath and without hesitation rammed it through the center of his chest. His death was instant. His body slowly toppled over and slid down the muddy hill.

Johnny left him there for the critters and 'gators of the unforgiving swamp. He traveled the rest of the night, arriving at his own village early in the morning.

As he approached, he could see Emot and Lawa, sitting with young Neil Carter around a smoking fire pit. They stood quickly, startled, as Johnny was covered with mud. Johnny stopped at the creek to wash himself off as the men approached him.

"Did you kill Tagah?" Neil asked.

"He killed himself just as I found him," answered Johnny. "He was already hurt really bad–he would rather die by his own knife than by mine."

"My daddy shot him," explained Neil, "but they still overpowered him. There was nothing I could do. I fought until they killed him, then I ran into the swamp. They all had spears and knives, and we were unarmed."

Young Neil's voice was trembling, and he burst into tears as Johnny placed his strong arms around the shoulders. "You did all you could do, my young friend. It is no shame to be afraid." Johnny clutched the boy tighter. "I, too, know the pain of losing someone."

Neil sobbed, hanging on to the big Indian as if he would never let go. The two remained united in their grief for a long time.

At last, the men had returned to sit by the fire pit. Johnny broke the silence. "Tell me, young Neil, can you write the white man's language?"

"Yes, sir, I can print it, if that's OK?"

"We must write a letter to the Armstrong's at the ranch and tell them of the death of your father, and a few things more I will explain to you. We can do this tomorrow when we have had a little time to mourn."

Suddenly, Johnny remembered his unfinished business. He turned to Emot. "Now, what have you done to those seven young men? Did you find them all?"

"We have all of them tied to trees down the creek a little way."

"We will decide their fate after Neil tells us if any of them killed Sam and the boys. Today we must rest, and tonight, if the hunting parties are successful, we will celebrate. It is a good day to be rid of that devil Tagah."

With that, Johnny turned and put his arm around Neil's shoulder. "Let's find you a hut, Neil. I understand if you want to be alone. I know how hard it is to lose your father–

he was a good man, and my friend also."

The rest of the day and night went as planned, and the hunting parties brought to the village several wild pigs. There was peace, and for once in a long time, no guards had to be posted.

The Following Morning

As dawn arrived, Emot built a small fire. Johnny joined him, and they discussed the fate of Tagah's seven young braves. The rest from the village slowly gathered around, and Emot sent for the seven to be brought before him. The seasoned warriors of the hunting party he had sent to fetch them wanted to see the traitorous young braves dead. They handled them roughly as they cut them from the trees. Not knowing their fate, and feeling they would surely die, the captives screamed and pleaded for their lives. Some were dragged by their hair and others were lashed with rawhide. On their arrival at the village circle, they were tied and placed on their knees. Emot sat in his usual chair by the small fire and chanted to the Great Spirit.

Then he commanded, "Bring young Neil to me!"

Several warriors ran to fetch the still-exhausted Neil, who was still asleep, and carried him, almost at a run, to the chief. Their rush caused Neil to panic a little. But Johnny put a calming hand on Neil's shoulder.

"It's all right, my young friend. This is our tradition. You will be fine."

Neil settled down as Emot ask him to identify the killers.

"Did these men kill your father? Show us which ones killed the other men."

Neil looked at the frightened young men. "No, we were just overpowered and taken by surprise by their numbers. Their leader, Tagah, did each killing, one at a time. He even beat one of his own men because he wouldn't kill us."

Emot looked at the ground for a long time, and then asked one of the older captives, "Why did you do such a thing?"

"We were terrified of Tagah," answered the brave. "We all have lived in fear–we knew he would kill you for the fun of killing you. He raped most of the young women in our village, and if anyone complained, he would kill them on the spot. Please don't kill us! We obeyed because we feared for our lives!"

"Lawa will talk to the Great Spirit, and if he says you die, you die. If he says you live, we will honor that."

Lawa walked to the top of the mound near the village and kneeled to begin his chant. He was there for about an hour while the captives waited in terror. At last, he walked to the seven youths who were now tied to the trees, and looked each one in the eyes as he slowly passed in front of them.

"The Great Spirit says they shall live and be free to return to their village to become better men and remember this day always. If they do not remember to be good men, they shall surely die."

"It is done," Emot decreed. "Cut them loose; give them food and water." He addressed the captives. "When you return to your people, tell them of this day, and that Tagah is dead."

The young braves all gave thanks to Lawa and Emot, and to the Great Spirit. They had listened very closely to Lawa, and promised they would work to bring their tribe back together as a people.

CHAPTER 35

That night at the campfire, Johnny explained how he would use the white man's gold to help the tribe. Lawa assured Emot that the curse would be lifted, only for the tribe.

Johnny planned to set the barge adrift and dive for the gold the way they once had with the Armstrong boys. He explained the procedure, but noticed that Lawa and Emot were acting kind of funny as he talked.

Finally, Emot spoke. "Johnny, we have something to show you in the morning. We will let Keena guide you." Keena, sitting as close as he could get, tapped on Johnny's shoulder and again pointed off in the direction of the huge rock bluffs in the distance.

Johnny didn't sleep well. The night was full of strange sounds and mystery. In the distance he could see small glowing objects crawling through the ancient Cypress trees. "The Wisp is restless tonight," he thought. "I wonder if it is searching for the souls of those killed by the barge?" The night stretched out endlessly, and he was relieved when the light of the sun peeked through the trees.

Then he grinned as he saw the urgent face of his young friend. "What are you doing up this time of morning, Keena?" smiled Johnny.

Keena pointed at the cliffs in the distance.

"What's up there, my little friend?"

Keena was persistent and urgently began tugging on Johnny's arm.

"OK, Keena, I'll go with you."

Keena excitedly took off, and Johnny followed, eventually ascending to the top of the cliffs. The moss on the rocks was very slippery, making the climb treacherous. When they reached a slight ledge about ten feet from the top, Keena stopped and pointed to a small hole between the rocks.

"Is that some kind of animal den?" Johnny guessed.

Keena motioned for Johnny to follow him as he crawled through the hole. The boy slid right in, but it was difficult for Johnny to fit his massive frame through the opening. After wiggling about ten feet or so, he was relieved to find that the opening widened. They were inside a large room. The sun shone through a long crack in the ceiling–a natural skylight.

Johnny was awestruck as the glimmering, almost blinding, reflection of gold bathed his clothing in a warm glow. Gold coins stacked to the ceiling lined the walls. As he took it all in, he heard a voice from behind.

"We uncovered these from the swamp years ago," explained Emot. "One year we had no rain, and the swamp was very low. Some children playing by an old tree found these there. We worked many days carrying it all up these steep cliffs. We knew that if the white men were to get knowledge of this, they might kill us all in their quest to have it."

Amazed, Johnny knew that he could use this to help the tribe. This was why Sam Carter had only found a few of the coins.

"Tomorrow we will set the barge adrift and set it on fire to hide any trace of where it was anchored," he murmured, still in shock at the turn of events.

"Yes," Emot agreed. "I would have told Sam Carter, but

I think there are still many coins there." He set his jaw. "Now, Lawa has removed the curse from this, and we will use it to better the life of our people. It came with a terrible price and the death of Sam Carter. We must be sure his son is taken care of. Get what you can carry, and let us return to the village. We have many plans to make, and a new life to provide for our people."

Before descending the cliff, the three sat down and looked over their beloved home. To most it was just a fearful swamp, but to the people of the tribe it was a beautiful place filled with enchantment and mystery.

Five Years Later in the Swamp

Johnny stood on the hill above the village reminiscing. Wonderful memories crowded his thoughts. He remembered the long journey westward, the adventures, the prairie, the ranch and the Armstrong boys. A tear trickled down his cheek as he recalled his beloved Carl and his faithful Cha-cha. Visions of O.C. and their long friendship flashed through his mind. He hoped one day he could reunite with Little Boy Horse, and wondered how his life had turned out in the far north. Someday, perhaps he would find out.

Johnny One Horn would remain a leader of the small village, along with Emot, for several more years. The village would prosper and the tribe would become friends with the surrounding white ranchers. It all came with a price, but with the amount of gold the tribe possessed, that was easy. There were many things to overcome, but with the wisdom of its leaders and integrity of its members, the lives of those within the tribe continued to prosper.

CHAPTER 36

The Prairie Drive

Marshal Tibbs was a few miles behind the Armstrong's cattle drive when he and his deputies decided to split apart and encircle the drive, so they could encounter each of the hands separately as they were doing their jobs. Each man would ride alone.

It was late afternoon when the marshal came upon a large cluster of rattlesnakes. His big buckskin horse was bitten several times and threw Tibbs off onto the large rocks and cactus and bolted away. Severely injured and unconscious, the man lay there all night before regaining consciousness.

The morning was cool, but Tibbs gradually realized he would die if he didn't get out where someone might see him. He felt for his pistol, but it was gone. The buckskin, with the canteen strapped to the saddle, was nowhere in sight.

The temperature rose, and the marshal struggled to raise his head above the rocks. His .44 was there, he saw, a few feet past his left boot. He painfully tried to move his leg a little, but as he moved, he could hear the rattlesnakes in the surrounding rocks. He eased his body back down to think.

As time passed, the sun seemed to be cooking his flesh and his mouth felt as dry as the dust. Hours went by as he baked in the blazing sun.

Meanwhile, several miles away, Nate noticed several of the cows breaking from the herd. "Probably them damn snakes!" he yelled, motioning for Lee and Darrel Cross to go after them.

The brothers found several cows, and Darrel told Lee to take them back while he made one more pass through the brushy draw. A flash of red caught his eye, and he was surprised to see what looked like a pile of rags among the scattered boulders and cactus. But when he rode closer, Darrel realized it was a man's body. He dismounted and gingerly walked closer, being careful to avoid the snakes along the way. Tibbs' face was bloody and swollen, and Darrel did not recognize him.

"Mister, can you hear me?"

Tibbs had drifted back into unconsciousness, but Darrel could clearly see he was still alive. He mounted his horse and raced back toward the herd. "Nate! There's a man back there that's injured bad! His horse probably threw him–he's layin' in the rocks. We need to help him!"

"Was he snake bit, Darrel?"

"I don't know, sir–he is awful bloody and I couldn't tell. He might be."

Nate told Jose to take a wagon and a couple of hands and help Darrel bring the man back.

The cowboys were relieved to see that no snakes were real close to Tibbs. They loaded him on the wagon. One of the other men drove back, as Jose was washing his face and trying to give him water. By the time they got back to the herd, he was awake and talking.

Lee Cross had found the buckskin, and he seemed to be all right, but with a really swollen back leg. Jose quickly lanced the leg and put axle grease on the wound.

The rest of the deputies started showing up, and explained that they were looking for the Cross brothers. Marshal Tibbs was alert now, and started to explain why the brothers were being hunted.

All the cowhands were on their horses, gathered around to hear the marshal's story, including Darrel and Lee Cross. Suddenly, Tibbs pointed to the brothers. "Those men killed a man in Garden City over a poker game. The law says they should be hanged!"

"Now, wait a minute," cautioned Nate. "Marshal Tibbs, these boys say that a card shark drew down on them, and they returned fire in self-defense."

"Yeah, well that's what they say," said Tibbs, "but old Brian Houx had a lot of friends there that all say different."

"Do you know who found you out there, sir?" Pete broke in. "It was Darrel Cross. He could have left you there to die if he was of a mind to. And another thing, sir–his brother found your horse. If it wasn't for these boys, you and your horse would have died for sure. Now, these don't sound like killers to me."

"Well, I still have a job to do," Tibbs insisted. "We'll make a camp here tonight and take the Cross brothers back to Garden City for trial in the morning." He motioned to his deputies and they hastened to take the brothers into custody. "Tie them to the wagon for tonight and we can leave at first light."

Tibbs slowly eased off the wagon and limped to where his horse was tied. Jose was rubbing the animal down. "Is he going to be all right, Jose? Your name is Jose, right?"

"Yes sir, it is. He will be as good as new in a few days," Jose assured him. Lee Cross found him just in time, or the rot would have set in, sir."

Tibbs patted the big buckskin on the neck and stared at the ground for a second. "Yep, I suppose he did, Jose, I suppose he did."

As hard a man as Tibbs was, he headed to the wagon where the Cross boys were tied. "I guess I owe you boys a thanks for saving my life–and for the best damn horse I ever had. I wish this didn't have to be, but the law is the law." He turned, limped around the wagon, and sat back down.

The Cross brothers never said a word. They just kept their heads down, looking at the ground.

Tibbs was staring at the ground too. "You know, Nate, sometimes I hate this job."

"I bet you do, Tibbs, I bet you do." Nate stood up and walked away.

The Next Morning

The sun was just a pink glow as the morning edged into view. Nate and Pete were the first to rise. Pete walked to the camp tri-pod to put the coffee on and noticed Marshal Tibbs and the deputies were already gone.

"Still not quite light," Pete said, curiously. "Wonder what time they left, Nate? I never heard a thing."

"About an hour ago. I heard a little shuffling from the horses–I guess it was then."

As Pete walked around the wagon, he heard someone say, "You think we might have a little swig of that coffee? You might have to cut us loose first."

"Well, I'll be damned! Nate, it's the Cross brothers and they're still here."

Nate walked around the wagon and cut the boys loose from the wagon wheels. "What in the hell happened, boys? We thought you were gone for sure!"

"Well, I don't know exactly. They just all loaded up and left," Darrel shrugged, rubbing his wrists. "I heard Marshal Tibbs say, 'Well, boys, let's be on our way. It's clear these boys are not the ones we're looking for.' I heard a couple of chuckles from the deputies and they just rode off."

"Damn, you boys are lucky." Pete whistled between his teeth, shaking his head. "I seen old Tibbs hang one of them Bennis boys and never look back as him and his horse walked away and stretched his neck."

The Cross boys just looked at each other for a minute and then exchanged a firm hug.

"Well, let's get them other boys off their asses and get some cattle watching started," Nate said.

Pete fired his .44 a couple of times in the air.

"Damn, Pete, you could stampede this whole herd, man!"

"Yeah, I could, but I didn't. That's about the only thing you can do to get that old cook out of bed."

Nate looked at Pete and laughed, "Man, you're something else, Pete–something else."

Pete motioned for the Cross boys to saddle up. "We got cattle to watch, boys! Let's circle the herd and see if any wandered off during the night."

As the Cross brothers saddled their mounts, Lee took a deep breath and leaned against his horse. "Damn, man, I'm tired. I didn't sleep any last night."

Darrel looked at Lee and nodded. "I didn't either, Lee, but I'm not going to complain. Not when we could be on our way to swing from some tree."

"Yeah, you're right, Darrel. I don't have a thing to complain about."

The day was long, hot, and humid, as the air had thickened. At sunset Nate noticed some lightning flashing from the west. "Boys, we better be on the alert tonight–it looks like a storm coming from the west. I hope we get the rain we need, but I sure don't want these cattle spread out all over the country! Jose, you take some of these boys and circle the herd tonight. If it doesn't get too bad, we'll trade off sometime tonight."

The wind was picking up to the point that the campfire was throwing sparks toward the dry prairie grass.

"Boys, get some buckets and put that damn fire out or we'll be in a hell of a mess!"

After the fire was out, Nate could see other fires in the distance ahead of the storm. "That lightning is setting its own fires to the west! I sure hope there's a lot of rain in this! Remember, O.C. got caught in a prairie fire? It damn near killed him."

As the front of the storm drew closer, the smell of rain grew strong. The rain hitting the dry dust made an eerie dust cloud. Miraculously, the herd stayed calm. Throughout the night, the wind calmed as the steady heavy rain persisted. Most of the hands traded off grabbing a little sleep at a time in the wagons. At sunrise everyone was amazed at the changes the rain had made to the surrounding prairie.

Over the next few days, the rains seemed to build and storms passed in a pattern that seemed typical in this part of the country. Late afternoon showers were persistent in this land this time of year.

CHAPTER 37

One week Later

Nate and Pete gazed in amazement at the new prairie grass.

"Holy Cow, would you look at that, Nate? I believe it's time to go home!"

"Jose," yelled Nate, "send one of the boys back to the ranch and tell Joe we're bringing the herd back! Tell him to expect us in six or seven days."

The Ranch

Within four days, the hand had arrived and delivered the news that the herd was coming home. Joe had been running the ranch with a very small crew for what had seemed like an eternity, but all together it had been less than a month. The rains had also drenched the ranch, and the hills and prairie were transformed into a glowing green. The river was rising fast, and would soon get back to or above normal.

Carl and his brothers Earl and James went to the river every day to visit the grave markers of OC., Jack Tunnie and their Uncle Carl. The boys would often talk to O.C. and the others as if they were alive and well. Sometimes Carl would get overwhelmed by his emotions and would have to turn away from his brothers. Tears would escape from his tightly squeezed eyelids, and he would feel the burn of sadness deep in his throat.

"The water will be clear soon, Earl, and maybe we can still catch those big flatheads," Carl said as he brought his thoughts back to the present.

"It won't be the same without Johnny One Horn," frowned Earl. "Do you think he will ever come back?"

"I think he might, Earl. Let's hope so. Everybody seems to miss him so much. This place just ain't the same anymore with everybody gone." Carl had to blink hard to keep the tears at bay. "Well, we better get back. You know Mom will throw a fit if we stay up here too long."

The herd arrived a few days later. Joe and the girls had planned a celebration–the girls were beyond excited to see their men come home. There would be music and a feast with beef cooked over the scrub oak fires. Cindy and Mariana were arranging the food, and Yolanda was setting up the park and gazebos.

The hands driving the herd were overjoyed to be welcomed with such gratitude. When all the cattle were within the fenced boundaries, the sun was already setting. The hands rushed to the showers by the water tank. An hour or so later, music and dance were in full swing.

Carl was sitting on the old oak stump where Johnny One Horn and his beloved Cha-cha used to watch the parties and tell the great stories of the far north. Carl was a sensitive young man, and it didn't take much before his eyes would show his sadness. He walked to the stable, and Johnny One Horn's beloved horse Coattail trotted to his side. The horse was older now, but still as spunky as ever. Carl climbed the wooden railing and slid on, bareback.

"You miss him too, don't you, boy? Well, I believe he may return one day." He talked to Coattail all the way to the cemetery. The moon shining on the water was almost fluorescent as the new rains filled the riverbanks.

Carl dismounted and Coattail followed close behind him, as if to guard him. He stood before the graves of O.C., Carl, and Jack Tunnie. A shadow standing at the water's edge moved toward him. Carl was surprised to see his father already there.

"Hi, Son. I was wondering when you would show. It's a beautiful night."

"There is just something about this night, Pop–I can almost hear Grandpa and all of them talking to me. I had a dream last night of Little Boy Horse and Johnny One Horn riding together across the plains. Then I saw my Uncle Carl, and now I know what he looked like. But I never miss a night without dreaming of Grandpa O.C."

Joe and Carl stood in the cemetery talking for an hour or more before Joe turned and hugged his son, tears streaming down his cheeks. "Well, Carl, the celebration is going on and your mother is probably worrying herself to death about now."

As they turned to head back home, the sound of several whippoorwills echoed between the canyon walls. Father and son turned and stared for a second, met each other's eyes, then just smiled and walked away.

THE END

There are many adventures of the These Characters lives left to be told, but these are different stories, to be told at a different time.

ABOUT THE AUTHOR

Jim and Susan Armstrong

James (Jim) Armstrong, originally from Southeast Missouri, now makes his home in the Ozarks with wife Susan, their two Boston Terriers and countless other creatures of the wild. He loves to spend time with grandkids, and when he's not doing that, he spends time in his music studio or writing.

As a, now retired, oil industry consultant and professional musician, through the ups and downs of the oil business, Jim spent many years bouncing back and forth between the two careers. His passion is music, and playing at Woodstock is one of his best all-time memories, yet that is a different story.

As the sixth son of a cotton sharecropper, he spent the first ten years of his life on a small farm near Steele, Missouri. Many spring storms rumbled across the boot heel of Missouri, and on those dark nights the family would spend time in their musty old dirt floored cellar. Jim remembers the smell from the kerosene lamp thickening the air. Aunts, uncles, and sometimes neighbors, would crowd in to weather the storms.

It was those nights that many stories were told. The tale

of the Wisp intrigued Jim the most. He dreamed of one day writing it just as he'd heard it as a child, and so he did, but the manuscript was destroyed in a fire.

Author's Note: It's taken five years to complete A Voice in the Wind. I hope you enjoy reading it as much as I did writing it.

About the Artist

James H. Hussey

Jim Hussey is a native of New Orleans who has become one of the country's artists of note. Born in 1936 Jim was educated in New Orleans, and upon completion of his academic training he began a career in the world of business. Later, in the summer of 1970, he decided to leave that career.

Equipped only with the paints and brushes his mother had left him, an interest in art from early childhood, and inspired by his surroundings, his family, his friends, and prominent artists, he decided to leave his successful career as a salesman and merchant to pursue his love for art on a full-time basis.

In order to refine his ideas, skills and techniques, in 1972 he attended the John McCrady School of Fine Arts. The decision to pursue art proved to be a wise one for his renditions of the Old South. Its many lazy bayous, and life along the Mississippi, shortly became wanted by many art collectors, galleries and museums throughout the world.

His paintings reflect personal feelings in the nostalgic and romantic moods, settings, and history of the South as seen through the eyes of numerous novelists and historians. Like most true artists, Jim is constantly driven toward self-improvement and growth through better interpretation, increased skill and authenticity in subject matter and composition.

"I believe when I display realism in a painting, it is as important to reflect my feeling on the mood of that subject, or to tell a story much as a poet, using all of the color and feeling of one's mind. Otherwise, one might just as well take a photograph.